W9-BFO-052

Ms. Renee Rosa
743 Graydon Ave.
Norfolk, VA 23507-1620

STRANGE BREW

ALSO BY KATHY HOGAN TROCHECK

STRANGE BREW

A CALLAHAN GARRITY MYSTERY

KATHY HOGAN TROCHECK

HarperCollinsPublishers

Although Candler Park, Little Five Points, and Hawkinsville, Georgia, are real places, and some of the other locations mentioned in this book are also real, many other locations in this book are fictional and the product of my own imagination. All of the situations that occur, and the characters to whom they occur, are fictional, and any resemblance to real people or to actual incidents is purely accidental and unintentional.

Designed by Elina D. Nudelman

ISBN 0-06-017542-7

For Celestine Sibley,
my treasured mentor and friend

ACKNOWLEDGMENTS

The author wishes to thank the following for their advice, suggestions, or assistance: Major Mickey Lloyd and Detective G. G. Carowan of the Atlanta Police Department; Glen Sprouse of Phoenix Brewing; management, staff, and patrons of the Euclid Avenue Yacht Club; Bill Ashton of Wax 'N' Facts in Little Five Points; Steve Akin of Alarm Depot; Don West of Albany, Georgia; Jane Crocker of the Georgia Pecan Growers' Association; Linda Christian, R.Ph., Harold Shumacher, and Steven Jasovitz of The Shumacher Group; Elliot Mackle; Audrey Newsome; David K. Secrest; and Tom Trocheck.

believes if she acts like she believes, something good could happen.

I believed it too, until the Sunday late last summer when my ideas about goodness and evil were shaken like one of those snow globes we put on the mantel every Christmas.

It was one of those unremarkable Sundays. Not unbearably hot, because we'd had an early afternoon shower. The windows were open, and I could hear the soft swish of a lawn sprinkler nearby. I was inside the house, watching an old gangster movie. I think George Raft was in it. Edna had put a chicken in the pressure cooker, and I was supposed to be listening for the steam to be sputtering good so I could turn down the heat. She was outside on the porch, probably dozing over the Sunday paper.

All of a sudden she let out a howl like a scalded dog. I went running out just in time to see her out in the yard, beating this poor old drunk with a dripping-wet floor mop.

She chased him down Oakdale, halfway to DeKalb Avenue, his pants still at half-mast around his knees, her pink terrycloth house shoes slapping against her bare feet, and all the while she was right behind him, jabbing the wet mop at him like a bayonet.

Her heart condition has slowed her down some in the past year. Otherwise, I believe Edna would have run that old wino to ground and pummeled him to death with that mop. As it was, she stopped chasing him only because I went after her and dragged her home by the arm.

"For God's sake," I told her, standing there on the sidewalk, panting for breath, hoping my own heart wouldn't give out, "that guy could have had a gun or a knife. What if he'd turned on you? What would you have done?"

"Son-of-a-bitch bums," she yelled, brandishing the mop in the direction he'd run off in. "The son of a bitch was using my yard as an outhouse. I saw him, Jules. He came right up to the edge of the porch and took a crap on my gardenia bush!"

I was pulling her along the sidewalk toward the house, trying to get her to come along quietly. But she had an audience now. Neighbors had heard her screams, and now dogs were barking and people were standing at the edge of the street or on their own porches to see what was going on.

Old Mr. Byerly across the street met us by the driveway. Homer, his Boston terrier, was barking and snarling and running in circles around Mr. Byerly's feet.

"I seen him, Callahan," Mr. Byerly said, working his toothless gums in agitation. "It's that same damned wino I caught sleeping in my car last week. Stank up the Buick so bad I had to use a whole bottle of Pine Sol on it. I think he's been sneaking around my back porch too, stealing Homer's food. Homer ain't never eat a whole box of Gainesburgers in one week. Have you, buddy?"

Homer lifted a black-and-white leg and directed a good-natured stream of urine at Mr. Byerly's work shoe.

"It's awful," Edna said. "Awful. Decent folk shouldn't have to put up with this. And I intend to put a stop to it." But her chest was heaving so hard, she couldn't say more. The chase had done her in.

I slipped my arm around her shoulder. "Come on, Ma," I said. "Let's go on inside and check on your chicken. You'll have a stroke standing around outside in this heat."

She pushed my arm away. "My gardenia," she said. "I've got to hose off that gardenia."

"I'll do it," I promised, steering her toward the porch.

"Soap and water," she said, pausing to rest after climbing the first step. "Otherwise, it'll be burned. Damned bum. I've been nursing that gardenia for four years. Longest I've ever been able to keep one going. Everybody says Atlanta's too cold for old-fashioned gardenias."

She eased down into her rocking chair, and I hustled into the house to turn off the pressure cooker, which was rattling and hissing and throwing off great clouds of steam inside the kitchen.

"The chicken's fine," I told her when I got back outside. She just nodded and pointed at the hose.

I squirted bright green liquid dish detergent all over the shrubs and breathed through my mouth and averted my eyes as I directed the spray at the neatly clipped azaleas, camellias, and sasanquas Edna had planted near the underpinnings of our little wood-frame bungalow. The shrubs made a frothy green hedge across the front of the house, and Edna always planted great swaths of pink and white impatiens in their shade so that it looked like a lady's lacy underpants peeking out from under her skirts. Never red, never orange. Every year since she'd moved into the bungalow with me eight years ago, she'd planted ten flats of pink and white "Gem" impatiens—and they had to be in the ground before Mother's Day. The shaggy green baskets of ferns had to be hanging from their hooks, two on each side of the front door, too, just as soon as it was warm enough in the spring to put them out there.

I'd owned the house on Oakdale for ten years, and poured untold buckets of sweat and money into making it livable in that time, but it was Edna who'd provided the grace notes— the glossy-leaved tea olive by the kitchen door, whose scent would waft into the house on the slightest breeze, the heavy brass knocker on the front door, which Edna herself polished every other week so that the engraved "Garrity" stood proud and businesslike, and, of course, the little fringe of grass out front, which she cosseted and babied and bullied into the deepest green velvet inside I-285.

Candler Park, where we live, isn't exactly the garden spot of Atlanta. We're a working-class kind of place, not country-clubby old money like Ansley Park, nor expensively remodeled historically significant Victorian yupnests like you have in Inman Park, just a mile west.

The only really significant thing about Candler Park is the fact that it's still here at all. There have been at least two attempts to build highways through the neighborhood, and at one time the state actually condemned and razed whole streets full of houses that looked like they might get in the way of some politician's idea of progress. Property values have waxed and waned over the past twenty years or so, but up until recently they've never jumped as dramatically as some of the trendier nearby areas, such as Virginia-Highland or Druid Hills.

Right now, there seems to be a renewed interest in our little pocket of heaven. You see more and more Volvos cruising slowly past the FOR SALE signs posted on Callan and Clifton and McLendon, women pushing babies in those pricey Italian jogger-strollers, and lots and lots of heavy-duty remodeling work going on. Houses that used to be rented by a half-dozen college students are now owned by Georgia Tech or Emory professors. In the last six months, we've lost two Korean-owned convenience stores and gained the same number of cappuccino cafés.

Of course, there's a downside to all the cheery news in Candler Park. The sudden transformation of crummy old boardinghouses and ramshackle rentals into $950-a-month townhouses, condos, and artists' lofts means that the most marginal of Candler Park citizens found themselves priced right out onto the streets.

My mother had been griping about the people she called "bums" all summer long. It appalled her to see somebody she considered able-bodied out on a street corner panhandling or, God forbid, sleeping in a doorway or picking through our garbage cans.

"We lived through the Depression, and my parents didn't have two nickels," she'd lecture me. "We ate a lot of rice and peanut butter, but we never asked anybody for anything. In those days, we didn't have food stamps or homeless shelters. People had pride!"

The day it all came to a head, I could hear my mother cursing to herself, rocking her chair back and forth so rapidly it was wearing a groove in the painted wooden floor.

When the disinfection process was complete, I coiled up the hose and stashed it on its reel by the faucet. Then I joined Edna on the porch. "You want a beer?" I certainly intended to have one for myself.

"What I want," she said, planting both feet in front of her to put the brakes on the rocker, "is a rocket launcher." Her eyes had that look. It was war.

2

"Look like it's really gonna blow this time," Baby said, pointing out the kitchen window at a sky the color of cheap new brass. "That be a for-real storm this time. See them clouds? Them's tornado clouds."

It was the last Friday of October, Halloween, and the weather was suitably scary. Summer had lingered through August and September, and even now, with November on its way, the air was relentlessly hot and sticky, so close you couldn't get your breath. Tornadoes had been ripping eastward out of Texas and Alabama all week long, bright blue skies alternating with ominous plum-colored thunderclouds. In short, the weather was as unpredictable as it always is this time of year in Atlanta.

I can remember one year when I was in college, Halloween was so warm I went to a toga party barefoot, dressed in my bikini top and a bedsheet. Edna still tells about the year I was six and there were snow flurries on Halloween. I refused to trick-or-treat with the other kids because I didn't want to spoil my Cinderella costume by wearing my ugly brown winter coat over it.

Sister went to the window and stood beside Baby, shouldering her out of the way. She squeezed her eyes shut and cocked her head toward where the wind rattled and snapped the glass in the old windowpanes. Then she pressed long bony fingertips to the glass and bobbled her head back and forth, like a human divining rod.

After a minute, she stepped away from the window. "No, ma'am," she said firmly. "You wrong, Baby Easterbrooks. That television weatherman fooled you again. That out there ain't no tornado. Little bitty old thunderstorm is all that is."

Neva Jean went to the refrigerator, reached in, and got a can of Mountain Dew. She popped the top, took a long swig, and then dabbed at her lips with the hem of her pink work smock. "Sister's right. It's a well-known fact that tornadoes never hit big cities like Atlanta. Swannelle was tellin' me about it this morning. It's like the really bad tornadoes get stopped over there in Carrollton or up in Cedartown before they can get to Atlanta. All them mobile homes just naturally attract tornadoes, and the skyscrapers downtown just naturally deflect 'em."

"I never heard that before," Ruby said, clutching her purse to her lap. Ruby always clutches her purse when she's nervous. She was waiting for a ride, anxious to be home but unwilling to venture out into the queer weather brewing outside our kitchen window. It had begun to rain an hour ago, hard slanting rain that stopped as suddenly as it started.

"I've been through at least one tornado in Atlanta," Ruby said. "You remember that last time a really big one came here, Edna?"

"Oh yes," Edna said. "That storm blew right through the Governor's Mansion and knocked it flat."

"People were killed," Ruby said, her voice solemn. "It was terrible. Our pastor's wife had her baby blown right out of her arms. Oh, mercy."

I went over and turned down the volume on the portable television we'd brought into the kitchen. The weather forecasters were starting to get on all our nerves with their non-stop predictions of Old Testament–type storms.

It was Friday afternoon, one o'clock, not even close to quitting time, but the National Weather Service had posted a tornado watch at noon, so I'd called all our personnel at their Friday afternoon jobs and told them to knock off early.

We used to call the employees at The House Mouse, our cleaning service, "the girls." We still do, when we forget, but since we hired our first man in September, we'd been trying to mend our ways. Cheezer, the new "boy," as the girls called him, was still out on a job. I'd beeped him an hour ago, but he hadn't called back. That was Cheezer. He didn't own a phone, and he lived out of his vehicle, an old U.S. Postal Service truck he'd bought at a government auction. He kept the mail truck parked behind an Egyptian Orthodox church not far from our house.

We're small, but we get the job done. Edna and I run the business out of our kitchen, and if somebody can't get to a job, we step in and do it ourselves.

"What do you think?" Edna asked. She was as antsy about the weather as I was, drumming her fingers, shuffling and reshuffling the deck of cards she keeps on the table for her nonstop hands of solitaire. "Think we better send everybody on home?"

"I'll run Ruby home," I said. "Neva Jean, would you give Baby and Sister a ride?"

"Sure," Neva Jean agreed. "Y'all mind making a couple stops? I gotta pick up stuff for the big party tonight."

The Easterbrooks sisters had finally, reluctantly given up

driving. Sister has been legally blind since I've known her, and Baby's hearing is faint at best. The only age they'd ever give was "old enough to know better." They live in a senior citizens' high-rise in Midtown, and cleaning a couple houses a week for us keeps them in lottery tickets and out of trouble. The only effect age seems to have on them is that they seem to shrink a little more every year. One day, I swear, they'll be small enough to ride around in my hip pocket.

Sister put on a bright yellow rain slicker and jammed a black knit cap onto her head. The oversized cap's brim rested on top of her Coke-bottle-thick glasses. The slicker's hem touched the floor, and its sleeves reached almost to her knees. Baby got both their pocketbooks and took Sister by the elbow, heading her toward the kitchen door.

"Where we going?" Baby asked. "You say something about a party? Me and Sister going to a Halloween party at the center tonight. Fuzzy dice, that's what we gonna be. Got black dancing girl tights and everything."

Sister pursed her mouth and tried to look disapproving. "Miss Thing there has to show off her legs for all the men," she said. "Got to show her behind to the world."

Neva Jean put an arm around Sister's shoulder and gently pulled the rain slicker off Sister's bony shoulders, replacing it with the moth-eaten red and black high school letter sweater Sister had worn to work in the morning.

"This here raincoat's too big for you, Miss Sister. See if this nice sweater doesn't fit a little better. See there?" She patted Sister's shoulder and put on her own rain slicker.

"Okay. We gotta stop at the grocery store so I can pick up some chips and dip, and then we gotta go to the package store."

"Hard liquor?" Edna raised her eyebrows. "That must be some party you're going to tonight. What are you going as?"

Neva Jean giggled and put a hand to her hair, which she

was currently wearing in a strawberry-blond Doris Day flip complete with bangs and a two-inch tease on top.

"I'm gonna be Raggedy Ann and Swannelle's gonna be Raggedy Andy. I've got the red yarn wigs and the outfits and everything. You should see the cute little short britches and striped stockings and Mary Janes I got for Swannelle. That's why I need the liquor. I figure it'll take about a quart of Jim Beam to get him into the outfit, and another pint to get him out of the truck and into the Moose Lodge."

Cheezer's truck came puttering up the driveway just as I was getting ready to back out in my van. It made for a colorful sight, his rusting lime green mail truck and my putrid-pink Chevy van. Psychedelic, almost.

Ruby beamed when he came around and poked his head in the car window. She's partial to boys anyway, having raised five of her sister's sons.

"Cheezer, where have you been?" she scolded. "There's a big storm coming on, and we were all worried about you. They're saying on TV it might come up a tornado."

He squinted up at the sky, which was still that weak yellow. "Tornado? For real?"

"That's why I beeped you," I said. "Don't you listen to the radio?"

He pointed to the portable CD player and headset on the seat beside him. "I listen to my tunes. Radio sucks, Callahan. Everybody knows that."

Now I was losing patience. "I gave you the beeper so you could keep in touch with us, Cheezer. We've been over this before. You're supposed to call me back after I beep you."

He dropped his eyes to his ground, hung his head, and sagged his shoulders. I felt like I'd kicked a sick puppy.

"I'm sorry," he said, his voice low. "I was in a groove, you know? This new house I was doing, the lady dentist over in Dunwoody? The kitchen's the size of a football field. It's awesome. And it's all white. I mean everything. I was trying out this new stuff I mixed up, it's a whitener, but no bleach. I meant to stop and call you, but once I got into it, I guess I lost track of the time."

How do you yell at somebody for being totally dedicated to his work? Especially somebody who looks like Cheezer? With his shoulder-length tangle of light brown curls, big dopey eyes, and wispy little goatee, he reminds me of a cocker spaniel. He was only twenty-one, just out of Georgia Tech with a degree in chemical engineering, when he answered my classified ad and all my prayers back in August.

"Never mind," I told him. "Just call next time, okay?"

He shrugged. "That's cool. Anyway, it's Halloween, right? You going to the Yacht Club tonight?"

"Mac is supposed to get back into town about four, and we were going to get some dinner before we headed over there. Guess I'll wait and see what happens with this tornado watch."

Cheezer pushed a stray curl out of his eyes. "Come on, Callahan. It's the biggest party night of the year. Wait till you see my costume. I been working on it all week."

"Well, now, you all need to just stay inside and be safe tonight," Ruby fussed. "No need to be out in the streets all hours of the night. Halloween. Huh! Devil night, I call it."

Cheezer gave me a broad conspiratorial wink. Ruby is deeply religious, doesn't approve of drinking, cursing, or rock 'n' roll. Even if there hadn't been a tornado watch, she wouldn't have wanted us out partying.

"Don't worry about us, Ruby," Cheezer said. "If the wind starts to pick up tonight and we see somebody dressed as the Wicked Witch of the West, we'll just click the ruby slippers and head for home."

"We need to head for home right now," Ruby said meaningfully.

I can take a hint. "Maybe I'll see you at the Yacht Club," I told Cheezer, starting the van up again. "Who should I look for?"

"It's a surprise," he said, waving good-bye to Ruby.

3

I took the longest, hottest shower I could stand, working on the old steambath theory that it would cause me to shed a couple of pounds before I had to get into my Halloween costume.

The long black wig hung down to my waist, the bangs brushing my eyebrows. I went a little crazy with the makeup: thick Cleopatra-like ribbons of eyeliner, shiny white metallic eye shadow, half-inch fake eyelashes, frosty pink lipstick. The effect was satisfyingly ghoulish.

But the bell bottoms were much tighter than I had anticipated. I could get them up over my hips, and the zipper zipped, but when I went to snap the waistband, which actually rode down a couple inches south of my belly button, my eyes bulged in an unattractive way.

"*This* ain't right," I muttered, grabbing a bottle of baby powder off the dresser. I sprinkled powder all over my abdomen, hips, and thighs, then lay down on my bed and began pulling the pants up again, knees bent, weight on my shoulders, my butt pushed up in the air.

"Jesus, Mary, Joseph, and all the saints."

Edna was standing in the bedroom door, her face etched with shock.

"What are you supposed to be? The bride of Frankenstein?"

I sucked in hard and snapped, then slid off the bed to survey myself in the mirror. Not bad, if I pulled my fringed buckskin jacket far enough down over my hips. The suede platform-heeled boots gave me another three inches of height, and with the right amount of blusher, I thought I looked appropriately hollow-cheeked.

"I'm Cher," I said, doing a little spin to give her the full effect.

"Say who?" she asked.

"Cher," I repeated. "You know, of Sonny and Cher? 'I Got You, Babe?' 'Gypsies, Tramps and Thieves'? Mac is supposed to be Sonny. I've even got a wig and a fake droopy mustache for him." I showed her the fringed leather vest I'd picked up for him at the Junkman's Daughter, one of the vintage clothing boutiques in Little Five Points. "Think he'll wear it without a shirt underneath?"

"Not this time," Edna said. "He came while you were in the shower."

I dropped the vest on the floor. "He's not going."

"It's the tornado," Edna said. "The Civil Defense people called some metro-wide emergency preparedness meeting down in Clayton County. He said he didn't know what time he'd get done."

"Don't those assholes know it's Halloween?" I gave the leather vest a vicious kick.

Andrew McAuliffe may be the man in my life, but he's also second-in-command at the Atlanta Regional Commission, the planning organization for the thirteen-county metropolitan Atlanta area. Mac is a not-so-civil civil engineer by training, but he spends most of his life trying to get all the disparate city and county governments around Atlanta to work for the good of the region instead of their own narrow interests.

"He dropped off Maybelline and Rufus," Edna added. "He doesn't want Maybelline staying out at the cabin alone this close to the time the puppies are due, and of course Rufus let out a howl when he put her in the Blazer, so he went on and brought them both into town to stay here. Lucky us."

My bedroom door opened a little wider and Rufus and Maybelline, Mac's black Labs, sauntered in and dropped to their favorite place beside my bed. I knelt down and scratched the special place between Maybelline's ears, and she raised her head and gave my hand a genteel lick. Rufus pounded a tattoo on the rug with his tail, demanding equal-opportunity head scratching.

"Guess now I'll go as postdivorce Cher."

"Go? You're not really going out, are you? The wind's picked up again. It's not safe."

I put four or five strands of love beads around my neck, then added a silver Aquarius medallion for effect. "It's just the Yacht Club," I said. "I'll be less than a mile from home. Besides, they called off the tornado watch for Atlanta. It already missed us."

Edna crossed her arms over her chest and pooched out her lower lip. If I hung around here, we'd have another fight.

I didn't feel like fighting. I felt like dressing up and playing pretend. Good sense, hard work, levelheadedness, where had they gotten me? I was nearly forty, never married, living with my mother, dateless on the biggest party night of the year.

Screw that. Tonight I was not Julia Callahan Garrity, former cop, cleaning-business owner, private detective. Tonight I was a raven-haired, bell-bottomed, tattooed rock goddess with exceedingly bad taste in men.

I picked up my fringed leather purse, slung it over my

shoulder, and marched past my mother, listing ever so slightly in the three-inch platform heels. "Don't wait up," I told her.

The crowd at the Euclid Avenue Yacht Club spilled out onto the sidewalk and the street. Four or five people were perched astride gleaming Harley choppers on the sidewalk, while a couple dozen people sat on the curb or leaned up against the bar and its next-door neighbor, an adult toy store called YoYos.

Frisbees were sailing back and forth across Euclid over the bumper-to-bumper line of cars cruising the street, and I could hear hard-driving guitar licks pumping out the open doors of the Star Bar back up across the street.

Parking was nonexistent. Little Five Points is always rocking on weekends, but when Halloween falls on a Friday, things get really dicey. I circled the block, down Euclid, across Colquitt to North Highland and back down to Moreland twice before I found an open slot in the lot beside a health food supermarket.

As I walked past YoYos, the front door opened and a cardboard carton came sailing out onto the sidewalk. I had to jump to avoid being bowled over by it.

"Hey!" I said sharply. The carton was heavy and had grazed me on the shin. If I'd fallen down in those tight bell bottoms it would have taken a crane to get me upright. Two more boxes came flying out the door, landing on the sidewalk and spilling their contents everywhere.

I opened the door to YoYos and poked my head inside.

"Wuvvy?"

YoYos specialized in all kinds of toys for grown-ups: yoyos, of course, but Frisbees, kites, Hacky Sacks, Hula Hoops, and jump ropes were among the heaps of stuff thrown all over the store.

Wuvvy sat on the floor in the midst of the heaps, legs crossed Indian-style, staring up at the ceiling. A tear worked its way down each of her plump brown cheeks. She brushed at the tears and at the tangled gray mass of hair that kept falling in her face.

She blinked when she saw me standing there, then picked up a sleek black plastic disc off the nearest stack, holding it out toward me.

"Callahan. Want a Frisbee?"

"No," I said, surprised. "No thanks. What's happening, Wuvvy? You almost knocked me down when you threw that box outside."

"Sorry." She held out the Frisbee again. "Go ahead. It's free. Take it. It's all free. Anything you want."

Her shoulders sagged. "A fuckin' free-for-all. That's what this is."

I looked around the dark, cavernous space. Once kites had hung from the high ceilings and Grateful Dead tunes played an endless loop on the store's sound system. Old rock concert posters from Atlanta landmarks like the Agora Ballroom and the Great Southeastern Music Hall had lined the walls behind displays of lava lamps and neon peace symbols, skateboards, and boomerangs.

The walls had been stripped now, and there was no music and the only light came from a single naked bulb hanging from the ceiling.

"Are you moving?"

A small brown-and-white dog trotted from a curtained-off area at the back of the store where I knew Wuvvy lived. He climbed nimbly over the stacks and deposited a battered red Frisbee in his mistress's lap.

"No, Brownie," Wuvvy told the dog. "No catch. Not right now." She brushed at another tear. "Yeah. I'm moving. Lost my lease. I'm moving on down the road."

What could I say? I didn't know Wuvvy well. I didn't even know if that was her real name. Mac and I sometimes saw her playing Frisbee with Brownie when we were walking Rufus and Maybelline in the park near my house. I knew she liked black Labs and cold beer. But she was a fixture in Little Five Points, and I was suddenly finding out how attached I was to the old order of life.

"Is business that bad?"

"Yeah," she said. "Shit happens. Usually to me. Landlord's kicking me out. Tonight's the last night."

"Where are you going?" I asked, wishing I'd never come inside the store.

Wuvvy put the dog down and struggled to her feet. "It's Halloween, Callahan. I'm gonna get fucked up." She grinned conspiratorially, reached in the breast pocket of her pink and purple tie-dyed T-shirt, and brought out a joint the size of a Cuban cigar. "Wanna get fucked up with Wuvvy? Last chance."

"No thanks," I said as she lit up. Dope gives me a headache. And besides, I was already wallowing in my own self-pity tonight. Wuvvy's idea of a party was too maudlin, even for my tastes.

"I'm going over to the Yacht Club," I said, gesturing down at my Cher outfit. "Costume contest. Come on over and I'll buy you a beer."

She took a long hit off the joint, pursed her lips, and sent a tendril of smoke curling toward the ceiling. "Maybe later."

I had my hand on the door, opened it, heard the jingle of the brass bells that announced customers, back when she had customers.

"Hey, Callahan?" She held Brownie out as an offering, the same way she'd done earlier with the Frisbee. "You like dogs?"

I thought about Rufus and Maybelline, at home on the rug

beside my bed. And I thought about the litter of black lab puppies that could come at any time.

"I've got a dog, Wuvvy," I said, as gently as I could.

She hugged the brown-and-white dog closely to her neck, kissed the top of his head. "Never mind. Brownie goes with me."

I'd just stepped outside YoYos and was looking up at the weirdly colored sky when somebody grabbed me around the waist from behind and squeezed tight.

"Ooh, Cher, baby, rock my world," he whispered in my ear, his breath hot and boozy.

I'd been mugged in L5P once, and what with that and my years as a cop, instinct took over. I pushed away, spun around, and had my knee drawn back for a wicked groin thrust when I realized I was about to assault a lady. Or something.

"Shit, Callahan, not in the nuts," a masculine voice said.

I took a good look. She was tall; maybe six-four, although the pale pink spike heels and the veiled pillbox hat probably added three or four inches to her stature. She wore a pale pink tweed Chanel-type suit, and her softly teased brunette hair came down to her shoulders. Black wraparound sunglasses obscured most of her face, but the startling thing was the blood—big hideous splatters of it all down the front of the suit.

"Bucky? Is that you?"

Bucky Deavers struck a pose. Of course. The five o'clock shadow on the jowls, the hairy forearms protruding from the too-short jacket sleeves. I will say that he looked pretty good as a woman. And he was managing a lot better in his heels than I was.

I first got to know Deavers back in the old days, when we were both detectives for the Atlanta Police Department, Bucky over in Vice, me on the burglary squad. Vice was perfect for Deavers—his favorite part of the job was dressing up as a pimp or a male hooker. I left seven years ago to start my own business as a private investigator. Bucky stuck it out, got transferred over to Homicide, and actually made sergeant last year.

"You get it?" he asked eagerly. "Who I am?"

"Fashion victim?" I asked. The skirt was *waaay* too tight, and with Bucky's olive skin tones, he should have avoided pastels like the plague.

"Come on," he urged, grabbing me by the arm to steer me toward the Yacht Club. "I want to make sure the judges get a good look before they give out the prizes for best costume."

"I still don't get who you're supposed to be," I said. "Give me a hint."

"Think early sixties," he said. "Motorcade. Dallas. The Texas School Book Depository."

Of course. "Jackie Kennedy," I said. "Deavers, you are one sick ticket."

"Thanks," he said. "Let's hope I'm sick enough for this crowd. First prize is five hundred bucks. I got plans for that money."

Deavers and I weren't alone on the sidewalk. Half a dozen people were standing around, picking through the boxes Wuvvy had thrown out.

"Vultures," I said under my breath.

Bucky shook his head. "Yeah. I heard. Wuvvy's closing shop. Today was her last day."

"She just told me," I said. "Doesn't seem right."

YoYos had been a L5P institution as long as I'd lived in the neighborhood. The shop had changed locations four or five times that I knew of, moving up and down Euclid and Moreland, but its stock always stayed the same; and with her tie-dyed wardrobe, long wiry gray hair, and year-round George Hamilton tan, Wuvvy was even more colorful than her merchandise, if that was possible.

"She wouldn't tell me where she's gonna go," I said.

Bucky pulled open the door of the Yacht Club, pushed me in front of him, and then squeezed the two of us into the jam-packed room. That's where our progress stopped. You couldn't move. The bar was five and six deep with people waiting for their drinks, all the tables were full, the music was so loud you couldn't hear yourself talk, and to add to the din, they were showing old black-and-white monster flicks with the volume turned all the way up on the wall-mounted televisions around the room.

Fortunately, Bucky Deavers doesn't faze easily. As a waitress with a trayful of Heinekens snaked her way past, Bucky grabbed two greenies off the tray and thrust a five-dollar bill at her. "Hey!" she protested. "These are for my table."

"Come back with two more in ten minutes," Bucky said, giving her a wink. "I'm a big tipper."

"You're a pain in the ass," she said, shoving past us.

I took a long drink of the Heineken. "What about Wuvvy?" I repeated. "Where's she moving?"

"Nobody knows. Not even her. I heard she was behind on her rent or something, and the building changed hands, so they evicted her. She just found out last week. Somebody said they're gonna put a microbrewery in the space."

"That sucks," I said loudly. "They can't just kick her out like that, can they? I mean, she's got a little apartment in the back there. She lives there with her dog, for crying out loud."

Bucky shrugged. "I guess they can if they want. The neighborhood's changing, Callahan. Going upscale. You can't fight progress. Besides, you living here, you ought to be glad. Not about Wuvvy, of course, but these new businesses, the cappuccino cafés, the new shops, the microbrewery, they're gonna raise property values for everybody. Get the scum cleaned out of here. The junkies, the winos, and the psychos, they got no business hanging around here."

"I happen to like this scum," I said stubbornly. "You want tasteful, go to Buckhead. This is Little Five Points, not Dunwoody."

"Drink your beer," Bucky said. "Wuvvy can take care of herself." He plucked two more bottles from the tray of another passing waitress and handed one to me.

Just then a blue bubble light hanging over the bar began flashing on and off, sirens started to blare, and Hap Rudabaugh, the Yacht Club's owner/bartender and unofficial mayor of the Republic of Little Five Points, climbed up on the bar and started waving his arms.

Hap was tall and lanky, with wire-rimmed glasses and a permanent stoop in his shoulders from bending over the bar and listening to his customer's troubles. He wore baggy shorts year-round, and was always doling out a couple bucks to whoever came up short. He had a "Semper Fi" tattoo on his left forearm; I'd heard he'd been a Marine in Vietnam.

"Listen up, everybody," he shouted, motioning for the waitresses to turn off the jukebox and the television.

"Good, they're gonna judge the contest," Bucky said. "Come on, we gotta get toward the front so the judges can get a good look at us."

He grabbed me by the fringed sleeve of my jacket and started tugging me toward the bar, using his spike heels on the instep of anybody who made the mistake of standing in our way. "Excuse me," Bucky said loudly. "Coming through. Make way for celebrities."

Hap was introducing the judges. Chief judge was himself, of course. His white-streaked ponytail fell down the back of a rusty black choir robe he'd thrown over his usual Hawaiian shirt and shorts, and he'd also donned a mask with a dangling rubber penis nose. Very magisterial. Miranda Varnedoe, his longtime girlfriend and business partner, was a judge too. Miranda was at least fifteen years younger than Hap, a hard worker who'd started as the Yacht Club's first waitress ten years ago and ended up as co-owner. For Halloween she'd rigged herself up as a Vegas showgirl's version of Satan in a tight red satin bustier, red fishnet stockings, a horned head-piece, and a long pointed tail that curled provocatively over the shoulder of her flowing cape.

The third judge was somebody I'd never seen before. He'd had the sense to ditch the jacket of his navy blue pinstriped business suit, roll up the sleeves of the white dress shirt, and loosen his tie, but he was still as out of place in the bar as a screen door in a submarine.

"This is our new neighbor Jackson Poole," Hap announced, throwing an arm around Poole's shoulder. Poole forced a smile and a brief wave. "Jackson here's starting up a microbrewery. Blind Possum Brewing," Hap continued. "And to show what a good neighbor he is, he's the one putting up the money for the costume contest tonight. Five hundred bucks. Not too shabby, huh?"

A huge prolonged cheer went up from the room, and Jackson started to look a little happier, throwing his own arm around Miranda, who was standing next to him on the battle-scarred oak bartop.

"What about Wuvvy?"

The voice came from the far back of the bar.

"You just gonna throw Wuvvy out into the street?"

Hap craned his neck and squinted his pale blue eyes, look-ing out into the darkness, trying to see who the speaker was. Jackson Poole dropped the arm that had been draped around Miranda.

"Yeah. What happens to me?"

It got very quiet in the bar. Then Wuvvy was pulling her-self up onto one of the rickety barstools. Backlit by the blue light atop the back bar, every frizzy strand of her steel gray hair seemed to jut straight out from her head. She stood there, swaying slightly, her red-rimmed eyes searching the crowd for a friendly face.

"What a long, strange trip," I murmured.

"Bad trip, if you ask me," Bucky said.

"Ask these fuckers why they kicked me out," Wuvvy cried, pointing a finger first at Hap and then at Poole. "Ask 'em where I'm supposed to go. Ask 'em why they turned on Wuvvy."

She swiveled on the barstool and put out a foot to try to climb onto the bar. But her foot slipped, and she would have fallen smack on her face, except that people were crowded together so tightly she merely landed on the shoulders of a group of guys who'd been standing near the front, jockeying for a good position in front of the judges. The guys were dressed in matching white shirts, red knit shorts, sneakers, and extravagant wigs. Their T-shirts proclaimed them to be the Black Widows. A cross-dressing girls' softball team.

"Sons of bitches," Wuvvy roared. "They sold me out. The yuppies are taking over, y'all. Ain't noplace in Little Five Points for a cosmic wanderer. It's the greedheads now. Yuppies and corporations and blind ambition—and greed-heads like Hap Rudabaugh."

Hap shook his head and laughed a little bit. "Okay, Wuvvy. You know we all love you. Doesn't everybody love Wuvvy?"

A loud cheer came up from the crowd. "We love you, Wuvvy!" a guy back by the dartboard screamed.

"They not only all love her, they've all fucked her," Bucky whispered in my ear.

"What's that supposed to mean?" I asked. Men are such gossips. Much more vicious than women. Especially when it comes to sexual innuendo. That's why I prefer hanging out with men.

"Just what it means," Bucky said. "You know Wuvvy. She'd just as soon screw as shake hands."

"All right," Hap was yelling. "To show Wuvvy we really do love her, the house is standing everybody to a round. How's that? Free drinks on the house!"

Miranda reached over and gave Wuvvy a big bear hug, but Wuvvy pulled away, stony-faced. Hap was whispering something in Wuvvy's ear then, but her expression didn't change.

"Fuck all of y'all," she shouted, then she slid down off the bar and melted into the crowd.

"What'll you have?" a waitress was at my elbow.

"A martini," Bucky said. "Stoli with a twist."

"Are you out of your mind?" I asked. "This is Little Five Points, not Buckhead."

"Wrong!" Bucky crowed. "Hap's got a martini menu going now. Cigars too. Miranda finally talked him into it. Pretty uptown, huh? If I win that prize tonight, I'll buy us a couple of Macanudos."

"That's a Stoli with a twist," the waitress repeated. "What about you?"

"Another greenie," I said gloomily. "I can't take all this change. What's next? Clean bathrooms? Valet parking?"

"Lighten up, will you?" Bucky said. "They're having people get up on the bar for the contest. Let's go."

"You go," I said, taking the beer the waitress was offering me. "I want to see if I can find Wuvvy."

"Waste of time," Bucky said.

A moment later he was parading up and down the bar, in between the cross-dressing girls' softball team, a woman got up in a black leotard with purple balloons pinned all over her (The Grapes of Wrath), and a guy dressed in a white disposable paper zip-front coverall, his face, hands, and neck swathed in white bandages, dark glasses covering his eyes. He kept telling the judges he was a Chernobyl survivor, urging them to write anti-nuclear messages on his jumpsuit.

Bucky was the crowd's obvious favorite. They cheered and

stomped every time he did one of his little Jackie moves. He would have won the money, too, if the biker bitch hadn't shown up at the last minute.

She came roaring up to the doorway of the Yacht Club on the back of a big black Harley Fatboy, sending spectators diving to get out of the way. The driver didn't get off, didn't remove his helmet or goggles. But his passenger did. She handed her helmet to the driver, shaking the long, oily blond hair over the shoulders of her black leather jacket. She strode over to the bar and pulled herself up onto it. She planted her black leather boots and with a single defiant gesture unzipped the jacket, writhing her shoulders and throwing her head back, so everybody could get a good look at the red and blue Harley-Davidson double eagle tattooed right across an amazingly ripe pair of bare breasts. They were Ds at the very least.

The place went nuts. Screams, catcalls, people reaching out to try to touch her. But there was more. She waited until the audience was in a fever pitch—the boobs were that good— and then she took a silver whistle that had been hanging on a lanyard on her neck and let out a long shrill *SHRREEEEE.*

That got everybody's attention.

With Hap and Jackson Poole standing there, their tongues hanging out, the biker bitch hooked the thumb of her left hand onto the waistband of the skin-tight blue jeans, dragging them down, way down below her belly button.

"Got something for you," the blonde announced. And with her right hand she unzipped the jeans, exposing what Bucky would later admit was her/his winning asset.

A collective gasp went through the audience. "That ain't real," a guy next to me hastened to tell his girlfriend.

A second later, the bitch had zipped up. She tossed her hair again and got right in Hap's face. "Gimme the money," she demanded, holding out one hand.

Hap bent over double laughing, then conferred with Jackson Poole, who nodded his agreement. Miranda pulled a stack of twenties from her cleavage and counted them out into the biker bitch's hand. Another cheer went up.

"Thanks," the bitch said. Then she reached up and pulled off the long blond wig.

"Cheezer?" I looked around for Bucky, who'd taken off his own wig and pillbox hat and thrown them to the floor in a fit of pique. "It's Cheezer!" I said.

"Big fucking deal." Bucky sulked, draining his martini. "Anybody can show off fake tits."

I would have tried out some words of condolence then, except I was too awed by the coup my employee had just pulled off. Besides, at that moment I saw Wuvvy slipping toward the bar's rear exit.

"Wuvvy," I called, "wait. I want to talk to you."

She shrugged, shook her head impatiently, but she didn't leave.

"What now?" Up close, I could see what a wreck Wuvvy was. Her eyes were dull and bloodshot, her skin dried and tanned to the consistency of an old boot, hands and nails grimy.

"Isn't there anything anybody can do?" I asked. "Take up a collection, something like that?"

"Like what?" she said dully. "I'm fucked. Even if they hadn't taken my store, everything's screwed up. It's like I can't get a break."

"What's been happening?"

She brushed a strand of hair out of her face. "Everything. Goddamn shoplifters. I'm losing a hundred dollars a month in pilferage. Break-ins. Three times in the past six months. Last time they just took a sledgehammer and knocked a hole in the wall. Cleaned me out, tore the shit out of my apartment, stole my CD player and microwave oven. Hell, I had a load of stuff stolen right off the UPS truck last month. My best suppliers, they cut off my credit. I got no stock to sell."

"Did you talk to the cops about the crime problem?"

"You're kiddin', right?"

"The Candler Park Commandos, I thought they'd gotten the cops to double manpower, start foot and bicycle patrols," I said. "I thought the merchants were a big part of that."

"Some people," she said sullenly, nodding her head in the direction of Hap and Miranda. "Not me. The cops fuckin' hate me. Especially that fuckhead Deavers. You know Deavers? Hangs around here all the time? Him and his cop buddies claim I'm selling drug paraphernalia. Just because I stock Grateful Dead shit and rolling papers. Had a uniformed cop standing around outside for a week, stopping everybody who came out of here, asking them about drugs and shit. It's harassment, but I can't do dick about it."

"Bucky Deavers has been harassing you?"

I found that hard to believe. Bucky worked in Homicide, not Vice. Why would he be bothering somebody like Wuvvy? Although, come to think of it, I'd wondered about the racks of rolling papers and bongs and pipes YoYos sold. Wuvvy kept the stuff in plain view on a glass counter near the door. Other shops in L5P sold much more blatant merchandise geared toward drug use, but then they were head shops, where you expected to find that kind of stuff.

"Fuckin' pigs," Wuvvy said. Her eyes were half shut, she was slurring her words, and she swayed as she talked. She was wrecked.

"You'll probably find another space pretty quickly," I said, trying to sound upbeat. "What about the place up the block, where they sold crystals and incense? I saw they've shut down."

"You know what kind of rent they want? Fifty dollars a square foot. Nobody in L5P can afford that kind of rent.

Nobody except Hap, maybe. And dear old Miranda. Fuckin'
greedheads."

Bedlam broke out again. It sounded like a jet engine had
landed right on Euclid Avenue. The real source of the problem was that Cheezer and his escort had wheeled the Harley
into the middle of the room and were busy revving the
engine to the delighted screams of the captive audience.

I turned around to watch the show. When I turned back,
Wuvvy was slipping out the back door. A woman I hadn't
noticed before was right behind her. She hesitated, looked
around, and then went out. Another refugee from the
Buckhead fern bar scene, probably. She had carefully coiffed,
light brown hair, a well-cut red business suit, heels, and
chunky gold earrings that matched her thick gold necklace.
A lawyer, I thought, or maybe an accountant.

4

By the time I caught up with Bucky at the bar, the crowd had thinned out considerably. The amateurs had gone home to count their candy; now it was just us professional night-crawlers. Bucky was snout-deep in what I estimated was his fourth martini. His short blond hair was matted to his head from the discarded wig, his lipstick was smeared, and he was puffing away on a thick black cigar. He looked more like Aristotle Onassis than Jackie Kennedy.

Bucky was immersed in discussion with one of the members of the cross-dressing women's softball team. "Call that a costume?" Bucky raged, glancing in Cheezer's direction. "That ain't a costume. That's perversion."

The softball player nodded vigorously, absentmindedly shifting the fake breasts under his tight white jersey.

I ordered myself a Heineken and squeezed into a space next to them. Bucky raised his martini glass in acknowledgment. "You know Callahan?" he asked the softball player. "She's s'posed to be Cher. She didn't win shit, either."

"Hi," I said, extending my hand.

"I'm Chuck," he said, taking my hand in his. "I like your jacket."

"Thanks," I said, eyeing his costume. "I was just wondering about the boobs, Chuck. They look pretty good. How'd you work out the nipples?"

"Yeah, how'd you do that?" Bucky demanded.

Chuck looked down at his chest like he'd forgotten about his newfound cleavage. "Oh yeah." He laughed. "That was my wife's idea. I used socks with golf tees. Pretty good, huh? Except the adhesive tape itches like crazy."

Bucky wasn't listening. He was watching somebody at the back of the room. "Look what the cat dragged back in," he said.

It was Wuvvy, making her way toward us, a swagger in her walk, a big grin pasted on her face.

Miranda and Hap had been standing at the back bar, their heads together, talking intently. They saw Wuvvy at about the same time I did.

"She's blitzed," I heard Miranda say. She started toward the other end of the bar. But Wuvvy intercepted her, catching her by the arm. "Where you goin', devil lady? The party's just startin'."

Miranda shook her off. "Go home, Wuvvy. You're drunk."

"Damn straight," Wuvvy said. She pulled a crumpled piece of paper from the pocket of her jeans and waved it under Miranda's nose.

"See this? It's a check. A check for three months' rent. And there's more where that came from. Where's that asshole Poole? Tell him his deal's off. Wuvvy ain't goin' nowhere."

"Tell him yourself," Miranda said. Then she twitched off in a swirl of red satin.

Hap stood behind the beer pulls watching, his arms crossed over his chest, his face expressionless.

Wuvvy lurched over to where I was standing. "Hap!" she shouted, right in my ear. "Gimme a beer. Didya hear? I'm not moving after all!"

"That's good, Wuv," Hap said. "Where'd you get the money?"

Wuvvy looked down at the check, frowned, then stuffed it back in her jeans. "None of your goddamn business, Hap Rudabaugh. Just you get me a beer. And tell that Poole I wanna see him."

Hap looked from me to Bucky to Wuvvy and he shrugged. "Sorry, Wuvvy. Poole left fifteen minutes ago. I think he was meeting some work crews next door."

"Son of a bitch," Wuvvy roared.

She hurried off toward the front door.

"Hey, Hap!"

One of the bartenders was down at the end of the bar, pointing up at the wall-mounted television, which somebody had tuned in to the weather.

The guy on Channel 3 was hopping up and down, pointing at the Doppler radar map, which looked like it had a case of glowing green measles.

"They're saying the tornado's coming this way, Hap," the girl called out. "No shit. A real tornado."

Hap hurried down to the opposite end of the bar and turned that television to Channel 6. He turned on the volume as high as it would go.

The Channel 6 weather guy had on a yellow rain slicker and was standing outside somewhere, hanging on to his yellow rain hat to keep it from blowing off in the sideways wind and rain.

"I'm live from East Point," he shouted into the camera. "A funnel cloud touched down here ten minutes ago, demolishing the East Point Pentecostal Church of God, injuring thirty teenagers who were attending a Halloween party here tonight. National Weather Service tracking devices report the storm system is moving north, packing heavy rain, golf-ball-sized hail, and winds of up to eighty miles an hour."

Hap motioned for somebody to turn off the sound system. Then he climbed back up on the bar and turned the flashing blue light and sirens on again.

"Okay, everybody," he yelled. "Party's over. There's a tornado heading this way. We're closed. Right now."

Bucky tossed back the last of his martini. "Screw that. Let's go to Manuel's."

"Not me. I'm gone," I said. Even rock goddesses know when the party's over.

Edna met me in the driveway, flashlight in hand.

The wind was whistling Dixie now, bits of leaves and tree branches whipping past. She had to shout to make herself heard. "I was just coming to get you. That tornado's headed right this way."

"I know," I hollered, trying to herd her back toward the house. "I'm sorry I made you worry."

"You been making me worry since you were in my womb," she said, keeping one hand each on Rufus and Maybelline's collars. The dogs were whining, pawing at the front door as we tried to back them away and close it.

"They've been like this since the wind picked up again," Edna said. "Not Maybelline so much, but Rufus has been whimpering and pacing till I think he'll wear a track in the floor."

I leaned down and took Rufus's muzzle between my hands. "You don't like storms, do you, boy?" His whole body was trembling.

For once, he didn't wag his tail in pleasure at being petted.

"I made some coffee and a pot of soup," Edna said, heading toward the kitchen. "Locked the garage up as good as I could.

And there's water and lanterns and stuff down in the basement, just in case."

The mention of the basement made me shudder. Ours is unfinished, with earthen walls and floors. My private idea of hell has nothing to do with fire and brimstone and everything to do with mildew and spiders and the kind of damp cold that invades your bones and never goes away.

When I'd gotten out of my Cher outfit and into some jeans and a sweatshirt, I joined my mother in the kitchen. She had the television on the Weather Channel, and the radar was showing a wall of showers and high winds headed like an arrow straight at the heart of Atlanta.

"So much for Swannelle's skyscraper theory," I said, sipping the coffee Edna handed me.

"Listen to that," Edna said.

The wind worried at our little wood-frame bungalow like a loose tooth. The glass in the windowpanes rattled, and we could hear the muffled *plink-plink* of sticks and pine cones hitting the side of the house.

Lightning cracked once, twice, very close, maybe a block away. Rufus whined and tried to burrow under the kitchen table.

BOOM! The kitchen was flooded with a dazzling silver light. The lights flickered off. Outside, we heard a slow, sickening splitting, then a terrific crash. The whole house shook. Then it was quiet again.

Edna's voice was shaky. "That was the oak tree out front. Had to be."

"Give me the lantern and I'll go see," I said.

"We'll both go see."

The living room was shrouded in dark. The streetlights were out. I pressed my face to the glass and saw nothing. Edna held the lantern up to the rain-spattered window. Leaves pressed against the glass. I ran to the front door and opened it and a shower of leaves blew right into my face. I could make out more branches, and the debris from the porch roof, and a dark solid mass that had to be the trunk of the old oak, laying smack across the porch.

"Holy shit," I said.

Edna came and stood beside me. A yellow light glimmered and sparked near the edge of the yard.

"Power line's down," she said, closing the door. "And if it's down, the phone line is too."

She picked up the lantern and sighed the sigh of a born martyr. "All right. Let's go. I put Kevin's old transistor radio and a stack of blankets down in the basement. We can listen to the weather report down there."

"You go right ahead," I told her. "Take the dogs down there with you. I'll ride it out up here."

"What if another tree falls on the house?" she demanded. "It's out of the question. I'm your mother and I forbid it. You can't stay up here alone during a tornado."

"I won't be alone," I said, opening the door of the small mahogany cabinet beside the sofa. "It'll be me and my friend Jack."

"Jack who?" she said suspiciously.

I held the bottle aloft. It still had a shiny gold Christmas ribbon wrapped around the neck. Present from a satisfied client. "Jack Daniel's."

Hunkered down in the den in a pile of blankets and pillows, we played double solitaire and drank bourbon until the hearts and spades and diamonds and clubs all began to look alike. We turned the transistor radio up loud, to drown out the whine of the wind, and sometime after midnight we both drifted off to sleep.

I felt the thud in my sleep, thought at first that I was still dreaming about the storm. But Rufus wasn't dreaming. He went into a frenzy, tearing around the room, knocking into furniture, barking and whining.

Edna's eyelids fluttered. "What?"

"Another tree, maybe. From the back of the house."

"That's what I was afraid of." Edna sank back down into the sofa cushions. "We'll check it in the morning." She was asleep as soon as her head hit the pillows.

I turned the radio off and went to the window and stared out at nothingness. The wind and rain seemed to have slacked off. So what was the thump?

I grabbed the lantern and went to the kitchen door with Rufus right on my heels. I opened the back door and a blast of frigid air slapped me right in the kisser. When had it gotten so cold? I could see my breath coming in little white puffs. I turned to the coat rack beside the door to get a jacket, and in that moment, Rufus shot past me out into the dark.

"Rufus!" I hollered, shoving my arms into the sleeves of the black leather bomber jacket. I could hear him barking at something in the front yard.

"Stupid dog."

The backyard looked like it had been clear-cut. At least four pine trees lay on their sides, along with too many dogwoods, crape myrtles, and smaller shrubs to count. I held the lantern in front of my face and saw that the thud had come from the old apple tree on the side of the garage. Its new resting place was on the garage roof.

There was no time to survey the rest of the damage. Rufus was still barking, but the barking was growing distant. He was off and running.

And so was I. The black Lab was Mac's oldest and best friend. Live power lines and broken glass were everywhere, and Rufus was bad spooked.

My first thought was to take the van to look for him. But it had a new hood ornament: a three-foot-thick tree branch draped across it. The Mousemobile windshield was shattered, the hood crumpled like a cigarette pack. Edna's big Buick was blanketed in pine needles and leaves but was otherwise unharmed. Unfortunately, I had her blocked in in the driveway.

"Stupid dog." I trotted past the van into the street, gingerly dodging the sparking power line. With relief, I saw that Mr. Byerly had managed to dodge the bullet. His collard patch had probably been blown all to hell, but even in the inky darkness I could see that the silhouette of his house appeared to be untouched by the storm.

I stood in the tree-strewn street and cupped my hands to my mouth. "Rufus! Come back!"

His barks were growing more distant, and now other dogs were joining in. Rufus could have been hot on the scent of a terrified possum or a stray cat or a chihuahua in heat. It didn't matter. Whatever that hound from hell was chasing was headed up the street toward McClendon. And I was right behind him.

My arm ached from holding the lantern out in front of me, my hands and arms and legs were scratched and bleeding from climbing over what seemed like an eternal Black Forest of downed trees, and I was hoarse from calling for Rufus.

Still, I trudged onward. Before I knew it, I'd walked to Little Five Points. The lights were off there too, but the going was easier, since there weren't that many trees to begin with in the business district. The sky was clearer now, but it was the new moon, and only the distant glimmer of a handful of stars dimpled the deep purple horizon.

I made the turn onto Euclid Avenue, still holding the lantern as a navigational guide. Maybe Hap or Miranda had stayed to look after the Yacht Club. Maybe they'd give me a Diet Coke or just some ice cubes to soothe my blistered throat. Maybe they'd drive me home.

Something wet brushed against my cheek. I swallowed a scream, dropped the lantern, and struck out at it with both hands. I heard the thing bounce against the sidewalk. I knelt down and picked it up and dropped it just as quickly, wiping my hands on the seat of my jeans. It was a filthy black high-top sneaker. I glanced up. The power lines crossing Euclid sagged deeply, only six or seven feet above the street. Dozens and dozens of pairs of sneakers dangled from the thick black lines, dripping rainwater like a busted gutter. It was some kind of L5P tradition, flinging old sneakers over the power lines.

I wiped rain off my face and kept walking toward the Yacht Club.

Orange and black cardboard cutouts of witches and black cats and pumpkins had been taped all across the front windows of the bar, and sodden crepe paper streamers hung limply from the roof overhang. Halloween seemed like something that had happened a long time ago. Trick or treat, y'all.

I pulled hard on the door, but it didn't budge. Locked. I banged on the door. "Hap? Miranda? Anybody?"

I pressed my face to the door. The only light came from the glowing red EXIT sign at the back of the room. Maybe Hap was in the office and couldn't hear me. The back door was worth a try.

The mercury was still dropping. I pulled up the collar of my jacket and shoved my hands in my pockets to keep them warm. Not even gale-force winds and torrential rains could wash away the stench that lingered in the alleys behind the bars and shops of L5P. The bouquet was unmistakable: rancid grease, stale beer, urine, and rot.

The cleaning lady in me wondered how many gallons of full-strength Clorox it would take to flush the place out, the ex-cop hoped nobody was lurking in that evil heart of darkness.

I had to step over drifts of garbage from blown-over trash cans and around the cans themselves, willing myself not to look too closely at what I was walking on.

The rear entrance to the Yacht Club was a battered fire door with an impressive-looking lock. Stenciled on the door were the words EAYC. NO SOLICITATIONS. NO DELIVERIES AFTER 5P.M. RING FOR ENTRY.

I leaned on the plastic doorbell, then remembered the power was off. "Come on," I muttered. "Open up. It's me. Callahan Garrity. Tracer of lost dogs."

It was no good. Rufus was gone, I was alone. I wasn't wearing a watch because I don't wear watches, but by my estimate it must have been around two A.M. The alley wasn't getting any lighter or any prettier.

YoYos' rear door was a flimsy wooden affair that had been crudely patched in a couple of places with bits of scrap lumber and silver duct tape. A pushover for anybody who wanted in bad enough. No wonder Wuvvy had been the target of so many burglaries. The door didn't even close properly. Cardboard boxes were thrown all around the alley near the back door.

I held the lantern close to one. It was splitting at the seams from the rain and it was full of old record albums. The one on top was a classic: Frank Zappa and the Mothers of Invention's immortal *Weasels Rip My Flesh.* The other boxes held clothes, mostly T-shirts and jeans, and some papers.

Wuvvy's stuff. All her earthly belongings, probably, left out in the rain. Had she been so stoned she'd abandoned everything? Even Frank Zappa?

"Wuvvy?"

I pulled at the door to YoYos and it swung open effortlessly.

"Wuvvy?"

Maybe she was inside, too wrecked from the booze and pot

to seek shelter from the storm. Maybe she'd been oblivious to the storm.

My voice echoed off the concrete floors. I pulled my jacket closer. It was colder inside than out. I swung the lantern around in an arc.

I was in a small walled-off back room. A dropped ceiling of water-stained acoustical tiles, a dingy pedestal sink and toilet in one corner, a homemade plywood platform for a deflated water bed in the other corner; this must have been Wuvvy's living quarters. Except for the bed, the place had been swept clean.

A curtain of red, yellow, and purple plastic beads hung in the doorway that led out of the apartment and into the store. Love beads. I'd had a curtain like that in my college dorm room. The beads clicked noisily against each other as I parted the curtain.

Now I really was time-traveling. A sweet ashy smell hung in the air. Incense and dope.

"Wuvvy?"

The room was packed with huge wooden crates, stacks of stainless steel vats and tubs, and lengths of rubber and steel pipes. No more toys. This was now the serious home of serious adults who planned to turn a profit from their efforts.

Just then I heard the click of a doorknob, then the silvery jingle of bells and the sound of the door closing. I swung the lantern that way, but the brewing equipment completely blocked my view of the front door. I tripped over something. It gave a hollow metal clang and rolled away, and I would have gone sprawling onto the floor if I hadn't grabbed hold of one of the packing crates.

After I'd steadied myself, I panned the lantern over the floor to see what I'd tripped over. It was a long piece of galvanized pipe. And it had come to rest against the only soft surface in the room.

"Christ!" I could see my own breath forming in the cold gray darkness. Which is more than you could say for the body of the man sprawled facedown on the floor. Even from where I stood I could tell this guy had breathed his last. Under his suit jacket, the collar of his starched white dress shirt was stained crimson. You don't see a lot of serious business suits in L5P. I'd seen this one only a few hours ago, right next door at the Euclid Avenue Yacht Club. Jackson Poole.

5

By the time I got out the door of YoYos and onto Euclid Avenue, nobody was in sight. The street was slick with standing rain, but the only thing reflected in the puddles were the dim stars overhead. I got that old eerie *Twilight Zone* sensation—like I was the last person left on earth after a nuclear holocaust.

I hiked over to the PitStop, the all-night convenience store across the street on Moreland. It was shuttered tight, the first time I'd ever seen the place closed. In addition to serving as a convenient community clearinghouse for beer, wine, junk food, and change for MARTA tokens, the PitStop has two pay phones out in the parking lot. Pay phones are a rare commodity in Little Five Points—Southern Bell takes it personally when their equipment is repeatedly ripped off.

I crossed my fingers when I picked up the receiver, and was rewarded for a sincere belief system by the comforting purr of a dial tone.

"Who ya gonna call?" I wondered aloud. Jackson Poole was, as the Munchkins said, really most sincerely dead. I hadn't gotten any closer to the body than I had to, but it didn't take a coroner to tell that the back of his skull had been bashed in. The right thing to do was to call 911 and report that a man had been killed. The cops would swarm the place, I'd be stuck for hours answering questions, Rufus would be left to wander the streets, and Edna, when she eventually slept off the bourbon, would think I'd been swallowed whole by the tornado.

I decided to call Bucky Deavers. What else are friends for?

"What?" Bucky sounded like he was speaking from his tomb.

"It's Callahan," I said. "You made it home okay?"

"You're calling me at three A.M. to see if I made curfew? Lose this number, Garrity."

"I wish I could," I said. "Bucky, listen. I'm at Little Five Points. I just found the body of Jackson Poole. His skull's been bashed in, and the body's at Wuvvy's store."

"Jackson Browne?" he groaned. "What the hell is he doing at Little Five Points? How does he know Wuvvy?"

"Not the rock 'n' roll guy, Jackson Browne. Jackson Poole. The guy who kicked Wuvvy out. He was at the Yacht Club last night, remember? The guy who's opening the micro-brewery where YoYos used to be?"

"You're serious," he said finally. "You think it's murder?"

"That's why I'm calling you," I said.

"Unbelievable," Bucky said. "I've got the king-hell of all hangovers. Couldn't you call 911 like a normal person? You know I don't go on until two o'clock tomorrow."

"Tomorrow is today," I said impatiently. "Besides, it's Wuvvy's store. Her stuff is scattered all around the place. You saw the big stink she made at the Yacht Club. What are the cops gonna think when they find Poole's body?"

"They'll think she killed the guy. All right. I'm on my way. Where'd you say you are?"

"I'm at the phone booth in the parking lot at the PitStop, over on Moreland," I said. "But it's closed. Everything's closed. There's a million trees down all over Candler Park and Inman Park, probably up on Ponce too. The power's off and it's freezing cold out here. I want to go home."

"If you're cold, go back over to YoYos to wait for me. But don't touch anything. I'm leaving right now."

He hung up before I could tell him I didn't keep company with corpses.

I hate waiting under the best of circumstances. Perched on the frame of a water bed in a dark unheated hovel with a dead man only a few feet away was the worst of circumstances. I didn't dare touch anything for fear of fouling up the crime scene more than I already had. So I sat and contemplated how hungry and thirsty and chilly I was.

Along with wishing for a Diet Coke and a cheeseburger and another pair of dry socks and maybe a blanket or two, I was also pining away for the comforting heft of my nine-millimeter Smith & Wesson. Time was when I kept it in the oatmeal box at home in my pantry. But that was before I found out the hard way how mean Atlanta's streets could really be. Now my gun is like my Visa card. I rarely leave home without it. Except this once.

Crime scenes be damned. I walked gingerly around the body of the late Jackson Poole, deliberately averting my eyes. I may be a former cop, but that doesn't make me any less twitchy about being alone with a corpse. I finally found a big ugly pipe wrench in the bottom of a toolbox in the front of the store, and propped it across my knees. If anybody except Bucky came in the store while I was there, I intended to become very handy.

*   *   *

Bucky brought some friends along. Two homicide detectives, the crime scene van, and three APD cruisers full of beat cops. Being Bucky, he also brought two dozen Krispy Kreme doughnuts and some coffee. I sat in the front seat of his big city-issue sedan scarfing donuts and swilling coffee with the heater turned up as high as it would go. Still, I could not get warm, and even after six cream-filled, chocolate-frosted fat grenades, I couldn't get full.

Bucky watched sympathetically. He knows how I get.

"You have no idea who was in the store when you got there?"

I chewed and thought. "Somebody quiet. If they hadn't had to open that door with the chimes on it, they could have slipped out without me even knowing they were there."

I shuddered. "Or bashed me over the head with the same piece of pipe they used on Jackson Poole."

"You know it was a piece of pipe?"

I shrugged. "I don't know it, no. Guess I just assumed."

"No sense of whether it was a man or a woman?"

"I didn't see anybody," I repeated. "The whole street was like a ghost town. It was like the storm sucked everybody down a sewer or something."

"What about Wuvvy?" Bucky asked. "When was the last time you saw her tonight?"

I'd been thinking about that. "I saw her after she came back in the bar and started mouthing off about how she'd gotten the money and wouldn't have to give up the store after all. I have no idea what time that was."

"You saw her leave the bar?" Bucky asked.

"Didn't you? She went out with a woman."

"What woman?" Bucky demanded.

"I never saw her before. She was white, probably middle-aged, conservatively dressed. Didn't look like Little Five Points material, that's for sure. I only saw her for an instant. Then she went out the back door with Wuvvy. I don't remember seeing her come back inside."

Bucky was scribbling away in his notebook. "Gimme a better description of the woman, Callahan."

I licked chocolate frosting off my fingers. "Mmm. Brown hair, sort of turned under, decent figure, medium height. Conservatively cut red business suit. Not knock-down gorgeous, but quietly attractive."

"Not the type you'd normally see with somebody like Wuvvy," he concluded.

"How do I know? It's not like I knew Wuvvy all that well. I knew her from YoYos, is all."

"Shit," I said, suddenly noticing the clock on the dashboard of the car. It was nearly five A.M.

"Can you give me a ride home?" I asked. "I'll answer all the questions you want later, but I gotta go now. My mother is probably awake by now and out of her mind with worry. Not to mention that Rufus took off last night, and I have no idea where he is right now."

"You lost your boyfriend's dog? In the middle of a tornado?"

"Just take me home, okay? I should have gone home after I found that body, but no, I had to be Miss Good Citizen and hang around and wait for you guys."

He got out of the car and went over to one of the detectives, who was watching while the crime-scene guys sprayed fingerprint goop all over the front door at YoYos.

"Can't wait to see the list of latents they lift off that door," Bucky said. "It'll be a who's who of Little Five Points lowlifes."

"Your print's probably on that door," I pointed out. "Mine too."

"There's exceptions to every rule," Bucky said.

As we pulled away from the curb I saw headlights in the rearview mirror. I turned around to see who the new arrival was. It was Hap's green army surplus jeep. He pulled the jeep up over the curb and onto the sidewalk, then went around to the passenger side and helped Miranda hop down. Their faces were pale, hair mussed like they'd been awakened from a sound sleep. Hap put an arm around Miranda's shoulder and scowled as the detective who'd been supervising the finger-printing strolled over to have a chat.

Hap caught sight of me in Bucky's car and gave a half-hearted wave.

"You called them down here in the middle of the night?" I gave Bucky a questioning look.

"You know the drill, Garrity," he said.

6

Rufus was lying across the kitchen doorstep when I got home, his muzzle on his paws, his big brown eyes accusing.

"Don't give me that look," I told him. "You're the one who ran away from home." He jumped up and planted a pair of muddy paws on my chest, then licked my chin.

"Okay," I told him. "I won't tell if you won't."

Edna must have had a bigger snootful of Jack Daniel's than I knew. She was still snoring blissfully away on the den sofa. Weren't mothers supposed to intuitively know when their children were in danger? Right now, mine didn't even know she had a child.

I stepped out of my filthy clothes, pulled on one of Mac's old football jerseys, and climbed into bed, surrounding myself with my biggest, squishiest pillows. I thought wistfully of how nice it would be to snuggle up to the warm curve of Mac's backside. And I said a little prayer that wherever Mac was, he was safe and warm—and sleeping alone.

I might have slept all day the next day. Instead, I was flung into consciousness by a high-pitched mechanical droning that seemed to echo off my bedroom walls. At first I thought I'd been dreaming of the dentist's office. Then it came. *AAAAHH-AAAHHH-AHHHH-BOOM!* The loud splinter of wood that followed seemed to come from right outside my window.

I jumped out of bed and ran over to the window. Three men in hard hats, work boots, and yellow rain slickers were attacking a gangly fallen pine with the biggest chainsaws I'd ever seen. Their slickers had writing on the back. Georgia Power. Wouldn't you know it? The one day the sons of bitches from the electric company choose to get efficient, they have to do it when I'm trying to sleep.

Edna came into the room and handed me a cup of coffee. "We've got sixteen trees down out there," she said, shaking her head.

I sipped the coffee. "How'd you manage coffee?"

"I've still got my old drip percolator from when I got married," she said proudly. "I knew there was a reason to keep that thing."

"Not bad," I admitted. "Thank God for gas stoves. Did the Georgia Power guys say anything about when we'll actually have electricity again?"

"They're just a tree crew," Edna said. "There's a bunch of linemen working up the street, but they couldn't tell me nothing. Phone's still out too. Haven't seen a Southern Bell truck."

She opened my closet door, got out my bathrobe, and tossed it onto the bed. "You got company. Bucky Deavers is here. He wouldn't tell me what he wants. Is he still single?"

"I know what he wants," I said. "And yes, he's single. You want me to set you up?"

"Smartass."

Bucky was sitting at the kitchen table, the sports section

spread out in front of him, drinking coffee and chatting on his little black flip-phone. He hung up as soon as I walked in. He was still wearing the clothes he'd been in at YoYos, not the Jackie Kennedy getup, but jeans and a Gold's Gym sweatshirt.

I spit on my finger and rubbed at a dark smudge under his eye. "You always wanna take your mascara off with cold cream before going to bed at night," I advised him. "Otherwise it makes your eyelashes fall out."

He pushed my hand away and started scrubbing at his face with a paper napkin. "Great. That means Major Mackey saw me with makeup. So much for any hopes of a promotion."

"It was your night off," I said. "What you do on your own time is none of his business."

Bucky made a face at me. We both knew Lloyd Mackey, the head of the Atlanta Police Department's criminal investigation division, thought everything his cops did, on or off duty, was his business.

"I thought you'd be interested," Bucky said. "They're doing the autopsy on Jackson Poole this morning, but the medical examiner already told me it looks like the cause of death was a blunt object blow to the skull. A no-brainer, you might say."

Edna poked her head around the kitchen doorway. "Anybody need anything?"

"You might as well come in here and listen instead of hanging around out there eavesdropping," I said. "I was going to tell you, but I didn't have time. Last night, after you went to sleep, Rufus ran off and I went out looking for him. I found a body instead. A guy named Jackson Poole. Nobody you know, but it was in YoYos, that little store right next door to the Yacht Club."

I looked at Bucky. "Has anybody talked to Wuvvy?"

"You mean Virginia Lee Mincey?"

"That's her real name? I never heard anybody call her anything but Wuvvy."

"Who's Wuvvy?" Edna demanded. "Is that the person who was killed?"

"No," I said patiently. "That's the woman who owns the store where I found the body. The dead guy's name was Jackson Poole. I never knew Wuvvy was really somebody named Virginia Lee."

"That's the name on the lease for the store," Bucky said. "We're still checking to see if that's her legal name. And no, we haven't talked to her."

"Virginia Lee," I repeated. "I never would have seen Wuvvy as a Virginia Lee. Such an old-fashioned name. What about Hap or Miranda? When did they last see Poole?"

Bucky shrugged. "They say he left right before they announced they were closing the Yacht Club. He wanted to go next door to his new property, make sure everything was secure, try to find some boards to put in the windows. Everything was crazy, they say they didn't even check on him before they left for home. Hap says they cleared everybody out around midnight, locked the place up, and headed for home. They live just around the corner on Elizabeth Street and they've got a lot of trees in the yard, so they were anxious to get home and try to board it up as best they could."

He opened a file folder and pushed some sheets of paper toward me. "I typed up your statement from my notes. You wanna read over that, see if you remember anything else?"

"All right," I said. Bucky's typing, spelling, and punctuation were all egregious, but his memory was close to flawless. He'd put it all down just the way I'd told it to him.

"This is all I know," I said, pushing the papers away. "What about the locks on the door at YoYos? Can you tell whether there was forced entry? Whoever slipped out that front door must have known it wasn't locked."

Bucky drained his coffee cup, then set it on the tabletop. "Both front and back doors had the hell beat out of them. But hey, she'd had multiple break-ins. The computers are all still down, but I talked to somebody over in Zone Five, he says he knows of at least three burglaries at YoYos in the past year."

"All of them unsolved," I guessed.

He nodded. "Neighborhood needs cleaning up."

"And now there's been a murder right around the corner from our house," Edna said. "I knew it would come to this. I'm just surprised it wasn't some old lady, murdered in her bed by one of these bums always wandering the street. Wait till the commandos hear about this."

"Ma," I protested. "They're not bums. They're homeless people."

The subject of homelessness was a touchy one for us. After the incident with the gardenia bush, Edna had spent the fall mobilizing her troops. She'd formed a group called the Candler Park Concerned Citizens' Organization, whose sole purpose was to keep the street people off our streets and out of our shrubbery.

It was a cause whose time had come. Besieged with what seemed like an endless stream of aggressively stoned, drunk, or psychotic homeless types, people in Atlanta who lived or worked where the homeless congregated had started to fight back.

In our neighborhood, the Candler Commandos, as the group quickly came to be called, was already a political force to be reckoned with.

In the fall, the Atlanta City Council had passed an anti-panhandler ordinance that made it a crime to panhandle, sleep, urinate, or defecate in a public place. Advocates for the poor called it a blatant attempt to criminalize poverty, but others said it was the only way to take back the city and make it livable for everybody.

In the meantime, Edna and her commandos called the cops whenever they spotted anybody in the neighborhood who even looked like he might want to take a leak outside.

"Someday you'll thank me for helping make this a safe place to live," Edna said, pushing away Rufus, who was trying to put his head in her lap.

"Someday you and your cronies will be ashamed of yourselves for putting people in jail just because they're poor," I countered.

"Here we go again," Edna said, throwing her hands in the air. "She's talking about Shirley," she told Bucky. "The crazy one with the filthy red hair and the rouged cheeks. She hangs out around Little Five Points Pharmacy."

"Last week, one of Edna's commandos called the cops on Shirley just because she spat on the sidewalk. I was coming out of the drugstore when they arrested her. They hauled her away kicking and screaming and cursing. Quite a show."

"I know Shirley," Bucky said. "Crazy old bag lady."

"Good riddance," Edna said smugly. "That woman's a damn nuisance. She stopped me and demanded that I give her a cigarette the other day, and when I said no, she called me an old bitch and spat on me. I could get a disease, for God's sake."

"She's mentally ill," I said sharply. "She needs help."

"She won't take any help," Edna retorted. "If she was hungry, she could go to the Methodist church up on Ponce de Leon and they'd feed her. If she wanted a place to sleep, there's a shelter. But the pharmacist in the drugstore said Shirley won't go. She just hangs around there because she doesn't want anybody telling her what to do. In the meantime, she shoplifts candy and cigarettes, sneaks into the bathrooms and makes a big stinky mess, and hangs around outside screaming and cursing, scaring off customers. What would you do if you owned that drugstore, Little Miss Bleeding Heart?"

"I wouldn't throw her in jail," I said. "Besides, I doubt that it was Shirley or any other homeless person who killed Jackson Poole."

"Bums," Bucky said decisively. "Winos, scumbags—a rose by any other name would stink just as bad. Your mother's right, Garrity. They're taking over this neighborhood. Ruining the place."

"See?" Edna said. She left off the I-told-you-so part. Fortunately for her.

I followed Bucky out to the front door, to try to get a word in private. "What about a motive, Bucky? What do you know about Jackson Poole? What was he doing before he decided to start a microbrewery in Little Five Points?"

"I know he's dead," Bucky said, holding up a finger on his left hand. "I know he had Wuvvy, I mean, Virginia Lee Mincey, evicted, not just from her business, but her home." He held up a second finger. "I know Virginia Lee Mincey had motive and opportunity, and I have witnesses who heard her make threats against him." Now he had three fingers raised. "And I know that nobody's seen Virginia Lee Mincey since about eleven P.M. last night."

He smirked. "Not bad for a white boy."

"Except that the last thing I heard Wuvvy say last night was that she'd gotten the money to pay her back rent," I pointed out. "She was waving a check around. Somebody had bailed her out."

"Or so she said," Bucky said. "Hap and Miranda didn't notice the woman you saw leaving with Wuvvy. Besides, it would have been too late. I talked to the leasing agent first thing this morning. Wuvvy was three months in arrears on her rent. They told her a month ago that somebody else had leased her space. No matter what, she had to get out. She might have acted like it was a big surprise, but the leasing agent says that was Wuvvy's little head game. Acting like she didn't know what was going on. Classic case of denial. Hell, she says Poole had contractors in and out of there for the past two weeks, getting bids on construction for the brewpub. She'd had a month to find a new place to live, but she just kept acting like it wouldn't happen. When it did, she flipped out. Picked up a pipe and killed the dude."

Bucky opened the front door. We both stared out at the tree that took up three-quarters of the doorway.

"I forgot about the tree," I said. It seemed bigger now than it had the night before.

"Denial," Bucky said. "Lot of it going around these days."

7

Bad storms flush out snakes, rodents, bugs, and disaster junkies. We had our share of them all after the Halloween tornado, but the disaster junkies were by far the biggest nuisance.

By noon Sunday, we'd chased away roofing contractors, tree trimmers, electricians, junk haulers, carpenters, and even a burglar alarm salesman. Once the city tree crews had cleared fallen trees from the streets, we were treated to a steady stream of cars cruising past the house, their occupants pointing fingers and even video cameras at our plight.

Edna and I saw them all, because we spent the whole weekend trying to clean up the mess the tornado had visited upon us. With old Mr. Byerly next door, we managed to drag most of the smaller branches and debris down to the curb, where it joined all the other piles of debris springing up along Oakdale. After one of the friendly "tree men" quoted us a price of $800 to chop up and remove the oak tree on the front porch and the one on the hood of my van, Edna decided to look up her family tree for help.

On Sunday afternoon, my brother Kevin and my sister
Maureen's husband, Steve, showed up with Kevin's chainsaw,
two six-packs of Old Milwaukee, and a portable radio only
slightly smaller than my van.

Steve spilled a gallon of gas on the front porch trying to
figure out how to get fuel into the chainsaw, while Kevin finished off two cans of beer just searching for the Falcons football game on the radio.

"I can't watch this," I told Edna, fleeing into the house.
Rufus loved all the excitement. Over the whine of the chainsaw, I could hear him outside, chasing around and around the
yard, barking happily at every car that passed by. Maybelline
had better sense. She hid under my bed. I went out in the
backyard for a while, making piles of brush, picking up shingles that had blown off the roof, and raking acres of leaves
that had swept in from Alabama, apparently. I tried to ignore
the mayhem taking place out front, telling myself that the
tree trimmers were family, after all, and they were doing us a
favor.

I'd gone into the house in search of Band-Aids for Steve,
who'd mistaken the tip of his pinkie for the branch of a dogwood, when the phone rang. The bleeding wasn't all that
bad, but Steve drives an ambulance for a living, which makes
him the equivalent of a neurosurgeon, in his own humble
opinion.

The phone's ringing was a welcome distraction. Finally, I
thought. The Southern Bell crews had been up and down the
street all day. We still didn't have any power, but at least we
had phones. Maybe I would be able to run my business come
Monday.

"Hello?" I was out of breath by the time I made it out of
the bathroom and into my bedroom and the nearest phone.

There was a long silence on the other end of the line.
Probably the phone company, testing out the repaired lines, I

thought. I was in the process of hanging up when I heard a voice.

"Don't hang up." It was a woman.

"I'm here," I said, putting the phone back to my ear.

"Callahan? Is this Callahan Garrity?"

"Yes," I said, ever cautious. Now that the phones were back in service, the aluminum-siding telemarketers wouldn't be far behind.

Outside, the chainsaws started up again. Steve must have started to clot. For him, this was an accomplishment. The woman's voice was faint; it sounded scratchy, sort of far off. "It's uumph," she said, swallowing the name. There was static on the line, and I could hear the muffled sounds of other people's conversations in the background.

"What's that?" I yelled. "You'll have to speak up. There's a lot of sawing going on around here."

"It's Wuvvy," she said, her voice only a little louder. "From YoYos."

"Where are you?" I asked bluntly.

"Nowhere," she said. "I mean, I'm around. That's all."

"Have the police talked to you? You heard about Jackson Poole, right? The police are wanting to talk to you, Wuvvy."

"I know he's dead," Wuvvy said. "At my place. The cops think I did it, right?"

"They want to talk to you," I said, trying to avoid the issue.

"I'm not talking to the pigs," Wuvvy said. "Look. I need a favor. Can you do me a favor, Callahan?"

"What kind of favor?"

"My stuff," she said mournfully. "All my stuff's over at the store. Everything. My albums, my clothes. All my Dead stuff, my Frisbees, shit, all my papers."

The word *dead* seemed to echo on the phone. "What dead stuff?"

"The Dead," she said, annoyed at my stupidity. "Grateful Dead. I've got T-shirts from every tour since the '67 Monterey Pop Festival. Except Watkins Glen. Then there's all my rock 'n' roll stuff. I got a poster from the first Atlanta Pop Festival. You remember that? 1969? Grand Funk Railroad played their first major concert right here in Atlanta."

"Uh, no," I said. "I was in junior high back then. I was more into the Monkees and the Archies. The Cowsills."

"Bubblegum," she said, her voice dripping contempt. "Hey. What about it? Think you can get my stuff for me?"

Talk about a space cadet. She was a suspect in a homicide and all she was worried about was some moldy old rock crap.

"A guy was murdered at your place Friday night, Wuvvy," I said. "The cops aren't going to let me come in there and take any of your stuff away. It's a crime scene. A homicide investigation. Besides, they want to talk to you."

"I didn't kill that fucker," she said. "Why can't people leave me alone?"

"You should probably get yourself a lawyer," I pointed out. "Then go talk to the cops. Talk to Bucky Deavers. He's the detective on the case. He's a good guy. Talk to him."

"I heard you're some kind of private eye," Wuvvy said. "I want to hire you. Get the police to leave me alone, okay?" Her voice had a pleading quality. "Tell Deavers I didn't do it. He's your friend. He'll believe you. Then you can get my stuff back for me."

"Callahan?" My idiot brother-in-law was standing in the hallway, his arm swathed, fingertip to elbow, in what looked like my best bath towel. "What about those Band-Aids? I'm gonna need a transfusion if you don't hurry up."

"I'm coming," I said, slamming my bedroom door in his face.

"Listen, Wuvvy," I said. "I gotta go. Call a lawyer and then call me back."

"So you'll do it, right? You'll get my stuff back? Tell the cops I didn't do it?" She still wasn't paying attention. She was still fixated on Grand Funk Railroad.

"Where are you?" I asked. "I need a phone number."

"I'll call you," she said, and she hung up.

"Hey, Callahan," Steve said, banging on my bedroom door. "You got some stuff that'll take blood out of carpet? I'm dripping here."

My mother invited Maureen and Steve and Kevin and his wife to come over for Sunday supper. Shortly before four, when they were all due back to eat, I decided it might be prudent to take a long walking tour of our tornado-stricken neighborhood. "Don't wait supper," I told Edna.

After I'd walked up to Ponce de Leon and back down to DeKalb Avenue to see the extent of the damage, I felt slightly guilty about my own fortune. Our house was still in one piece, but there were whole blocks of Candler Park with houses whose roofs or porches had been torn off. Huge old oaks had smashed onto cars, houses, and garages. I saw two concrete foundations that had been swept clean of their houses. The tornado had skipped to and fro like a mischievous kindergartner, wreaking havoc in no pattern I could discern.

"God," I found myself muttering. "We really did miss the big one."

After an hour of wandering and muttering, I realized I was headed in the direction of Little Five Points. If I went home now, I rationalized, Steve would be sitting in my favorite chair in the den, staring at professional wrestling on television, Kevin would be tanked out of his gourd on Old Milwaukee, and my sister and sister-in-law would be discussing the fine points of ovulation. And the dinner dishes would all still be stacked in the sink, waiting for me.

They could just wait a little longer.

The late afternoon light did a funny thing at Little Five Points. The amber sunlight burnished and softened the old storefronts, giving them a romantic Old World quality. If you overlooked the knots of skinheads hanging around in front of the bars, you could mistake L5P for a quaint little village, maybe in the South of France or Brussels or Tuscany someplace. Not that I've ever been to any of those places. But I've seen pictures.

The front door of YoYos was open, and two men were carrying out plastic garbage bins full of Sheetrock and wood lathe, loading them onto a flatbed truck that was pulled up on the sidewalk. The bed of the truck was piled high with construction debris, and the sounds of hammering and power saws echoed from inside the store. From the look of things, it would take more than a pesky little murder to stop the progress of Blind Possum Brewing.

"I knew you'd be back over here."

Deavers stepped out of the doorway, dodging around one of the garbage cans. He had plaster dust in his hair and a Polaroid camera hung from a strap around his neck.

"Just out for an evening stroll," I said. "How about you? Is this the APD's new crime-scene unit I've been reading about in the paper? What do you do, take the whole building apart and run it through the state crime lab?"

Deavers kicked at a chunk of concrete with the toe of a dusty cowboy boot and sent it spinning down the sidewalk. He didn't look happy.

"We had a warrant, got what we needed. Or what we think we need. The building's new owner has been ragging on us since yesterday to let his contractor back in. He called his friendly local city councilwoman this morning to complain that we were holding up construction on a valuable new addition to her district. Juanita Davis called the chief. The chief called Major Mackey, Major Mackey called me. We signed off two hours ago, and when I got down here to see if any loose ends needed tying up, these clowns were already in there, ripping out the walls."

"I'm confused," I said. "I thought the new owner was your homicide victim. Jackson Poole."

"Co-owner," Bucky said. "Blind Possum Brewing turns out to be an outfit out of Houston. They're putting these brewpubs in six different cities this year. Poole was owner-manager for this one."

"But not the money person," I said.

He shrugged. "He was living in a three-hundred-thousand-dollar condo overlooking Piedmont Park. Very nice. I'd say Mr. Poole was not hurting for money."

I popped my head inside the storefront. If the contractors had been on the job for only a couple of hours, they were the world's fastest workers. The walls inside had been stripped down to the old brick, and the water-stained acoustical-tile ceiling lay in a pile on the floor. A man in a dust mask and a hard hat looked up from a set of drawings he'd spread across a sheet of plywood nailed to some sawhorses.

"Wow," I said, inviting myself inside. The stacks of crates and pipes I'd seen Friday night had been shoved into a corner, and the wall separating the toy store from the living quarters had been demolished. It was all one big, high-ceilinged space now. The scarred brick walls were already begging for fern baskets and blackboard menus.

There was no sign of any of the previous tenant's pitiful rain-soaked cardboard cartons.

"What happened to all of Wuvvy's stuff?" I asked.

"Who wants to know?" Deavers has a very suspicious mind. It's what makes him such a good cop.

"Just wondering," I said, walking quickly toward the rear of the store.

The man in the hard hat frowned and flipped off his dust mask. "Detective, I thought you people were done in here. I got a construction site, and I can't have your people just wandering around getting in my sub's way."

"We're done," Bucky assured him. He caught me by the elbow, but I kept walking toward the back door, which had been propped open.

A huge Dumpster was parked outside in the alley. The local street people would be very pleased. It had a lid and a big window on the side. Four or five of them could happily take up residence in it.

"What are you doing, Garrity?" Bucky asked. "What are you looking for?"

"Nothing," I said. "I found a body here Friday night. I used to be a cop. I'm curious, that's all. Shop talk. Humor me, can't you?"

"You know where Wuvvy is," Bucky said flatly. "That's what this is about."

"I don't have any idea where Wuvvy is," I said. It was the truth.

"Don't get cute," Bucky said. "Wuvvy's a suspect in a homicide investigation. The base of Jackson Poole's skull was bashed in with something blunt. At least four blows, by the way the blood spatters look. This wasn't some little harmless shove or love tap, Callahan. The bitch meant business. She meant to kill him. I want her."

I let out a sigh and thought about my obligation to Wuvvy. She wasn't really a client. I hadn't agreed to do anything for her. Besides, I didn't really know anything.

"She called me about an hour ago," I admitted. "But she wouldn't say where she was. All she did was ask me to get her stuff back for her."

"You're working for her? You are nuts."

"I'm *not* working for her," I said. "She claims she didn't do it, you know. All she's worried about is getting her Grateful Dead shit back. Have you considered that maybe somebody else whacked Poole?"

"She did it," Bucky said grimly. "If she calls back, tell her to give me a call. I've got her shit down at headquarters, locked up tight in the evidence room. She wants it, she's gonna have to give me a statement. You tell her that."

8

Bucky stood in the alley and watched me walk away. I turned around and watched him watching me.

It was then that I noticed Hap's jeep, the one with the EAYC logo on the door, parked by the Yacht Club's back door.

I started walking back.

"What now?" he asked. "You're not going back inside Wuvvy's."

I could have argued with him. After all, the crime scene tape was down, and the new owners were in charge, not him.

Instead, I told him what was on my mind.

"This alley was completely empty when I found the body. So where was Jackson Poole's car? He didn't strike me as somebody who would have Rollerbladed over here from Midtown."

"No comment."

"Come on, Bucky," I said. "It's me, Callahan. Not the press."

Bucky looked around the alley. "He had a Lexus. Or rather, the company had one. It was leased to Blind Possum Brewing. We found it in the parking lot over at Sevananda."

"How'd you know it was his?" I asked. I was thinking about that expensive-looking suit Jackson Poole had been wearing Friday night. And about all the attention it would have drawn from the skinheads and bikers in the neighborhood.

"We're the cops," Bucky said. "That's what we do." He was getting testy, defensive.

"Was his wallet on him?" I asked. "Car keys? How about cash?"

"We didn't find a wallet," Bucky admitted. "So what? I'm not carrying a wallet right now." He knew what I was thinking.

"But your shield and ID are stuck in the visor of your city unit," I pointed out. "You still didn't tell me about the car keys. How'd you figure out the Lexus was Poole's?"

Bucky started massaging his temples with his fingertips. The nails were still painted a discreet Jackie shade of pale pink. I wondered if anybody else had noticed, but I decided not to mention it. I didn't need to antagonize Deavers right at this moment. Not on purpose, anyway.

"How stupid do you think we are, Garrity?" he snapped. "It was the only car left in the lot at four A.M. when you called us."

He knew what I was getting at, but he was being deliberately obtuse.

"No wallet, no keys, no cash on the body," I said. "Doesn't that look more like a robbery-murder than the kind of spite murder you're trying to hang on Wuvvy? Look around you, Bucky. You said it yourself. Every kind of lowlife in the world hangs out around Little Five Points. What about that homicide last year? Where the German guy was strangled and his body dumped down the street at the old Bass High School building? You guys never closed that one, did you?"

"Totally different deal," Bucky said. "The German guy was gay. He thought he'd picked himself up a date in the Yacht Club. Somebody saw him leave with a leather type around two A.M. It was an S & M thing gone wrong. We've got a Vice guy working that one, along with another similar homicide at Ansley Mall. In both those cases it was clearly rough sex. There's nothing like that here. So don't even try to suggest it."

I wasn't convinced. "Were the S & M victims robbed?"

"The German guy was, but with the Ansley Mall case we're not sure. The victim's a John Doe. Kid was a baby, no more than eighteen. Street hustler, probably, but we've never made an ID on him."

"What if I got Wuvvy to talk to you?" I asked. "Would you at least listen? Keep looking around for the real killer?"

Bucky raised an eyebrow. "The case is still open. We're still questioning people. If Wuvvy's got some information, I'd like to hear it. In the meantime, the sooner we hear from her, the better off she'll be."

"I'll do what I can," I told him. "In the meantime, you might want to stop at a drugstore on the way back to the shop. Pick up some nail polish remover. 'Cause that pink is definitely too dressy for daytime."

He held up his hands, and a look of horror flashed across his face. I strolled off, happy to have been of service.

When I got home Mac was busy blowing gusts of leaves and dirt and sawdust off what was left of the front porch. Edna was silhouetted in the open doorway, a beer bottle in her right hand, cheering him on.

I felt like cheering myself.

We sat out on the front steps and ate leftovers off the same plate. Talk about romantic. I did insist, however, on having my own beer. Rufus and Maybelline sat at Mac's feet, watching anxiously as he ate.

"They missed you," I told him, snuggling closer.

"They just like Edna's cooking," he said. He took a piece of meat and tossed it to Rufus, who gulped it down in midair.

"Equal opportunity for the women," I said, throwing a bigger piece to Maybelline. "Besides, I think she's getting ready to have those puppies. Poor thing, it must be hell, dragging around a bellyful of squirming babies."

"She's a class act," Mac said, scratching the white place under Maybelline's chin. "She'll do fine. Won't you, girl?"

A pair of mourning doves had settled themselves on the bottom limb of a dogwood that had somehow escaped the tornado, and with darkness and a lull in power saws and other heavy equipment, the two of them called out to each other. "WOO-EE-OOH-WOO-OOH-OOH."

"You ever notice how they always say the same thing?" I asked, pointing into the shadows of the tree limbs.

"Sounds like Indian signals," Mac agreed, sipping his beer.

We sat there and listened to the doves and watched while the streetlights came on. You could see a lot more of the street with the trees gone. The whole front of the house was bathed in a pool of yellow from the streetlight at the curb. It wasn't a view I welcomed. Edna and I always liked the idea of peeping out at the world from behind the screen of our landscaping. Now the world was right up in our faces. No wonder Mac preferred living out in the woods.

Mac had heard about Jackson Poole's murder on the radio driving back to Atlanta, but thankfully there'd been no mention of how the body was found. I filled him in on the gruesome details and tried to jog his memory about having met Wuvvy in the park, but Mac is hopeless with that kind of thing. He remembers every bend in every river he's ever crossed, every hair on every kind of fishing fly he's ever tied, but he couldn't tell you the name of a person he met last week, not even if his life depended on it.

"Sorry," he said. "I remember somebody playing Frisbee with a dog in Candler Park, but that's about it. Anyway, what more do you know about this Wuvvy person? I never heard you talk about her, did I?"

"Probably not," I said. "I didn't even know her real name until Bucky told me. It's Virginia Lee Mincey."

Mac stretched and yawned. "Mincey. That's a good Southern name. There's a crew of Minceys out in Douglas County. Leroy Mincey was county commissioner back in the eighties."

He stood up and whistled. The dogs got up and moved to his side. "Let's go, guys," he said. "I wanna see if we still have a roof over our heads."

I didn't bother to try to hide my disappointment. "Can't you stay? It's dark already. Too late to try to fix anything if there is damage. Your suitcase is still in the Blazer, right? So you can head out early in the morning. You owe me for standing me up on Halloween, you know."

"I'll have to leave by six A.M." he said. "Early meeting. The dogs would have to stay here another day."

"We'll try to bear up," I said, squeezing his hand. "Come on. There's half a chocolate cake on the kitchen counter. We can have dessert in bed."

He put both hands on my butt and pulled me close, so that his beard brushed the top of my head. "I was counting on dessert in your bed. We can have the cake for breakfast."

*   *   *

It had been a tough couple of days. I decided I deserved dessert and sex *and* cake for breakfast.

We were doing a little chocolate fingerpainting when the phone rang. I licked some frosting off Mac's fingers, sighed happily, and reached for the phone.

"Let it ring," he said, pushing the phone away from his side of the bed. He dabbed some frosting on my breast with his forefinger. "Now it's my turn."

It wouldn't have been fair to have him miss his turn. Especially when he played so nicely.

I let the phone ring six times, and it finally stopped. "That's better," he murmured.

"Much better," I agreed. Mac was really an artist with that chocolate frosting. Around and around and around until . . .

The damn phone started ringing again. "Keep going," I whispered. On the tenth ring, I was starting to lose my concentration.

"Shit!" I scrambled across Mac and picked up the phone. "What?"

"That's not a very nice way to talk to the police." It was Bucky. "Did you talk to Wuvvy?"

"She's not my client," I said. "Anyway, I can't talk right now."

"She's not Virginia Lee Mincey, either," Bucky said quickly. "Thought you'd want to know."

"Who is it?" Mac asked. He was running a line of frosting down between my shoulder blades, down my spine. God. Who knew chocolate was that good?

"It's Deavers," I said, holding my hand over the receiver.

"Tell him you're having dessert," Mac said. He was following the frosting with his tongue.

"Bucky, I gotta go," I said, trying not to giggle.

"Callahan," he said urgently. "The GCIC computer finally kicked on again. We found a Social Security number in some of Wuvvy's papers. The number comes up as Virginia Lee Poole. Does that name sound familiar to you?"

"Poole?" I said, brushing Mac's hand away. "As in Jackson Poole? They were related?"

"Only by marriage," Bucky said. He was enjoying himself now. "You don't recognize the name? Virginia Lee Poole? Think about it, Callahan. You're older than I am. You should remember the name."

"I never heard of Virginia Lee Poole," I said. "Why should I?"

"I have," Mac said.

I put my hand over the receiver again. These three-way conversations were tricky. "Who is she?"

He picked up his plate and took a bite of cake. "Shot her husband in the face with a shotgun. Must have been back in the seventies. Broward Poole. He was the biggest pecan grower in the state. Down in Hawkinsville, I think was where it was."

"You remember that far back?" Some days I wasn't sure he remembered my name.

"Sure," he said. "Gorgeous young wife blows her rich, prominent husband away with a shotgun, tries to claim it was an accident? You know what I remember best? She tried to say the husband had been out in the pecan grove, shooting at crows, when he stumbled and shot himself."

I could hear Bucky laughing on the other end of the line.

"What's so funny?" I demanded, pulling the sheets up over my chest. I knew it was impossible, but I had the feeling he knew what he'd interrupted.

"Sounds like you got company. Mac remembers Broward Poole, doesn't he?"

"He remembers some gorgeous sexy young wife," I said. "That can't be Wuvvy."

"Ten years in prison will work some changes on a person," Bucky said. "Jury gave her a life sentence, but the governor commuted it to time served in '87. Call me tomorrow, or come by the homicide unit after noon. The district attorney down in Pulaski County is faxing me the case file tonight, but the photo quality sucks. He's having a sheriff's deputy hand-deliver the rest of the file tomorrow. Even with the fax, if you look close enough, you can see a little bit of Wuvvy in Virginia Lee Mincey. Way before she got rode hard and put up wet."

I hung up the phone and looked at Mac. He'd finished the cake and was now eyeing me hungrily. He has a very healthy appetite, Mac does.

"Wuvvy an ex-con. A murderer. Somebody's trophy wife. Who knew?"

He pulled the sheet down and slipped his arms around my neck.

"Did you miss me?"

"Oh yes," I said, savoring the moment.

We'd only been back together for a few months now. That was following a painful breakup that had taken a year to heal. It probably wasn't all the way healed yet. We'd been working our way back toward a new relationship, but the process was taking time.

"I worried about you guys," Mac said, taking my hand and kissing my fingertips one by one. "The meeting got moved to Butts County and I started home as soon as it broke up, but they had the Georgia State Patrol set up roadblocks on I-75 at Forsyth, and they wouldn't let me get any farther north. I kept trying to call you, but the lines were down."

"We were all right," I said, breathing in the smell of him: chocolate and the salt of sweat and aftershave and even an undercurrent of Ben-Gay. "Nothing I couldn't handle."

He sighed. "There's nothing you can't handle, Julia Callahan Garrity. Hell or high water. So what do you need me for?"

I ran my hand down his belly and was rewarded by his involuntary shiver of pleasure.

"Stud service," I told him. "And heavy lifting. I have highly specialized needs, you know."

"I know all about your needs," he said, pulling me to him again. And that part was true.

9

When I staggered out to the kitchen with an armload of chocolate-covered sheets for the washing machine the next morning, Edna was already on the phone.

"Oh yes, ma'am," she said in a voice oozing concern. "Mrs. Isom mentioned you'd be calling. I'm so sorry about your home. Fortunately, the House Mouse is running a natural disaster special this week. Three hundred dollars. That includes your basic sweeping, mopping, and dusting, plus glass and storm water cleanup and removal of interior storm debris."

"What?" I screeched, dumping the sheets in the washing machine. "Are you out of your mind?"

Edna made a hand signal telling me to pipe down.

"Yes. That's one of our specialists for a minimum of three hours. But no windows, no carpet or drape removal, and oven and refrigerator cleaning will be a hundred dollars extra, this week only."

Edna scribbled furiously on a sheet of paper. "Yes, I think we can have someone over there by noon. Fine. And you understand, since this is a one-time service, that payment will be in cash?"

She hung up the phone, her eyes shining greedily. "Make hay while the sun shines," she told me.

"That's three times our going rate," I said. "Nobody in their right mind will pay that."

But nobody was in their right mind that day. The phone rang off the hook all morning long. Edna's natural disaster special was a winner. We called Cheezer and gave him three houses to hit right away, diverted Ruby from her regular Monday morning job, and called Neva Jean and left a message for her to report ASAP.

"I'll take one of these jobs," Edna said, plucking a piece of paper from her stack of assignments.

"No you won't," I said, snatching it out of her hand. "You stay here and run the office. Or I'll sic your doctor on you."

We were still arguing about whether or not Edna was allowed to vacuum when Baby and Sister yoo-hooed from the back door.

They were both dressed in conspicuously new clothes: colorful cotton blouses with the price tags still dangling from the sleeves, stiffly creased oversized jeans cinched around their waists with what looked like pieces of clothesline, and sparkling white cotton tennis shoes. Miss Sister had topped off her ensemble with an Atlanta Braves baseball cap. They were both jaunty and in high spirits.

"Well, look at you two," I said, giving them both a hug. "I guess you came through the tornado all right."

"I guess we sure did," Miss Sister said. "See these new duds we got? Red Cross give us these new clothes. Give us breakfast at McDonald's too. Had me an Egg McMuffin and the cutest little cup of orange juice you ever saw. Got the cup right here." She pulled the disposable plastic cup out of the front of her blouse and waved it under my nose so that I could see it.

"Did you get evacuated?" Edna asked.

"Oh no," Miss Baby said proudly. "My bowels held up real good. They made us leave the senior-citizen high-rise on account of some of them peoples don't walk so good, and they was afraid somebody might have a heart attack or something."

"She said EVACUATED, not CONSTIPATED," Sister said, her black eyes snapping from behind her thick-lensed eyeglasses. "We did so get evacuated. Took us all in ambulances to a Holiday Inn way out there near Conyers. Ooh, me and Baby had the nicest hotel room."

Baby helped her sister to a kitchen chair. "Guess who nearly got us kicked out on account of ordering room service when she didn't have twelve dollars to spend on a hamburger sandwich and a Coca-Cola?" Baby taunted.

"Whose idea was it to watch that nudie movie on the Nice 'n' Nasty channel?" Sister countered. "You think a Christian woman needs to look at a movie called *Cheerleaders in Chains*? That's the devil's work."

"I thought it was a movie about football," Baby replied, shamefaced. "As soon as I seen them little cheerleader girls didn't wear no panties under their little-bitty skirts I turned that TV off. I surely did. Called downstairs and told them people they had pornography coming in that hotel."

"Not 'til it was over, she didn't," Sister insisted. "She watched that movie clear through to the end. Would have watched another one too, except the pastor's wife knocked on the door to see if we wanted to have Bible study."

Edna poured mugs of coffee for both the girls and added two teaspoons of sugar to each cup. "We're just glad you made out all right," Edna said. "How did you get over here this morning?"

"Red Cross van brought us right up your driveway and dropped us off," Sister said. "Me and Baby need to make us a little spending money. You got some work today?"

"Gotta pay for those hamburgers and Coca-Colas," Baby said darkly.

Edna flipped open the appointment book. "We do have lots of work," she said. "When Neva Jean gets here, she can drop you off at Judy Knight's house. You think you feel up to that today?"

"Better call over there and tell her to lock that chihuahua of hers up in the bathroom," Baby said. "Last time we was to that house, Miss You-Know-Who thought that dog was a big ole rat and kept smacking it over the head with a flyswatter. Like to knocked that dog silly before I made her stop."

A horn tooted from the driveway. "That should be Neva Jean," Edna said. The horn tooted three more times.

We all trooped outside to see what the ruckus was about.

Swannelle and Neva Jean were perched on the hood of a bright blue tow truck I'd never seen before. The hand-lettered sign on the driver's-side door said McCOMB AUTO BODY. Swannelle was grinning like a man who'd just broken the bank at Monte Carlo.

"Where'd you get the tow truck?" I asked as Neva Jean hopped off the hood.

"We bought it after the storm, on Saturday," Neva Jean said. "Swannelle's cousin Rooney Deebs knew a man who wanted to sell, and we been wanting a second tow truck. We pulled thirty-seven cars into the shop between Saturday morning and last night. You know how many cars there are in this town that got hit by trees or telephone poles during that tornado?"

"I know about one car, personally," I said, pointing at my Mousemobile van.

Swannelle eyed the van critically. "That there is a teetotal, Callahan," he said.

"Not according to the insurance adjuster," I said. "He says it's an eight-hundred-dollar repair job."

Swannelle snorted. "I been in auto body for thirty years,

and I'm tellin' you, eight hundred dollars ain't gonna cut it on this baby. For one thing, every body shop inside the Perimeter's maxed out with storm work. Ain't nobody gonna take on that hunk of junk."

Neva Jean poked him in the ribs. "You could fix it."

"Yeah," he laughed. "If I didn't have thirty-seven other cars to fix first. Cars I can make some real money off of insurance companies."

I'd always dreaded the prospect of a moment like this—the moment I'd have to grovel before Swannelle McComb.

"Please," I said, gritting my teeth. "I've got too much money invested in the van to total it out. Custom-made racks to hold the cleaning equipment, new upholstery on the seats. . . ."

"Rebuilt transmission and a new fuel pump," Neva Jean added. "You should have traded that van in a long time ago, Callahan."

I gave Swannelle my most hangdog look. "Can you fix it or not?"

"Take a while," Swannelle said. "But since it's you, I reckon I can move you up the list."

"I'll need a loaner," I said. "Can you handle that?"

"Sure," Neva Jean volunteered. "McComb Auto Body is a full-service shop. We'll fix you right up."

Swannelle's idea of a loaner was a yellow 1985 Lincoln.

Its interior had once been white leather, but now everything was stained yellow-orange and stank of nicotine.

"Where'd you get this car?" I asked, choking from the fumes. "Joe Camel?"

"Only thing I got to spare," Swannelle said, handing me the keys. He pointed out a case of Quaker State 10W40 on the floor of the passenger side. "It's kinda bad to burn oil. You want to put in a quart every time you fill up."

"I'm not planning to keep it that long," I said. "You promised you'd have the van fixed in a couple of days."

He smiled, ran his fingers through his graying pompadour. "Give or take a day or two."

I opened the trunk and filled it with my grimebusters kit: plastic caddy of cleaning supplies, mop, broom, industrial-strength vacuum cleaner, heavy-duty hand vac, buckets, and a box of black plastic trash bags. As an afterthought, I talked Swannelle into letting me borrow his wet-dry shop vac.

I had two houses to hit, both in Peachtree Corners, an expensive suburb in Gwinnett County. The houses were supposed to be right next door to each other on a cul-de-sac.

"Two hours apiece and no more," Edna had promised me.

"You told the homeowners they'd get three hours minimum," I said.

"That was earlier," she said. "Before we knew the demand. Now it's three hundred and fifty dollars and two hours. The woman in the first house, Jean Miller, is a friend of Barbara Heckart's. She's Neva Jean's regular Tuesday job."

"I can't believe you're gouging storm victims," I said.

"It's not gouging," Edna insisted. "Besides, since they're referrals, I did agree to let these two pay by check."

It was a good thing I'd brought the shop vac. The Peachtree Corners houses were knee-deep in broken glass, rainwater, and despair.

I pulled on my heaviest rubber gloves and waded into the first house. I had to shovel up the first layer of mud and broken glass from the marble hallway, where the high winds had blown out the windows and blown in half their front yard.

It took closer to three hours, but I got up all the water and most of the glass, and despite Edna's new rules, I pulled down Jean Miller's drapes, pulled up her area rugs, and dumped them in her garage, where they could be sent to a commercial cleaner. Then I hauled twelve garbage bags full of debris down to the curb. The Millers' house was going to need major painting and fixing up, but at least it wouldn't resemble a swamp anymore.

Jean Miller wrote me a check with tears in her eyes. I tucked it in the pocket of my jeans, then I went next door and did the same thing all over again.

By six P.M. I was filthy dirty and physically exhausted, but I felt strangely exhilarated. The good thing about cleaning is the immediate results. I'd hit these two houses like a second tornado, imposing order where there had been chaos, shine where there had been grit.

I called the house to check in with Edna before I left for home.

"Your friend Bucky Deavers called. Wants to know why you didn't stop by the police department today. Said he had some stuff for you to look at. I thought you were done with all that stuff over there in Little Five Points."

"I am," I promised her.

"Better be. Because the roofer says it's gonna cost eight thousand dollars to fix all that tree damage. So you got no time to be working for deadbeats like that Wuvvy."

"I'm not," I said.

I hung up and called Deavers.

"Have you heard from your client today?" Bucky asked.

"I've heard from all my clients today," I said. "They all want their houses cleaned, yesterday."

"I meant Wuvvy," he said. "Virginia Lee Poole."

"No," I said. "Guess you'll have to make like a cop and find her yourself."

"Screw you," he said cheerfully. "And here I was all set to invite you out to dinner tonight."

"Take one of your little girlfriends," I suggested. "What's the new one's name? Chloe?"

"It's Zoey," he said. "She was my first choice, believe me, but she can't make it."

"Her mom won't let her go out on school nights, huh?" I clucked my tongue sympathetically.

"You're a riot, Callahan," Bucky said. "Actually, this is sort of a business dinner. I thought you might be interested in touring the Blind Possum Brewery. The one up in Roswell."

"How come you're inviting me?" I wanted to know. "You're always telling me to keep my nose out of your cases. Now you want me to play Watson to your Sherlock Holmes?"

"Christ," Bucky said. "Okay, look. It's not really an official interview. They don't know I'm coming. I just want to look around a little bit. Get the feel of the business. I thought it would seem more casual if I was, like, with a date. You know, just a couple out on the town, sucking down some homemade brew."

"And asking questions about the murder of one of their executives," I said. "That's pretty casual. I'm sure the guy in charge of this brewery won't have any idea you're a cop and I'm a PI."

"You leave the questions to me," Bucky said. "And the guy in charge is actually a woman. This thing they're having tonight is the Brewmaster's Dinner. It's sort of a private party, if you reserve ahead of time, which I did. The dinner starts at eight. You want me to pick you up, or not?"

"You're paying?"

"The City of Atlanta is paying," Bucky said. "See you at seven-thirty."

10

"You better come out and look at this," Edna hollered, pounding on the door of my bathroom. "That Wuvvy woman is on the news."

I shut off the shower, wrapped a towel around myself, and dashed into the kitchen, where Edna had stationed herself in front of the portable black-and-white television we keep on the counter.

"It's on all three local channels," Edna said.

The "it" Edna was referring to was a blurry photograph of a woman, kneeling down beside a brown-and-white dog with a Frisbee in its mouth. The woman looked a lot like Wuvvy.

"Police are searching for this woman, Virginia Lee Poole, a convicted murderer, in connection with the weekend slaying of Atlanta businessman Jackson Poole," the news anchor said. "Authorities say Virginia Lee Poole, who was convicted of the 1977 shotgun killing of her husband, wealthy Hawkinsville pecan plantation owner Broward Poole, had been living under an assumed name and running her own business in the

Little Five Points area of Atlanta since the governor of Georgia commuted her life prison sentence ten years ago, citing new evidence that Poole killed her husband only after years of battering and sexual abuse.

"Jackson Poole, twenty-eight, was one of the owners of the Blind Possum Brewery of Atlanta, and was Virginia Lee Poole's stepson," she continued. "Police believe revenge was the motive for the slaying of the younger Poole, whose business was taking over space previously leased by Virginia Lee Poole. Anyone having any information about the whereabouts of this woman is asked to call the Atlanta Police Department ."

Edna sniffed disparagingly. "Battered wife. Abused child. Misunderstood adult. Everybody's got an excuse nowadays, and nobody's responsible for nothing."

"Even a whipped dog will bite back eventually," I reminded her. "You and Daddy taught me that yourselves." I hitched up my towel more securely and went back to my room to get dressed.

I had finished drying my hair and was pulling a turtleneck shirt over my head when I heard it: a faint scratching noise. Coming from behind the bed? I shoved my feet into the nearest pair of shoes. We'd seen a snake and a couple of rats out in the yard after the tornado; if there was something behind my bed I didn't want it to jump out and bite me on the toe.

The scratching came again, only this time it was definitely from the window beside the bed. I ran to the window and pushed the curtain aside. The sky outside was purplish-blue, with white clouds still visible through the treetops. The big mophead hydrangea underneath my window had branches that rubbed against the glass sometimes, but there wasn't even the hint of a breeze right now.

I let the curtain fall back into place, picked up my purse, and pulled out my pistol, a nine-millimeter Smith & Wesson.

With hands shaking from haste and nervousness, I loaded the gun, tucked it in the waistband of my jeans, and pulled my shirt out to hide it.

Edna was still watching the news when I whizzed by on the way out the back door. "Stay right where you are," I ordered her. "There's somebody out in the yard. Stay inside."

I dashed around to the side of the house where my bedroom is. A thick privet hedge ran the length of our lot, ten feet away from the window. It curved and ran along the back of the lot too, so high and so effective as a privacy fence that we've never even met the neighbors who live behind us. At the back corner of the lot, a piece of shrubbery moved, leaves crunched, and a twig snapped.

"Who's out there?" I called, sounding braver than I felt. I pulled my gun out and held it loosely by my side. "I've got a gun," I called. "Who's there?"

By the time I got to the back of the lot, I could hear footsteps crashing through the undergrowth, and I glimpsed a flash of white, like a shirt or a jacket. Whoever had been creeping around out there had a head start now. I walked slowly back to my bedroom window.

The hydrangea bush had hairy, fleshy leaves the size of basketballs. They had started turning a russet color, and the blue mophead flowers were turning crimson too. I knelt down beside the bush and pawed around to get a better view of the ground. Some of the lower branches had been mashed flat against the pinestraw mulch. I could see a medium-sized footprint in the soft, damp soil. Somebody had been here only moments ago, peeking in my bedroom window at me. I could feel the hairs on the back of my neck bristle, feel goose bumps under the snug sleeves of my turtleneck.

I stood up slowly and brushed pine needles from the knees of my black jeans. My sockless feet felt suddenly cold and wet through the thin leather of my shoes. I was cold all over, shivering uncontrollably. Someone had been peeking into my bedroom, watching me. For who knows how long? Bile rose in the back of my throat. I held on to the window frame while waves of nausea washed over me. Who? Who was watching me? A stranger, or someone I knew?

Edna stood at the back door. "What's wrong?" she called. "Should I call the police? Was there really somebody there?"

"Kids, probably," I said, taking a deep breath. I tugged once at the window sash. It was locked from the inside, but I wanted to check. It didn't budge. "Whoever it was, they're gone now."

"I'm calling the police," Edna said.

A horn honked from the front of the house.

"That's Bucky," I told her. "I'll talk to him about it. He can send over a detective in the morning. If we call now, they'll just send over a uniformed officer. And for what? The guy's gone. He knows I heard him out there. He probably won't be back. You worried about being here alone tonight?"

"Hell no," Edna said. "I'm gonna call Mr. Byerly and tell him to call the other block captains. Let 'em know we got a Peeping Tom prowling around the neighborhood. Maybe somebody will catch the little bastard."

I followed her inside the kitchen so I could fetch my purse. I noticed how carefully she locked and dead-bolted the back door, and switched on all the outside lights. She ran her fingers over all the kitchen windows too, making sure they were locked tight.

Bucky honked his horn again. I took the gun out of my waistband, hesitated, then laid it on the hall table. "I'm leaving you this," I said. "It's loaded. You want me to show you how to use it?"

"Take it with you," Edna said grimly. "I've got my own."

"A gun?" I yelped. "You don't know anything about guns. Where is it?"

"None of your business," Edna said. "It's a thirty-eight. I've got a permit and you better believe I know how to use it. Now go ahead on. I'm not helpless, Jules," she said. "Never have been."

I looked over my shoulder at our little aqua bungalow as I went out the front door, locking it carefully. Inside, Edna threw the catch on the deadbolt. She jiggled the doorknob to make sure the door was locked tight. So that was how it was. We were two women living alone. Armed and dangerous. God help anybody who stepped foot on our property tonight.

11

"My mother's got a gun," I said glumly.

We were in Bucky's personal car, a tiny red Miata convertible, headed north out of the city. The car was cute and totally impractical, the perfect cure for a midlife crisis. Only Bucky wasn't old enough yet to earn a midlife crisis. The car zipped in and out of traffic on the interstate like a nimble little bug.

"What's wrong with Edna having a gun?" Bucky asked. "It's in the second amendment, Callahan. Mothers have the right to bear arms too, you know. It's a dangerous world out there."

"Mothers aren't supposed to have guns," I said. "Mothers are supposed to teach Sunday school and crochet and stuff. You know what my mother does? She gambles. She heads up the neighborhood vigilante committee. And now she packs heat."

Bucky shrugged. "What brought all this on? Same old neighborhood crime-wave stuff?"

I hesitated. "Somebody was peeping in my window tonight. Watching me."

He looked startled. "You sure?"

"I heard a noise," I said. "Ran outside, but you know how slow I am. He got a head start and ran through the hedge at the back of the yard. I saw a bit of white, like a jacket or something, and heard him running through the woods. When I checked by the window, I could see where he'd trampled the hydrangea bush. There was a footprint."

"I don't suppose you called the cops?" Bucky said.

"You're a cop," I pointed out. "Think you could get somebody over to the house to take a look around?"

He picked up the cell phone from its cradle on the dashboard of the Miata. "I'll call Burglary. Get somebody over there tonight. In the meantime, you ever thought about getting a security system? That neighborhood's not safe, Garrity."

"I started thinking about a security system as soon as I saw the guy's footsteps under my bedroom window," I admitted. "It gave me a serious case of the creeps. Tell whoever goes by the house to call first and let Edna know they're coming. Otherwise, she's likely to blow somebody's head off."

We got off I-285 and onto Georgia 400 and took it north, crossing over the Chattahoochee River, past exits for Roswell and Alpharetta, past Holcombe Bridge Road and Haynes Bridge Road and a lot of other exits I'd never heard of, until we got to Webb Bridge Road.

A couple miles ahead, past cow pastures dotted with new subdivision signs, Bucky turned off Webb Bridge and onto a bumpy county-maintained road. The road curved and dipped, and suddenly Bucky whipped the Miata into a gravel parking lot. Directly in front of us stood a hulking pile of red bricks.

"It was a gristmill after the Civil War," Bucky said. "Cool, huh?"

They'd left the fading white paint letters on the mill facade,

WEBB BRIDGE MILL, only now there were uplights mounted on the flat brick facade to illuminate the sign. Below the Mill sign there was a new sign. Five-foot-high pink neon letters over the arched oak plank front door said BLIND POSSUM BREWERY. A barn-red cylindrical grain silo stood on four legs and a pipeline ran from it to the mill building.

"Very rustic. Very picturesque," I said. "Very expensive, too. Where's all the money coming from for these restaurants? Did Jackson Poole have financial backers?"

"We're looking into that," Bucky said. He got out, came around, and opened my door. "When we get inside, do me a favor," Bucky said. "Just keep your mouth shut for a while. Remember, you're on a date."

"In your dreams," I told him, pushing the oak door open.

The fellow standing at the maitre d' stand looked like somebody who'd just abandoned his mule and plow out in the back forty. He was big and solidly built, with a meaty face ringed by a wispy gray beard that spilled down the front of his blue work shirt.

He picked up a stack of menus when he saw us walk in.

"Welcome to Blind Possum," he said, his smile showing uneven yellow teeth. "Y'all here for the Brewmaster's Dinner?"

"That's right," Bucky said.

"They're just starting the tour of the brewery," the host said. "Go on down through those doors there, and you'll see the brewhouse through the glass wall to your right."

The combined scent of beer and cigar smoke seemed to permeate the mill's old brick walls. Bucky inhaled deeply as we moved down the hallway. "Man. Smell that. Beer and cigars. I'm getting buzzed just standing here."

His voice echoed in the high-ceilinged hall. The floors were of a darker, polished brick, and the walls were lined with floor-to-ceiling glass cases crammed with a treasure trove of beer and brewing memorabilia.

"Hey," Bucky said, putting his finger on one of the glass cases. "Look at that. Hudepohl. Bet you never heard of that before. My granddad up in Cincinnati used to drink Hudepohl beer. He had an old wooden icebox down in the cellar, and when you opened that door, you'd hear those bottles clinking against each other." He grinned. "I snuck my first Hudepohl when I was ten."

"Good?" I asked.

"Nah," he said. "Well, I was only ten at the time. I remember thinking it tasted like piss smelled."

My eyes scanned the shelves of beer bottles, labels, bottle caps. I saw Grolsch, Streilitz, Yuengling, and dozens more I'd never heard of. There were beers brewed and bottled in Akron, Pittsburgh, Chicago, Boston, Detroit, Waukegan, Buffalo, Minneapolis, hell, every Rust Belt town in the United States. Even Atlanta, it turned out, had its own brewery.

A neatly typed card on the top shelf of the display explained why those regional beers had gone the way of the collar pin and the butter churn.

> In 1914 there were more than 1,400 breweries employing more than 75,000 people. The single most destructive force in U.S. brewing history was the 1920 enactment of the Volstead Act—known as Prohibition.
>
> Following the repeal of Prohibition in 1929 only 400 or so U.S. breweries were in operation. By the 1970s only about two dozen regional breweries were still in operation in the U.S.
>
> Today, 80 percent of all beer produced in the U.S. is brewed by four giant breweries: Anheuser-Busch, Miller, Coors, and Stroh's. Only about 2 percent of U.S. beer is craft brewed, but that amount is on the rise.

Bucky walked on to the next display, an even bigger glass case filled with old-time beer advertising giveaways. There were lithographed tin bar trays, coasters, glasses, mugs, oil paintings, neon signs, scale-model tin replicas of beer trucks, tiny wooden beer kegs, and dozens of intricate porcelain steins.

"Cool," he breathed.

A group of people was gathered up ahead in the hallway, peering through a plateglass wall. I could hear a woman's voice.

"Hey," I said, elbowing Bucky, "don't you want to see how they make beer?"

"I just want to drink beer, I don't want to dissect it," he said, but he followed me anyway.

A short bar was set up at the end of the hallway, just past the entrance to the brewroom. A college-aged kid was setting glasses on the bar, filling them from various taps. There were at least eight "in-house" brands, along with the fancy beers I was used to seeing in upscale bars: Sam Adams, Löwenbräu, Beck's, and others.

"All right!" Bucky said, pointing at the bar. "That's more what I had in mind. You ready for a cold one?"

"Start without me," I said. "I want to see the brewing operation."

Twenty or so people were standing in a semicircle around the young woman who appeared to be the tour guide. I inched my way closer so that I could hear what she was saying.

The woman pointed through the window at a pair of gleaming copper and stainless steel vats connected by a shared stainless steel stairway. "That's the lauter tun you're seeing there on the left," the woman said.

She was a tiny thing, barely over five feet tall, and the huge vats behind her made her seem even more toylike. She had glossy reddish-brown hair in a thick braid that hung down her back, a sprinkling of freckles across her thin, angular face, and dark blue eyes. Floppy black rubber fisherman's boots swallowed the lower half of her body, and she wore jeans and a tight black T-shirt with a blind, blissed-out possum embroidered over her breast.

When she turned around to point out how the grains were shoveled into a lid in the tank I saw what was written on the back of her shirt:

WE MAKE IT, WE DRINK IT, WE SELL WHAT'S LEFT

"The grains are cracked here, between a set of metal rollers calibrated for just the right consistency. We don't want to mash it so much we turn it into flour, but the grain does need to be crushed enough to allow for optimum extraction of the sugars that allow fermentation," the woman said. "We use a combination of wheat, corn, barley, and other grains, according to the recipe the brewmaster is using."

She moved along a few feet and pointed to the other vat. "In this vat, we've piped in water and we're cooking the crushed grain, or grist, with water heated to one hundred and fifty-five degrees."

Inside the brewroom, a muscular black man who wore the same type garb as our guide pulled the door open.

A bittersweet barley scent wafted out as we filed into the brewroom. The air was warm and yeasty, like the inside of my Grandma Garrity's kitchen after a day of baking. I closed my eyes and filled my lungs with the scent.

"Beer's simple," the girl continued after we were all inside. "We use four basic raw materials. Malted barley, water, hops, and yeast. Believe it or not, water is the biggest ingredient, and the most important to the taste of our beer."

"Atlanta has good water for beer?" asked a man standing next to me. He was short and dressed for business in a dark suit and a subdued red silk tie.

"Atlanta's water is just fine," she said soothingly. "I wouldn't use it if I didn't think so."

"You're the brewer?" I asked. It sounded sexist, but I couldn't help being surprised. I'd sort of assumed the Paul Bunyan–looking guy at the door was the brewer.

"Brewmaster," she corrected me. "My name is Anna Frisch. I make all the beers here at Blind Possum."

A couple of the guys standing around me snickered softly. Anna Frisch whirled around, clearly annoyed.

"Beer's come to be thought of as a macho drink through the advertising efforts of Miller and Budweiser," Anna said. "But believe me, in the early history of beer, especially in Northern Europe, brewing was always done by the women— it was a part of their life, like baking bread or spinning yarn."

Someone was squeezing my arm. Bucky.

"I thought you were just going to taste beer and keep your mouth shut," he hissed, handing me a pilsner glass full of a noxiously foamy red liquid.

"Just one little question," I said, taking a sip of the beer. It was ice cold, slightly bitter, and surprisingly fruity. I could have sworn I smelled raspberries or cherries.

"That's our Red Roadkill," Anna Frisch said, nodding toward me. "What do you think?"

"Different," I said, taking another sip.

"You're probably not used to craft-brewed beers," she said, resuming her lecture voice.

"The majority of American beer drinkers have grown up with beers made by the big brewers—Miller, Budweiser, Stroh's, Coors. Their beers are made with much more corn and rice and much less barley and hops, meaning a paler, wimpier beer. Our philosophy here is to make the kind of robust, distinctive beers small-town craft brewers made all over the U.S. before the Prohibition."

"And yet I notice you sell beers made by other breweries," I said, ignoring Bucky's elbow in my ribs. "Isn't that hurting your own business?"

"Not at all," Anna said smoothly. "Restaurants have to carry the premium beers. We have to have something to offer all our customers. Hopefully, though, they'll taste our Blind Possum beers and see the difference."

Bucky took a long pull of his own beer, which was a thick, coffee-colored potion with a thin creamy head on it.

"What's that sludge?" I asked.

"Blind Possum Black and Tan," he said. "It's a mixture of stout and lager. Probably too muscular for the likes of you, Garrity."

I took the glass from him and tasted cautiously. I wrinkled my nose and handed it back. "This stuff tastes like the stuff Edna used to rub on my chest when I had a cold," I said.

He took another long drink of the black and tan. "You got no nose for beer, Garrity. Better stick to the wussy stuff."

"Gladly," I said.

Anna Frisch was walking around the brewroom with the rest of us following slowly in her wake. She explained how the cracked grains were cooked long enough to allow the naturally occurring enzymes to convert the starch in the grains into sugar and showed us how the resulting thick porridge was strained and piped to a fifteen-barrel stainless steel brew kettle, where the mixture, called "wort," was brought to a rolling boil before the hops were added.

"Hops," Anna said, looking around her for approval from her students, "is the spice that give the beer its distinct pleasing bitterness. And it also acts as a natural preservative. And not least of the important properties of hops is that it balances the sweetness of the barley."

I tasted my Red Roadkill again and this time let it linger

on my tongue a little. Okay. Hops. Barley. I could be educated. I was a bourbon kind of gal. But that didn't mean I couldn't enjoy a decent beer.

"Brew day is a big day around here," Anna continued. She walked over to a third tank at the back of the room and patted its stainless steel side.

"At the end of the boil we take the bitter wort and let the hops settle out of it for about half an hour. Then we pump it through a heat exchanger on the way to the fermenting tank. This cools it down to the right temperature for the yeast.

"Does anybody here want to guess what the yeast does?" Anna asked, gazing at her students, who were beginning to drift away in the direction of the taps.

"It makes it booze," somebody offered.

Anna frowned. "Sort of. The yeast consumes the sugars in the wort and produces ethyl alcohol, which also produces carbon dioxide gas. We let the carbon dioxide bubble out, and then, in the fermentation tanks, the wort is again cooled with chilled water until it attains a temperature of about thirty-five degrees. That's the aging temperature. We let the beer age for fourteen days, and when I've done some sugar readings and other tests, including taste tests, the beer is done."

Anna looked pleased with herself. Three or four people applauded halfheartedly. I joined in too until Bucky squeezed my arm again.

"Any questions?" Anna looked around hopefully.

People were staring in the direction of the bar and the adjoining dining room. The main, unasked question was "When do we eat?"

"Fine," Anna said, pushing the brewroom door open. "Let's see what the chefs have cooked up for us tonight. And see how those dishes match with the five Blind Possum beers you'll be tasting tonight."

*   *   *

Bucky took a last bite of the apple-stuffed pork loin and dipped it in the raspberry-pecan relish. He chewed for a while, swallowed, washed it down with the Blond Possum pale ale he was drinking. He sat back and let out a long, self-satisfied belch.

Nobody at the table even glanced his way.

"Peasant," I said, managing just one more tiny bite of my garlic mashed potatoes.

"It's a brewer's dinner," Bucky said, snitching a forkful of my potatoes. "It would be an insult to our hosts not to burp."

I surveyed the table. Somehow, we'd managed to work our way through four courses: an appetizer of beer-poached Tybee Island shrimp, a trio of wild mushroom and goat cheese dumplings served with something called 'Winter Ale,' entrees of pork loin for Bucky and pecan-crusted baked brook trout for me, and now a waiter was setting the dessert, a decadent-looking apple strudel with warm caramel sauce and vanilla bean ice cream, down on the table. There was another kind of beer too, something the waiter described as 'Sweet Dream Cream Stout.'

"Take it away," I groaned. "I never want to see food again."

"Hi, folks!" Anna Frisch stood directly behind my chair. I was too gorged to move, my jaws weak from so much chewing and sipping.

"Did you enjoy the dinner?" she asked, moving around the table and eyeing the rows of half-full beer glasses.

"It was awesome," Bucky said. "I never knew there were so many kinds of beers before. This stuff is totally different."

"I'm glad you liked it," Anna said, her cheeks flushed pink with pleasure. "Tell your friends about us. We're planning to do these dinners every month."

"I'm fascinated with all these new microbreweries," I said.

"Yeah," Bucky said, cutting me off. He stood up and pulled out a chair for Anna.

"Can you sit down? I mean, if you're not too busy or anything." With Anna's back turned to me, Bucky gave me the zip-your-lips sign.

"Well . . ." Anna looked around the dining room. People were talking softly, forks clicking against china. Half a dozen guys sat at the bar, puffing away at inch-thick cigars. A willowy blonde dressed all in black had joined them, cupping a heavy crystal ashtray in one hand while she held her cigar aloft in the other hand, blowing a puffy tendril of smoke with crimson, pursed lips. The testosterone level was reaching locker-room level. Any minute now, I'd be wishing I had my own set of balls to scratch.

"Come on," Bucky said, giving Anna his boyish, aw-shucks grin.

"Just for a few minutes," she said.

Anna Frisch had changed out of her brewmaster duds and unfastened her braid. Now the thick paprika-colored hair fell over the shoulders of a snug-fitting sage green tunic worn over brown velvet jeans tucked into soft leather boots. She looked like a wood sprite.

She waved in the direction of the bar and called to the bartender.

"Jason, could you bring us a pitcher of the Belgian strong ale?"

"None for me," I said hastily. My temples were starting to throb from the night's excesses.

Bucky groaned. "I've got to drive home. Better not."

"Just a little sip," Anna insisted. "It's the house specialty. I've been tinkering with this recipe for a couple years now. I'm pretty proud of it."

Jason brought the pitcher and three clean glasses. Anna

poured maybe three ounces into each of our glasses.

"There's an art to tasting beer, you know," she said, holding her glass up to the light and tilting it from side to side. "Look at it first. Since this is a Belgian strong ale, it's probably darker than beers you've been used to drinking. That means the flavor will be richer and heartier."

Bucky and I held up our glasses to the light, as Anna had done. It looked like beer to me, but what did I know?

"Now smell," Anna said. "Can you tell what makes a Belgian ale different? Smell the apples and pears?"

"Sort of," Bucky said, sniffing at the rim of the glass.

"Take a small mouthful," she said. "Watch."

She took a sip and rolled it around in her mouth before swallowing. "You're looking for both the flavor and the feel of the beer," Anna said, her eyes shining with intensity. "Belgian strong ale should be medium-bodied, which this is. You should be able to discern the faint fruity notes. Then swallow, take a quick sip of air, and you'll notice the aftertaste, or what we like to call finish, of the beer resonating in the back of your throat and up into your nasal passages.

"Got it?"

"I think so," I said. Not bad, this Belgian stuff.

"Excellent," Bucky pronounced, slamming his glass on the table. "I could drink this stuff all night, but I better not.

"So," he said, leaning closer to Anna. "How did a nice girl like you end up making beer in a place like this?"

Anna made a sour face. "Do you realize how many times a day I get asked that question?"

"It's still a good question," Bucky persisted. "It's better than 'What's your sign?' or 'Come here often?'"

"Since you asked," Anna said quietly, "there really aren't all that many women brewmasters these days. There were only two in my class at brewschool."

"You have to go to a brewschool?" I asked.

"If you want to learn to do it right," Anna said. "My great-uncle and grandfather were brewmasters up in Pennsylvania. They had their own bottling line, even. But that closed in 1962. Way before I was ever born."

"Is that where you got interested in making beer?" I asked.

She shrugged. "Not really. My family has been out of beer a long time. I was working as a bartender at a nightclub in Oregon about five years ago. They got bored with country and western line dancing, decided to turn the dance floor into a brewhouse."

She ran a finger around the fine tracery of white foam left in the glass. "They didn't know squat about beer. Spent half a million dollars to buy their setup, then brought in a corporate guy from California and proceeded to make six different kinds of Bud Lite."

"That's bad?" I happen to like Bud Lite.

"Why not just buy Bud Lite, if that's what you want?" Anna said. "The whole point of craft-brewing is to go back to the great beers that used to be made before everything got pasteurized and sanitized. Beers with regional differences. Something unique."

"Where did you go to brewschool?" I asked. My own version of brewschool had been the time I'd spent at the University of Georgia, where I'd experienced a four-year-long keg party. Not that I remembered all that much of it.

"UC Davis," Anna said proudly.

"That's California?" Bucky looked confused. "I thought they were into wine out there."

"Beer, too," Anna said. "You'd be surprised. They grow hops in California, you know. In some places, people are ripping out their grapevines and planting hop vines in their place."

"It's a brew-volution," Bucky said jokingly.

She gave him a level gaze. The chick was serious about this beer business.

"It *is* a revolution," she said. "Microbrewing is the major restaurant trend of the nineties."

"I believe you," Bucky said. He looked around the room. "You've got some setup here. Are you, like, one of the owners?"

"Sort of," she said, following his gaze. "You could say that."

"Who does own it?" I asked, unable to keep my curiosity at bay. The Blind Possum reeked not just of hops and cigar smoke, but money. Lots of money. Anna Frisch hadn't seen thirty yet. Where did a chick who'd been a barmaid only five years ago suddenly get the money to buy into something like Blind Possum? A whole string of places, if what Bucky said was true.

"Blind Possum is owned by Blind Possum Brewers, Inc.," Anna said. "Just some people who know food and restaurants. And me—because I know how to make beer."

She stood up, tossed her hair over her shoulder. "Time to circulate."

"What about Jackson Poole?" I blurted. "Did he know about the restaurant business? Is that why he was involved in Blind Possum?"

Her hand jerked and sent one of the half-full beer glasses spinning over the varnished tabletop. Beer pooled over the remains of our dinner and began dripping to the floor.

"Jackson? You knew him?"

"We met," I said. "Before he was killed."

Anna hurried to the bar and came back with a stack of paper towels. She started mopping up the beer, stacking plates and silver haphazardly on top of each other. "How did you know Jackson was involved in Blind Possum? He was in charge of the Little Five Points store. It wasn't even open yet."

"I live in the neighborhood," I volunteered.

"Here," Bucky said, standing up to get out of her way. "Let me help."

"What about you?" she asked him. "Why are you so interested in craft-brewing? You didn't really know Jackson, did you?" The flirty little smile had suddenly turned flinty.

"I'm a police detective," Bucky said. He took his billfold out of his hip pocket and handed her a business card. Much more discreet than flashing a badge.

She snatched the card away from him, and as she read it, her face paled.

"Aren't you supposed to tell people you're a police officer before you start interrogating them?"

Bucky shrugged. "Interrogating? Nah. We were drinking beer, talking shop."

She bit her lip. "The company's lawyers told us we shouldn't talk without consulting them . . ." A strand of the long hair fell across her face and she brushed it away impatiently.

"I can't discuss Jackson," she said sharply. "I've got to check my fermentation barrels."

She threw the beer-soaked towels onto the stack of plates and walked quickly away, back toward the brewroom.

"That was subtle," Bucky said, turning on me.

"You notice how quickly she got busy once I brought up the subject of Jackson Poole?" I asked.

"I noticed she was friendly and helpful right until the moment you stepped up and opened your big mouth," he said. "Great timing, Garrity."

12

The silence in the car was glacial. Bucky's jaw muscles were taut, but he was too angry at me to speak. Until we saw the throbbing blue glow of the lights from the police cruisers at the corner of McLendon and Moreland. Then we heard the sirens. "Sounds like at least three units," I said.

"Four," Bucky corrected me. "What now?"

He stomped on the accelerator and the Miata responded accordingly. Bucky was still talking to the dispatcher on the car radio when we pulled up to the intersection at Little Five Points. The two cruisers were parked across McLendon at Moreland, and two more were parked across Euclid. A uniformed officer was directing the line of backed-up cars away from the intersection, which was clogged with people.

Bucky swung around the line of cars in front of us and pulled into the middle of the intersection, holding his shield out the window so that the cop could see his ID.

The uniformed officer, a trim black woman with a gold cap

on her front tooth, bent down and looked in the window, frowning until she recognized Bucky.

"Hey there, Tanya," Bucky said. "What's going on?'

Tanya Peeples pointed across Euclid, in the direction of the Yacht Club. "Got a body in a van, back there in the alley. White female. That's all I know."

But I knew. I knew whose van was in this alley, whose body had been found.

"Christ," I said. "It's Wuvvy."

"Who's working it?" Bucky asked Peeples.

"Major Mackey showed up as soon as they called in the homicide. I heard he was looking for you."

Bucky glanced over at me, his face set. "Here's where you get out," he said.

I knew better than to argue. I wasn't even out of the car completely before the Miata was rolling through the intersection, heading up Euclid toward the Yacht Club. I tucked my pocketbook under my arm like a football and sprinted across McLendon, right behind his car.

I had to push my way through the crowd on the sidewalk. The night was unexpectedly warm, the air greasy and stale. A guy with dreadlocks was sitting on the curb, whaling away at a set of African drums; somebody else was tooting away on a flute. It was all just annoying background music to accompany the buzz of shock and excitement death brings when it happens in a public way.

Hap and Miranda stood outside the Yacht Club, huddled close together, watching the street circus as it whirled around them. Hap had a protective arm drawn around Miranda's shoulder; her eyes were red-rimmed, and the hand that held a cigarette out to her side was shaking badly.

"Wuvvy?" I asked.

Hap nodded. Miranda tossed the cigarette to the pavement

and ground it out with the toe of her boot. She gave me a half-smile, turned, and walked back inside the bar.

"Miranda found her," Hap said. "Christ, what a mess."

"What happened?"

"We had a case of lemons go bad. It was stinking up the whole kitchen. Miranda took it out to toss it in the Dumpster. She saw the van nosed back in those woods on the other side of the alley. There's a little sort of pull-through in back of the Dumpster, but it's all grown up with weeds and shit. People from the neighborhood think it's their private dump, always leaving old refrigerators and mattresses and tires and shit the city won't pick up. We have to pay to have it hauled off, and it ain't cheap. Miranda didn't realize at first that it was Wuvvy's van. Then she walked around to the back of it, to see if there was still a tag on it, and that's when she realized whose van it was. She took a look, ran inside, and called me."

Hap rubbed his jaw. He needed a shave, and I noticed the stubble on his chin was mostly gray. It was November, but he still wore baggy cotton shorts, a faded Yacht Club T-shirt, and leather Birkenstock sandals. His arms and legs were thin, covered with fine dark hair. He reminded me of some old pirate, marooned on a desert island.

"She blamed me for losing the store," Hap said. "You heard her in here Friday night, didn't you?"

I nodded. "She was drunk. Stoned too."

He sighed. "We've been friends a long time. I never knew she'd been in prison. I never knew any of that shit. Not that it would have mattered. I'd have helped her if she'd asked. You know that, right?"

I hesitated. "Was it suicide?"

"Carbon monoxide, I guess. There was a piece of hose attached to the exhaust pipe. She'd run it in through the window. I guess she'd been there a while, 'cause the motor wasn't running when we found her. When I saw the hose, I didn't get any closer. Came in the bar and called 911."

A burly guy in a Harley-Davidson T-shirt came bustling up the sidewalk toward us, his head swinging from side to side, taking it all in. He held his hand out to shake Hap's.

"Hap! Man, what's goin' on?"

Hap kept his hand in the pockets of his shorts. "You know Wuvvy? The chick who owned YoYos?"

"Nah," the biker said. "I just come over here to drink." He laughed at his own little joke.

"She killed herself tonight," Hap said bluntly.

The biker blinked. "Radical," he said. He turned and pushed through the door of the Yacht Club.

More cruisers blocked the entrance to the alley, and a uniformed officer was stationed at the Yacht Club's rear entrance. I could see Bucky over near the Dumpster, walking around, squatting, taking notes. It was as close as I could get. I stood at the edge of the crowd, watching, finding myself becoming oddly detached from the fact of Wuvvy's death.

It got colder, and finally people moved on. One of the uniformed officers remembered me from my days on the burglary squad, and let me move to a spot out of the wind, close to the Yacht Club's back door. Around one A.M., two paramedics wheeled a gurney carrying a neatly zipped body bag out to the waiting ambulance and loaded it aboard. It pulled out of the alley, lights flashing but no siren. No real emergency now, after all.

Bucky finished his note-taking and had a final chat with Major Mackey. Mackey got in his unmarked city unit and drove away too. Bucky looked over in my direction and gestured for me to join him.

"You need a ride home?"

"Yeah," I said. "Like you said, the neighborhood's going to hell."

A dozen questions ran through my head, but I couldn't think what to ask first. Bucky saved me the trouble.

"Asphyxiation," he said, sliding behind the Miata's steering wheel. "She wasn't taking any chances either. The attendant at the gas station across the street said she pulled in around eight o'clock, bought twenty-four dollars' worth of high test. He said he'd never known her to buy more than five dollars' worth of gas before."

"Was there a note?"

"Not really. She had a plastic bag fixed up, left it on the passenger seat. Her papers, I guess. The letter from the governor, commuting her prison sentence, title to the van, her high school diploma, stuff like that. Like she wanted to make sure her body was properly ID'd."

"It *was* Wuvvy, right?"

"It was her," Bucky said. "You know she had an old eight-track player in that van? The tape was still playing when the first uniform got here."

"What was the tape?"

"Rolling Stones," Bucky said. "*Sympathy for the Devil.*"

An Atlanta Police cruiser was parked at the curb, across the street from my house. A silhouetted figure waved at us. Bucky waved back.

"He's gonna stay till he gets off shift at seven," Bucky said, nodding at the car. "Best I could do."

"I appreciate it," I said, touching him on the shoulder. I've never minded depending on the kindness of friends. Especially when the friend is a cop and the boogeyman has been sniffing around my windows.

13

An Atlanta Police cruiser was parked at the curb, across the street from my house. A silhouetted figure waved at us. Bucky waved back.

"He's gonna stay till he gets off shift at seven," Bucky said, nodding at the car. "Best I could do."

"I appreciate it," I said, touching him on the shoulder. I've never minded depending on the kindness of friends. Especially when the friend is a cop and the boogeyman has been sniffing around my windows.

"What happens with the Jackson Poole investigation now that Wuvvy's dead?" I asked.

"Mackey wants it finished up," Bucky said. "We talked about it before he left tonight. I've got a couple more interviews, some loose ends to tie up, but as soon as that's taken care of, he thinks, and I agree, that Wuvvy killed Poole. She's dead now, the coroner's gonna call it suicide. By the end of the week, the case is closed."

He braced both hands on the steering wheel. "You're not

gonna dog me about this, are you? I mean, it's not like you had a client. You said yourself you weren't working for Wuvvy. Even if you were, she's dead now."

"What's your hurry?" I asked. "It's not like this is a cold case. Jackson Poole's only been dead three days. There are still tons of leads that could be followed up. Like that business at the Blind Possum tonight, for instance. Aren't you the least bit curious about Anna Frisch's reluctance to cooperate with a homicide investigation?"

He sighed. "I knew you were gonna get jammed up in this."

"I found Jackson Poole's body, remember?"

Bucky leaned over and unlocked my door. "Mackey wants this case cleared. I've got four other active cases going right now and two trials coming up. We've got a new assistant chief, Marge Fitzgerald. Heard of her?"

"I thought she was in charge of public relations," I said.

"She's in charge of everything as of this week," Bucky said ruefully. "And Fitzgerald is a number cruncher. She wants weekly case-clearance reports. Homicide reports are due Friday."

"So this is about numbers?"

"It's about keeping my job," Bucky said, refusing to get riled. "Under the old system, a murder was a murder, even if the perp killed somebody in front of a whole streetful of witnesses. We had a ninety-three percent clearance rate when you counted it that way. But now Fitzgerald, she separates out the whodunits from the Saturday-night knife and gun stuff, and we've only got a forty-three percent clearance rate on whodunits. Mackey wants that rate up—yesterday."

"I see," I said. "Thanks for an interesting evening."

"You're welcome," he told me. "You're gonna see about getting a security system installed first thing—right?"

"Yeah," I said earnestly. "First thing."

*　　　*　　　*

A note dangled from the hall light, right inside the front door, just at eye level. It was from Edna.

> *Callahan:*
>
> *Gone to spend the night at Maureen's. Took my gun with me, so don't bother to look. Don't forget to lock the doors.*
>
> *Love, Mom*

Just like my sister. Once she heard that we'd had a Peeping Tom, she'd insist it wasn't safe for Edna to stay in the house. Of course, she didn't give a tinker's damn about me staying there alone.

"Fine," I muttered to myself. I locked the deadbolt and peered out the window to see that my guardian cop was still in place. Which he was.

I walked through the house checking on all the windows and snapping off lights. Jittery? Oh yeah.

My bedroom was the last stop. I took my gun out of my purse and put it on the nightstand, for once not bothering to unload it. Then I got undressed in the closet, draping myself in my longest, thickest flannel nightgown.

It wasn't until I'd gotten into bed that I noticed the red flashing light on my answering machine.

I punched the play button and sank back into my pillows. "Callahan?"

I sat upright, reaching unthinkingly for my pistol.

The voice wasn't Maureen's. It wasn't even anybody who was alive. It was the voice of Wuvvy. I still couldn't visualize her as a Virginia Lee. I gripped the gun with both hands, a talisman to ward off whatever demons haunted that voice on the other end of the line.

I could hear faint background music. Very faint. But it sounded like "Keep on Trucking," the Deadhead national anthem.

"It's me," the voice said. "Wuvvy. I guess you saw me on the six o'clock news. Everybody in Atlanta has seen it by now."

There was a long pause. "Don't hang up," I said aloud. "Tell me why you did it."

"I don't know why I'm calling you," Wuvvy continued. "Hell, I can't think of anybody I should call, so you'll have to do."

Wuvvy's words came tumbling out in a torrent. "It's like I'm an outlaw or something. They've already got me tried and convicted." Her voice cracked, trailed off into nowhere. "Channel 10 even had a picture of me, me and Broward and Jackson. Back before. They used my old name," Wuvvy said bitterly. "Dug up all that old stuff. You wonder why I was hiding? That's why. Once a killer, always a killer, that's how people think. It's a police state, Callahan. I spent ten years in prison. I did everything I was supposed to do, but people still wouldn't leave me alone.

"You know when the last time was I saw Jackson Poole? Before Friday night? Twenty years ago. He was a nine-year-old kid. I never saw him again until Friday night. Not in all those years. I helped raise him. Broward didn't care anything about that boy. Nobody did. So what happens? I finally get my act together, he hunts me down and ruins my life all over again. He's dead and I might as well be. So fuck it. Nobody cares about the truth. Nobody ever did."

The tape kept running, but Wuvvy had said what she had to say. She didn't even bother to hang up, just kept on truckin'.

14

"Smell this."

Before I could protest, Cheezer was spritzing the back of my hand with a plastic pump-action spray bottle.

I sniffed my hand, rubbing at the wet spot. "Peppermint? What's it for?"

"Spearmint," Cheezer said. "It's an all-purpose spray cleaner. My theory is that America is tired of lemon- and pine-scented cleaners. Whaddya think?"

"I think you better not be spraying me with any more chemicals," I said, getting up from the kitchen table and rinsing my hand under the tap.

"Yeah," Edna chimed in. "You could put somebody's eye out with that stuff."

Cheezer held the bottle up to his face and misted his face with the cleanser. "Not really," he said, wiping the liquid from his eyes. "See? The ingredients are totally nontoxic. Earth-friendly."

"Yeah, but does it work?" Edna demanded.

He sprayed the kitchen countertop and swiped at it with a paper towel. Edna and I bent close to inspect the results.

"Not bad," I had to admit. The forty-year-old scratched and stained Formica gleamed in the late afternoon sun.

"Pretty decent," Edna agreed. "What else does it do?"

Cheezer beamed. "It really is all-purpose. Glass, metal, plastic, tile, laminate, even painted surfaces." His voice dropped to a whisper. "I'm still not happy with the results on wood, though. It's leaving a slightly dull film. I've got to do some more tinkering on my formula."

"That's real good, sweetie," Edna said, patting his shoulder. She put on a sweater and picked up her purse, hooking the strap over her shoulders. "You run along home now," she said. "All the other House Mice are long gone."

She was right. It was Thursday, after six P.M. We'd been running ourselves ragged trying to get a handle on all the new business the storm had generated. Cheezer and I had cleaned four houses that day, Neva Jean had done three, Ruby two, and Baby and Sister had pitched in with Edna to clean two condos.

"We've still got the Stoutamires to go," I said wearily. The Stoutamires owned a huge three-story Victorian heap over on Spruce Street in Inman Park. They were some of Neva Jean's original clients.

"That's an all-day job," Edna said. "Call them up and tell them we'll have to cancel today. See if they want to rebook for Friday."

"I could do it," Cheezer volunteered. "I went with Neva Jean last time."

"You've done enough today," I said.

He sprayed some more of the cleaner and dabbed at a perfectly clean spot on the counter. "I could use the money," he said quietly.

"You do what you want," Edna said, buttoning her sweater. "I'm tired of working for a living. I've got to pick up

Baby and Sister, and then I'm fixing to go win me ten thousand dollars."

"Wow," Cheezer said. "How?"

"Rollover jackpot at the Knights of Columbus bingo," Edna said smugly. "It's early bird night tonight, and I'm on a streak. I won twenty-five dollars on a Lotto scratch-off ticket yesterday, and last week I won a hundred dollars on a four-corners game at the Piedmont Park American Legion."

"I'm surprised you're letting Baby and Sister horn in on the action," I said teasingly.

"They mostly just go for all-you-can-eat spaghetti for a dollar," Edna said. "And they don't play their own cards. They just help me with mine."

"How many cards do you play?" Cheezer asked.

"Depends," Edna said. "I gotta be going now." She headed for the door.

"Well, how many, approximately?" I asked.

She had her hand on the doorknob. "Anywhere from four to forty-eight, Miss Snoop," she said.

"Geez," I said. When my mother started going to bingo a year ago, I'd encouraged her new interest as a way to keep her mind off smoking. Who knew she'd found a new addiction?

She read my mind, as usual. "I can stop any time I want to," she said stubbornly. "And it's my money, and how I spend it is none of your beeswax." With that, she flounced out the door.

Even with both of us working like whirling dervishes, using what seemed like ten gallons of Cheezer's miracle mint spray, we didn't get done with the Stoutamires' house until past eleven o'clock.

"You hungry?" I asked as we were leaving the house. "We could stop and get a bite. My treat," I added hastily.

"Whatever," Cheezer said.

I turned the Lincoln up Moreland Avenue out of habit. As always, I was amazed by the number of kids hanging around Little Five Points at that hour of the night. There were dozens and dozens of them; teenagers mostly, some who looked like they'd barely reached puberty. They lolled against the street lamps, perched on the curb, dirty bare feet sticking out into the street, puffing on cigarettes, some taking furtive sips from brown paper bags. As usual, a big circle of kids stood on the sidewalk in front of The Point, playing Hacky Sack. As usual, there were four or five older men, street types, asleep or passed out, slumped in the doorways of storefronts that had closed for the night.

"Doesn't anybody have parents anymore?" I sounded like a forty-year-old fuddy-duddy. "How do they survive?" I asked. "Where do they sleep? Get money for food? Hell, where do they use the bathroom?"

He laughed. "Take a look around, Callahan. This is where they sleep and shit. Right here. Although usually Hap and some of the other store owners let 'em use their bathrooms. Anyway, you don't really want to know how they live."

"Why not?" I asked, bristling a little. "I'm not all that old. Believe it or not, Cheezer, I wasn't born middle-aged."

"I didn't say that," Cheezer protested. "Okay. They live off the streets. Day to day. The girls, some of 'em, turn tricks, not for money so much, but for food or dope, or maybe a place to stay when the weather's bad. A lot of them do a little dealing. Nothing major. Some of the guys hustle, but not that much. There's still kinda a stigma to being a queer."

Queer. One of those words that makes us tolerant types shudder in the nineties. Cheezer said the nasty word matter-of-factly.

"Depressing," I said, looking up and down the street for a parking spot. "It's like it was back in the seventies when I was a teenager. The only difference is, back then, kids ran away to the strip."

"The strip?" Cheezer raised an eyebrow. "Like Sunset Strip? Hollywood?"

I spotted a parking space in front of the Baker's Café, pulled the Lincoln abreast of the car in front of the slot, and started trying to remember how to parallel park. I spun the Lincoln's steering wheel all the way clockwise, edged the gas pedal a little, and inched forward and backwards, spinning the wheel and craning my neck to check how I was doing.

After five minutes of craning and cursing, the Lincoln's rear was still sticking four inches out into the street. I realized what Cheezer had asked me. About the strip. Obviously it was a generational thing.

"The strip was right here in midtown Atlanta," I told him. "Peachtree and Tenth Street. Ground zero for the age of Aquarius. Peace, love and drugs."

"Your rear end is sticking out," Cheezer said, looking over his shoulder.

"For a long time," I agreed. "Let's eat."

I ordered the gumbo and Cheezer ordered the shrimp étouffée. We ate a whole loaf of french bread while we were waiting for the food. I knocked back two Dixie beers, and Cheezer sipped on a big glass of iced tea.

"This is great," he said when our food came. He plowed into the étouffée with no pretense at manners. "Kinda like a place in the Garden District, only they put okra in their étouffée, and I'd always pick it out. Okra sucks."

"You lived in New Orleans?" I asked.

"For a couple years," Cheezer said, dipping a piece of bread in my bowl of gumbo. The waitress had seated us at a table in front of the window. He pointed across the street. "Isn't that your cop friend?"

I looked. It was Bucky Deavers. He was crossing Euclid Avenue, walking toward us but not looking at the Baker's Café, not seeing us in the nearly empty restaurant.

Bucky was dressed in a suit, and he was unfastening his tie as he walked, stopping to take it off and stuff it in the breast pocket of his jacket.

"Must be just getting off work," I said. "Headed for the Yacht Club. All that number crunching makes for a big thirst."

I thought about Wuvvy for the first time that day, thought about her last phone call to me, the music in the background, the finality of what she'd decided to do.

They'd taught us about carbon-monoxide poisoning at the Police Academy. What happens is, carbon-monoxide atoms attach themselves onto a red blood cell, displace the oxygen needed for normal circulation, and keep the red blood cells from being able to carry oxygen to the tissues. It's a slow suffocation, really. The thing I remembered most succinctly was the cherry-red color of the blood of people poisoned by carbon monoxide, and the fact that the victim's face is flushed, as though sunburned.

Wuvvy always had a George Hamilton tan, summer and winter, from playing Frisbee outdoors year-round. Had the poison flush shown under her tan? I tried to push the thought from my mind, finished my beer in one gulp, and pushed the empty bottle away, my mouth puckered from the sour taste.

"You want the rest of this?" I asked, gesturing toward my nearly full bowl of gumbo.

He nodded. I pushed the bowl toward his side of the table, took a twenty-dollar bill out of my purse, and placed it under the edge of the bowl. "You stay and eat," I said. "Come over to the Yacht Club and get me when you're done."

Cheezer kept chewing but nodded his head.

The sidewalk in front of the Yacht Club and YoYos was littered with construction debris. Light and plaster dust flooded out the open door of Wuvvy's old storefront. The high drone of a power saw was punctuated by the banging of hammers. Somebody had draped a canvas banner across the dust-streaked window.

BLIND POSSUM BREWPUB GRAND OPENING IN ONE WEEK! the banner announced.

Neither Jackson Poole's nor Virginia Lee Mincey's death could slow down the inexorable wheels of corporate progress.

I pushed the door of the Yacht Club open. It was quiet inside. Three guys played darts at the back of the room, a few booths held scattered occupants. Four people were seated at the bar, their backs to me. Bucky was hunched over his beer, reading the *Constitution*'s sports pages.

I sat down next to him. He glanced up.

"Want a beer?"

"I've had enough, thanks," I said. "Hard day at the office?"

"Mackey signed off on Jackson Poole and Wuvvy. Both cases are closed, Virginia Lee Mincey responsible for the homicide. That's what you want to know, right?"

"I guess." Hap came over and stood in front of me. "Hey, Callahan," he said. "Whatcha having?"

"Just a glass of water," I said. He nodded, filled a glass with crushed ice from the cooler, and filled it up with water, put it in front of me, then wandered away down the bar.

"Where'd she get the hose?" I asked.

"What?" Bucky looked startled.

"The hose," I repeated. "The one she hooked up from the

van's tailpipe. Wuvvy didn't have a yard. She lived in a store. Where'd the hose come from?"

Bucky drummed his fingertips on the scarred wooden bar. He shook his head and made a *tsk-tsk* sound. "Wuvvy had a water bed. You fill up a water bed with a hose, right?"

Maybe I wasn't so clever. "I didn't think about the water bed."

He sipped his beer, wiped away a fleck of foam from his upper lip.

"It was a suicide," he said, enunciating each word. "No doubt about it. I saw the autopsy report. No trauma to the body, nothing. Some pills in her system. Wuvvy liked her pharmaceuticals. Everybody knew that. Face it, Callahan. Wuvvy killed a guy and she knew she was going back to prison. So she hooked up that hose, fired up the van, popped in a Rolling Stones tape, and then went off to sleep. That's all there is to it. I swear. You know I wouldn't agree to closing the cases if I didn't believe that. Right?"

His dark eyes searched my face for some sign of trust.

"I guess," I said reluctantly.

Bucky swiveled around on his barstool so that he was facing the window. I turned, too.

"You see all the action next door?" he asked.

"How could I miss it?"

With his beer bottle, he gestured down the bar at Hap, who was loading a cooler with bottles of beer. "A brewpub right next door, that's gonna take some business away from the Yacht Club. Wonder how Hap feels about that?"

"Whole different kind of customer," I said. "Yuppies. They'll flock here from Virginia-Highland and Buckhead. Maybe Hap will get some spillover. You said yourself, it's a good thing for the neighborhood."

"It is," Bucky said. "Definitely."

Cheezer came in the front door then, but he didn't really come inside. Just stood there and gave me a half-wave.

"I gotta go," I told Bucky. "What happens now? To Wuvvy, I mean."

He knew what I meant.

"We couldn't find any next of kin. Hell, she killed 'em all, her husband and her stepson. We found a lawyer's business card in with all that shit of hers. Turns out she's an old friend from Hawkinsville. She's taking care of the arrangements."

"Will there be a memorial service or something?" It was the last thing I wanted to do, go to a funeral for Wuvvy. Still, it's the Southern way.

"Don't know," Bucky said. "We released the body to a funeral home down there today. Dubberly Brothers Mortuary."

I found a pen in my purse and wrote down the name. "I could call there. Or I could call the lawyer. Ask her about a service. What's her name?"

He scratched his chin and his eyes got vacant. "Hell, I don't know. Call me at the office tomorrow, I'll see if I can find the business card."

"What about all of Wuvvy's stuff?" I asked. "That's why she called me in the first place. To see if I could get her stuff back."

"It goes in the Dumpster, I guess. That friend of hers said we should just dispose of it."

"All of it?" I couldn't believe it. "Wuvvy talked like she had some really valuable rock 'n' roll memorabilia."

Bucky snorted. "There's nothing anybody but Wuvvy would think was valuable in that shit—unless there's some underground market for Fritz the Cat roach clips and boxes of those yellow smiley-face buttons."

"Can I take a look?" I asked, glancing toward the door. Cheezer was leaning up against the window, playing the patient martyr.

"There's nothing there," Bucky said.

"I just want to look."

"Come by in the morning," he said finally. "I'll have the lawyer's name for you by then."

15

I heard the chorus of snores as soon as I opened my bedroom door. Two tiny dark heads were nestled on my pillows, my favorite quilt pulled up around their noses. Miss Baby had bobby-pinned spit curls covering her head, a pink chiffon scarf tied around her coiffure. Miss Sister, always cold, had a pale blue crocheted cap pulled down around her forehead. Baby's snores were wheezy and high-pitched, Sister's deeper, like a tree frog.

I got a pillow and another quilt out of the linen closet in the hall and made myself a bed on the foldout sofa in the den. I was a licensed private detective, intelligent, intuitive. Someday I'd have to solve the mystery of why I spend so much time sleeping on makeshift beds in my own home.

The Easterbrooks sisters apparently slept sounder than I did. By the time I woke up Friday morning, I could hear soft singing and cooking sounds coming from the kitchen.

I got dressed and went to investigate.

Baby stood on an old wooden Coke crate in front of the stove, wrapped neck to ankles in one of Edna's old gingham aprons. She had three burners going, a black skillet full of sausage patties that sputtered and sizzled, a bubbling pot of grits, and a third skillet into which she was cracking eggs.

She dipped a spoon in the grits pot. "Over my head," she sang softly, "there's trouble in the air."

Sister stood nearby at the counter, deftly slicing cinnamon-and-sugar-dough pinwheels and patting them into place on a cookie sheet. "There must be a God somewhere," she said, joining in Baby's song. Sister was dusted with flour from fingertip to elbows, her face smudged with butter and cinnamon, and she patted her foot as she sang. She beamed when she saw me standing there, listening to their gospel concert.

"Good morning, sleepyhead," Sister said. "Did you ever taste my cinnamon rolls before?"

"My cinnamon rolls, you mean," Baby corrected her sharply. "I'm the one Mama gave the recipe to."

"You the one makes cinnamon rolls taste like roofing shingles," Sister said. She shook her head disapprovingly. "Baby got a real heavy hand with dough. Can't make pie crust to save her soul."

Edna did not look up from where she sat at the table, her head buried in the morning paper.

"I take it you didn't win the ten thousand dollars last night," I said, pouring myself a cup of coffee and sitting down across from her.

"No," she said, getting up and going to the refrigerator. She stood there with the door open, poking around among the milk cartons and the foil-wrapped containers of leftovers.

I helped myself to the section of the newspaper she'd abandoned.

"This is a nice surprise," I said. "If I'd known y'all were planning a pajama party last night, I'd have come home earlier."

Baby and Sister exchanged guilty looks.

"Edna invited us," Sister said. "'Cause, uh, it was so late when we got home last night, she didn't feel like going all the way over to the senior citizen high-rise."

"The girls are working this morning," Edna said, closing the refrigerator door and moving over to the pantry. I heard her rearranging cans and boxes of cereal, but could see only her polyester-clad rear end, protruding through the open pantry door. "Mrs. Draper asked for them, special."

"Okay," I said, turning rapidly through the newspaper pages. "I've got an errand to run this morning, then I'll check in with you."

She came out of the pantry with a bag of flour in one hand and a can of tomato sauce in the other. "What kind of errand?"

I looked up at her and nearly did a double take. Her right cheek was crimson, her right eye blackened and swollen, and there were long, bloodied scratches along her right cheekbone.

"What happened to you?" I asked, rushing over to get a better look.

"Nothing," she said, ducking back into the pantry. "Leave me alone. I'm fine."

I took her by the shoulder and turned her around to face me. She winced at the touch of my hand on her arm.

"You're not fine," I said, alarmed. "You're hurt. What happened, Ma?"

She tried to wriggle out of my grip. "I got up in the middle of the night to go to the bathroom and I bumped into the doorway, that's all."

I let go of her arm, but turned to the girls.

"Miss Baby, Miss Sister, you better tell me what happened

to Edna. I know y'all didn't spend the night because it was so late. Tell me the truth," I said sternly. "Did Edna get you all mixed up in a fistfight at the Knights of Columbus?"

Baby turned off the fire under her pots and pans and put a lid on the grits pot. "Better go on and tell her. You know the Bible says the truth shall set you free."

Sister wiped her flour-flecked hands on a dishtowel. "Your mama was robbed!" she said. "That white boy put a knife in her face and called her ugly names and liked to have slapped her into the next county."

"We seen it," Baby said. "Sitting right there in your driveway, in Edna's car. He didn't see us, though, 'cause it was so dark. He'd have seen us, we might all be dead and in our graves."

"Dear God," I whispered, setting my coffee cup down with shaky hands. "Tell me what happened."

Edna's shoulders drooped.

"All right. I'll tell you. But promise you won't get excited."

"Go over there and sit down," I said, pushing her toward the kitchen table.

She looked even worse sitting there in the full daylight by the big window that looks out onto our backyard. Now I could see that her right hand and wrist were bruised and cut, and she had bruises on her neck.

Edna twisted the worn gold wedding band on her left hand.

"I was mugged," she said finally. "Last night. He got my purse. And my winnings. I won the second game of the night. Two hundred dollars."

"Stole her good pocketbook you done give her for Mother's Day, too," Baby said. "That pretty leather one with all them zipper pockets. Took that knife and cut the strap like it was butter."

Edna looked like she'd done some crying last night and could break out again at any moment. "He took the St. Christopher's medal your daddy gave me right before he died." She looked up at me defiantly. "You might as well know. They got my gun, too. It was in my purse."

I looked over at Baby and Sister. "Are you girls all right? He didn't hurt you?"

"No, ma'am," Sister said. "Edna was just going to run in the house and hide that money she won before she took us home. She was just walking to the back door when that boy jumped out of the bushes and started grabbing at her."

"We scared him off," Baby said proudly. "Rolled down the windows, and me and Sister screamed some bad words at that boy. Honked the horn, too."

"Thank God they were there," Edna said. "He really could have killed me. He was crazy. Hopped up on drugs, I reckon."

Her hand wandered to her neck, to the place where she'd always worn the little gold chain that held the St. Christopher's medal. Now it was ringed with bruises.

"I guess I was thinking about how I was gonna spend that two hundred dollars, because I didn't even see this little piss-ant until I was halfway to the back door. Goddamn punk. Had a little old paring knife he must have stole off some other old lady. He kept jabbing it at me, telling me to give him my purse."

I reached out and touched the swollen cheek, and she flinched in pain. "Why didn't you just give him the purse?" I asked.

"It was my purse. My money. My gold medal. He didn't have any right to it," Edna said stubbornly. "Besides, he called me bitch. 'Hand it over, you old bitch,' he said. It made me mad. I jerked my purse away and tried to run. I was hollering my fool head off, thinking Mr. Byerly across the street would hear me. I forgot he's deaf as a post."

"What happened next?"

"He caught me, of course," Edna said wryly. "My running days are over. He like to have ripped my arm out of the socket yanking that purse. And when I still wouldn't let go, he slapped me, then he socked me, right in the face. I fell down then or he never would have got my purse away from me."

"That's when we started the commotion," Baby said loudly. "Wish I'd have had a gun on me."

"Thank God you didn't," I said fervently. "He could have killed all three of you. Why didn't you call the cops? Why didn't you at least tell me when I got home?"

"She wouldn't let us tell," Sister said, shaking a finger at Edna. "I tole her and tole her, we shoulda called the police. But she told me to mind my own business. Best we could do was make her let us spend the night. Me and Baby, we watched her good until you got home."

Edna looked down at her hands, which were scratched and bruised. "It's embarrassing," she said in a low voice. "I felt like a fool, all bloody and boo-hooing." She bit her lip. "I wet my pants, I was so scared. After Baby and Sister ran him off, at first I was scared, then I was mad. Then I wanted to die. I felt old, Callahan. Old and helpless. Useless. Baby and Sister made me a hot toddy, then I took a bath and I got in the bed, but I didn't sleep until I heard you come in. Tell you the truth, I didn't sleep much, period, last night."

I reached for the phone. "We've got to report this to the cops. First the other night with the Peeping Tom, now this. I'm sorry, Ma. I should have seen about the burglar alarm right away. It just kinda got away from me."

Edna pulled the phone back toward her side of the oak table. "Don't call the cops."

"Oh yes," I said. "We're calling the cops, and I'm calling Bucky, too. See if he can get somebody to get some mug shots for you to look at. What did the creep look like?"

"He was a white boy," Baby said. She extended her arm over her head. "About so high. He was white, but he had them long greasy pigtails like the black kids wear."

"Dreadlocks," I said. "What about his face?"

"That boy was ugly," Sister said. "Even a blind woman could see his ugliness."

"That's right," Baby agreed. "Skinny and ugly. And he had a purple-and-white-striped crocheted cap, pulled down low on his ugly face."

"The gun, Jules," Edna said. "I didn't have a permit for that gun."

I stared at her. "You said you did have a permit."

"I lied," she said. "If you call the cops, I'll have to tell them about the gun. They could arrest me for carrying a gun without a permit. Just let it go. We'll get the Candler Commandos to handle this."

"You must have a concussion," I told her. "Brain damage. This thug had a knife to begin with; now he has a gun. He's violent, beats up women. Now let me have the phone."

She took her hand off the phone and crossed her arms over her chest. It was the old Edna Mae Garrity "I'll take my stand" posture. Not a good sign for anyone taking the opposite posture.

"You can call the FBI, and the GBI, and the CIA, if you want," she said, narrowing her eyes. "I'm not filing a report. There are no other witnesses."

She glared at Baby and Sister. "Nobody saw a thing. It's my word against yours. Now I thought you had an errand to run. In the meantime, I'm going to eat my breakfast, and then I've got to get Baby and Sister over to Mrs. Draper's house."

"Don't you worry about your mama, Callahan," Baby said. "We gon' look after her real good. Stay right with her and watch out for that ugly white boy."

"That's right," Sister said. She pulled a nickel-plated police whistle out of the pocket of her apron. "And I'm gonna give a blast on this if anybody even looks at her cross-eyed."

"No cops," Edna repeated. "See? I've got my own body-guards."

I locked my eyes on hers. "I'm calling C. W. Hunsecker this morning. First thing after my errand," I said. "Get him to come out here and put in a security system. Alarms, motion sensors, everything."

"Who's paying for that?" she demanded.

"Remember what you told me last night?" I asked her. "What I do with my money is none of your business."

16

The Atlanta Police Department's Homicide Task Force was created back in 1982, when black children started disappearing all over the city. Eventually there were twenty-one "official" missing-and-murdered cases. Hundreds of local and federal cops worked the case, eventually causing the creation of a homicide task force and a separate office.

Unlike Atlanta City Hall, where the local politicians had built themselves an airy, elegant municipal palace complete with an atrium with $8,500 worth of potted palms, the APD's white brick building downtown on Decatur Street was dark, cramped, and crappy-looking. And the homicide unit's "new" digs were just as bad: a one-story mustard-colored cinderblock affair on a quiet street off Ponce de Leon in Midtown.

The receptionist at the front desk buzzed me through, but told me that Sergeant Deavers was in a meeting. "They're all in meetings. All the time," she said, rolling her eyes.

I sat at Bucky's desk in the communal squad room, looked

around to make sure nobody was watching. Nobody was. There was plenty of crime to go around. I leafed through a couple of case folders on Bucky's desk. Boring stuff. Clerk shot dead during a robbery at a liquor store on Martin Luther King Drive, eighteen-year-old mother of two shot to death by her boyfriend in an argument over who got the drumsticks out of a bucket of fried chicken.

There was a stack of pink telephone message slips on the desktop. Which reminded me. I picked up Bucky's phone and dialed 9, then the number for Hunsecker & Associates Security.

C. W. Hunsecker was my old cop buddy, a captain in the homicide unit before the shooting. He'd taken disability leave from the APD two years ago, after my carelessness got him shot, almost killed, paralyzed. He runs a security business these days, and helps me out with an occasional case. We'd been in some tight places together, and I knew that once I told him about what had been going on in our neighborhood, he'd give me a decent price on a security system.

C.W. answered the phone himself. We exchanged pleasantries: I asked him about his wife, Linda Nickells, a good friend of mine, and their preschool-aged son, Wash; he asked me about Mac and the family. Then I told him about the boogeymen who'd come sniffing 'round our door.

"Man," he said softly. "I hate to hear about somebody doing your mama that way. Sounds to me like the cops need to get over there and knock some heads together."

"I hate it, too," I said. "It's funny. With all her organization of this community-action patrol, you'd think Edna would want the police involved. But she doesn't. She won't even file a report. She's humiliated. I'm gonna talk to Bucky about it, see if he'll talk to the captain over at Zone Five, but in the meantime, I think we're going to have to get a security system for the house."

"Best money you could spend," C.W. said heartily. "Haven't I been telling you that neighborhood ain't safe?"

"I hate the idea of living behind burglar alarms and camera monitors," I told him. "How much is this thing gonna cost?"

"Won't be that bad," C.W. said. I heard him tapping on the keys of a calculator. "I'll give you the equipment at my cost, install it myself. You'll want silent and audible alarms, contact switches and motion detectors on the doors and windows . . ." He droned on, and I could hear the numbers adding up. I doodled on the margins of Bucky's desk blotter. Dollar signs, moneybags, barred windows. All very Freudian.

"Okay," C.W. said finally. "I think we can get you wired for the basics for about a thousand dollars. But I'd suggest one more thing. A closed-circuit video cam on the front door, with a monitor inside the house, probably the kitchen, so you can see who's at the door before they see you. That's another five hundred. I got most of the stuff in stock. I could come out there tomorrow morning. That suit you?"

"On your day off?" I asked, wincing. "Linda will wring my neck. She says you're never home as it is. No, better just get me your regular installer."

"You know what my installation guys get paid?" C.W. said, hooting. "You'll wish you'd gone to trade school instead of college. Naw. I'll do it. Linda can help. She's getting really good at wiring. You and Edna can run herd on Wash."

"You drive a hard bargain," I said. "See you Saturday."

"See who on Saturday?" Bucky said, looming over me.

I hadn't seen him come out of his meeting. He had a stack of files tucked under his arm and was wearing glasses I'd never seen before.

I got up hastily. "C. W. Hunsecker. He's gonna come out and install a security system on the house."

Bucky took off the glasses and tucked them in his shirt pocket. He nodded his approval. "Good. Peepers are nothing to mess with."

"It's more than a Peeping Tom now," I said. "Edna was mugged in the front yard last night. At knifepoint. Guy beat her up bad and snatched her purse. Baby and Sister scared him off or he could have killed her."

Bucky pulled up a chair from the vacant desk next to his. "You don't just need a security system, Garrity, you need a new address. Is Edna all right?"

I shrugged. "She says she's fine. But she's bruised and battered and mad as hell. I think this whole thing has left her feeling really vulnerable for the first time in her life." I hesitated. "Her gun was in her purse. Along with her bingo winnings."

"You called it in, right?"

"She wouldn't let me. Turns out she didn't have a carry permit. When I left the house this morning, Baby and Sister were playing bodyguard, and she was trying to act like the whole thing was a joke, but we both know it's not. I got a description of the guy. Sounds like a street kid."

Bucky was writing as I talked. "I'll talk to Jeff Kaczynski over at Zone Five. They've got a nice gallery of mug shots of the locals. He can take it by the house, have a chat with your mother, try to talk her into doing the right thing. A crazy with a gun is nothing to mess with. It was a thirty-eight, right?"

"Right. Good luck to Kaczynski," I said ruefully. "You know my mother. She's no pushover, not after she makes up her mind."

"Edna will like Kaczynski," Bucky said. "He's got that Southern accent, calls people 'ma'am' and 'sir,' takes off his hat when he comes in the house. Not a barbarian, like the rest of us."

"I feel better already," I said. "Now what about that business card you promised me? For Wuvvy's lawyer friend? And you said I could look through Wuvvy's stuff."

He opened a drawer in his desk, brought out a stack of business cards, fanning them out in his hand. He plucked one from the bunch and handed it to me.

Catherine Rhyne, attorney at law, it said. Offices in the Peachtree Promenade building in Midtown Atlanta.

Catherine Rhyne's secretary said she wasn't in, did I want to be connected to her voice mail to leave a message?

No, I said. Did she know anything about one of Catherine's clients, Virginia Lee Mincey?

"Would that be the lady who died?" the secretary asked. "From Ms. Rhyne's hometown?"

"Yes," I said. "Did she go to Hawkinsville already?"

The secretary hesitated. "She went down there this morning, to see that everything was taken care of."

"This morning?" I said, alarmed. "When are the services?"

"At two o'clock today," the secretary said. "Shall I leave a message for Ms. Rhyne?"

"I'll talk to her down there," I said.

"Where's Hawkinsville?" I asked, swiveling the chair around to face Bucky.

"South Georgia. Near Macon somewhere," he said.

"Never mind, I've got a map in the car. When can I look at Wuvvy's stuff?"

Bucky patted my hand. "You can *have* the stuff, for all I care." He motioned toward a stack of cartons in the corner of the squad room.

"I checked them out of the evidence room. Major Mackey gave the okay. If you're that interested, help yourself."

"Help me put them in my car?" I asked, fluttering my eyelashes in my best imitation of a helpless Southern belle.

*　　　*　　　*

My AAA map of Georgia showed me that Hawkinsville was a straight shot south of Atlanta down I-75. Exit in Perry, get on State Road 341, Hawkinsville was due east. If I could get my loaner Lincoln's speedometer to inch past fifty miles an hour, I should be able to make it in just about two hours.

But first I had to go home and change my clothes. Blue jeans were fine for domestic engineering and even for private investigation fieldwork, but they'd never do for a sympathy call to a south Georgia funeral home. Not even for a memorial service for a die-hard hippie like Wuvvy.

My charcoal pinstripe pantsuit was the closest thing I owned to a proper dress. With a cream silk blouse, black suede flats, and my good gold earrings, I thought I looked fairly tasteful.

I gritted my teeth and got ready to call Maureen to ask her to take custody of Edna until I got back. But Edna, Baby, and Sister pulled into the driveway before I could complete the call.

"Where you goin' all gussied up?" Edna asked.

"Look like funeral clothes," Baby said, running her fingers down the wool of my blazer.

"As a matter of fact," I said, "I'm going to run down to Hawkinsville. Pay my respects to Wuvvy. The memorial service is at two. So I thought you could go over to Maureen's until I got back. I shouldn't be much later than six o'clock . . . "

"No ma'am," Edna said quickly. "I don't want Maureen knowing anything about what happened to me last night. She'd have my bags packed and me in a hospital room in a New York second."

She looked at Baby and Sister, who smiled at me expectantly.

It didn't take her long to make up her mind. "Wait just a

minute till I get into something decent," Edna said, unbuttoning her pink House Mouse smock. "A little day trip in the country's just what I been needing. How about you girls? Y'all wanna go to Hawkinsville?"

"That'd be so nice," Sister said. "Me and Baby love to drive in that big yellow car of Callahan's."

"Can we spend the night at a motel?" Baby asked.

While Edna and the girls chattered about scenery, south Georgia, and the possibility of loading up on pecans for the Christmas baking, I finally had time to consider my motives for going off on a nearly two-hundred-mile wild-goose chase. Why was I going?

To see a woman I barely knew be buried? To pay my last respects to someone who wasn't a friend, wasn't even really a client? A nice forty-dollar FTD bouquet would have been more than sufficient.

But if I sent an anonymous bouquet of flowers, I'd miss the opportunity to stick my nose in somebody else's business. Virginia Lee Mincey had admitted to killing her husband and had been implicated in the murder of her long-lost stepson. If the cops were satisfied with those conclusions, why shouldn't I be?

Because you're not, I told myself. You're never satisfied.

17

We stopped three times in the first hour we were on the road, twice each for the girls to "powder their noses" and a third time so I could feed the Lincoln another quart of oil.

After the third stop all the girls drifted off to sleep and I had the road and my thoughts to myself. Somewhere south of Macon I sensed rather than knew that we were past the fall line, the geographer's delineation that divides north Georgia from south Georgia.

Gradually the soil in the roadside fields changed color—from the rusty red clay of the state's Piedmont to the sandy soil of the lower half of the state. The topography flattened out as though smoothed by an unseen hand, and I noticed that the trees still had leaves, while the trees around Atlanta had been denuded by the tornado that had swept through town.

Down here the golden and russet leaves of live oaks, dogwoods, and sweet gums still clung to the trees, although most of the landscape ran to spindly pines and endless fields of some low-growing green crop punctuated with scattered clumps of cattle.

The Lincoln's top speed worked out to about forty-eight miles per hour. I pushed the wobbly accelerator all the way to the floor and kept it there until I saw the exit sign for Perry and State Road 341.

It was a bright, sunny afternoon, comfortably warm. Fall could stay this way, I thought, even though the sun slanted directly into my eyes, making me squint to see where I was going.

In deference to the posted speed limits, I slowed down to thirty going through Perry. I felt guilty about rushing through such a nice little town without waking my mother. Edna loved Perry. There was a big old-timey hotel on the out-skirts of town, the New Perry. We'd stopped there once, on a long-ago family vacation to Florida, and thirty years later she still talked wistfully about the New Perry's homemade cream of celery soup scattered with puffy little oyster crackers and the magical quality of their squash soufflé.

No time to stop now, though. Not to gawk at the hand-some white-painted Victorians, nor at the prosperous-looking downtown business district.

After Perry, huge old trees crowded close to the edge of the two-lane road, their twisted black branches reaching out jagged fingertips to touch in the middle, each of the finger-tips clustered with dozens of open catkins. Pecan trees.

The pecan groves ran along both sides of the road, stretch-ing as far back as I could see. The trees were enormous, some probably sixty or eighty feet tall, with long arching limbs whose canopies stretched fifty feet in diameter. Machinery was scattered about in the groves, and every once in a while I glimpsed weatherbeaten wooden outbuildings tucked away among the trees.

Wuvvy's husband, Broward Poole, had been a big pecan

grower, Mac had said. One of the biggest in the state. Had these fields been his? I wondered.

The pecan groves gave way to the trappings of small-town life: a hardware store, a steakhouse, a pecan warehouse, a farm equipment dealership, even a tiny mom-and-pop motel court.

Then, abruptly, I was in downtown Hawkinsville. It was Perry's country cousin, a little shabbier, a bit more marginal. Storefronts along the main street, Lumpkin, were dust-streaked, and at least half the buildings were either long vacant or only halfheartedly still in business.

Dubberly Brothers Mortuary was easy to spot. It was the second-biggest building in town. The biggest, the Pulaski County Courthouse, was conveniently right across the street. The funeral home was a sprawling three-story white clap-board affair, with sagging white columns and a wraparound front porch. A pair of dispirited palm trees flanked the front walkway leading to the porch, where two men in dark suits stood looking out at the street, chatting and smoking.

Of course, the clock in the Lincoln didn't work and, as usual, I wasn't wearing a watch. It turned out I didn't need one. As I was nosing the Lincoln into a parking space in front of the courthouse, chimes began pealing out. Past the tower-ing magnolia trees on the lawn, past the Confederate memor-ial with its cross-eyed Robert E. Lee and startled Stonewall Jackson, a bell tower had been built onto the old stucco court-house. One, two, three, it finally chimed out fourteen times. Two o'clock. I was right on time.

Edna heard the chimes first. She woke with a start, sat up, stretched, looked around. "We there already?"

"Miss Baby, Miss Sister," I called, turning around to look at the girls.

"What's that?" Sister said. "Where we at?"

Baby yawned and covered her mouth. "This Hawkinsville. Remember, Sister, we come to Hawkinsville for the Eastern Star district meeting, long time ago."

"You talkin' about when Mama was inducted as Worshipful Matron?" Sister said, blinking. "Was that 1967 or 1968?"

"Girls," I said urgently. "I've got to go on into the memorial service now. I'll probably be an hour or so."

Edna unfastened her seat belt. "Go ahead on," she directed me. "The girls and I want to get some lunch, find the best place to buy pecans. We'll take the car, come back and pick you up."

The men on the front porch at Dubberly Brothers stopped talking when they saw the four of us, two white women and two black women, in the huge yellow Lincoln. They kept on smoking, but they didn't bother to hide their stares. It was still a small town, and this was still the Deep South. We must have looked like their idea of a traveling sideshow.

I had an idea.

"You want to do a little detecting, maybe?"

"Yes, ma'am," Sister said, punching Baby's arm. "You hear that? We gone do some private investigating for Callahan."

"You think I'll need a gun?" Edna asked, her hand straying to the bruises on her neck.

"This isn't Dodge City, Ma," I said. "I just want you all to do what you do naturally at home. Poke around town. Give folks a chance to gossip about Virginia Lee Mincey and Broward Poole and his son Jackson. Broward Poole's murder was probably the biggest news to ever hit this town. See what you can find out about their lawyer, too, a woman named Catherine Rhyne."

Edna and the girls nodded in unison. Then Edna held out her hands. I put the car keys in them, but she left her hand extended. "We'll need expense money," she said.

I got out my wallet.

"Twenty apiece would be nice," she added.

I winced but handed over the money and got out of the car. Edna slid over to the driver's side. "See you in a couple hours," she said, waving as she pulled away from the curb.

The front room of the Dubberly Brothers Mortuary smelled like Easter lilies and breath mints. The walls were painted a dark forest green, the carpet was green with little pink flowers, and a tiled fireplace had a gas fire going unnecessarily with the room temperature hovering at eighty-five degrees. With its spindly reproduction Early American settees and chairs and polished mahogany tables, Dubberly Brothers reminded me of a Holiday Inn lobby in Hahira. Only instead of listing wedding receptions and business meetings, the discreet black easel displayed the day's schedule of funerals. Neely, eleven A.M., Dogwood Parlour, Carden, twelve-thirty P.M., Magnolia Room, Mincey, two P.M., Cherokee Rose Room.

I suppressed the desire to tiptoe, and instead walked down the thickly carpeted main hallway. Each of the doors opening off the hall had small brass nameplates beside it. Dogwood, Azalea, Camellia, and at the end of the hall, the Cherokee Rose Room, whose door was slightly ajar.

The Cherokee Rose Room must have been Dubberly Brothers' smallest chapel. A balding man in a black clerical collar stood behind a wooden lectern. Over near the wall stood a silver-colored coffin draped with an arrangement of white and pink carnations. There were three other small flower arrangements, but it was the carnations that nearly made me choke. Pink carnations for Wuvvy? Red hibiscus would have been better. Or sunflowers, big as a dinner plate.

Four women sat in the middle row of folding chairs. Three of them were elderly, with carefully curled white hair, sensible shoes, and flowered Sunday school dresses. The fourth woman was my age, maybe a little older. She wore a well-tailored chalk-striped navy blue business suit that probably cost more than the sum total of my whole wardrobe of "good" stuff, and she was staring down at her hands, which she'd folded in her lap.

The minister cleared his throat, read a passage of Scripture.

"Virginia Lee Mincey is with our precious Lord," he said. "She is perfect in his eyes. She is forgiven."

Nobody in the room cried, nobody coughed. The old ladies nodded their heads in unison; the younger one, whom I assumed to be Catherine Rhyne, sat still as a statue.

I heard the door open behind me and turned, along with the others, to see who the latecomer was.

Hap Rudabaugh slid into a seat on the aisle in the back row, nodded in my direction, then fixed his eyes on the minister. The old ladies frowned at the sight of him; ponytails and Hawaiian shirts probably weren't de rigueur for funerals in Hawkinsville, but for Hap, who'd left off his customary hiking shorts and flip-flops, this was the equivalent of black tie and tails.

We'd all just settled ourselves again when there was another stir from the back of the room. Now we all frowned in unison.

It took me a while to put the face with the correct name and context. I'd last seen the woman edging past Hap into the next chair at the Blind Possum brewmaster's dinner. Anna Frisch's long auburn hair hung down her back, she was dressed in a perfectly stunning long-sleeved eggplant-colored dress that swirled around her ankles, and she looked as exotic in this setting as an orchid in a pumpkin patch.

Geez, I thought, we could have had a car pool with all this crowd from Atlanta. I spent the next fifteen minutes considering all the possibilities in this roomful of mourners.

It wasn't all that odd that Hap had showed up for Wuvvy's service. He and Wuvvy had been longtime friends, neighbors in the tight-knit Little Five Points Community. Wuvvy had accused Hap of selling her out, but that seemed like a long time ago now.

Anna Frisch was a different story. Blind Possum had made a displaced person of Wuvvy, and Wuvvy had probably killed Jackson Poole, Anna's colleague and a co-owner of Blind Possum. What was she doing here?

"Amen," the pastor said. I jerked my head up. The others were standing, milling around and talking quietly. Even Hap edged forward and spoke to the minister, shaking his hand.

Anna Frisch and I were the only ones to hang back. She slipped out of the room and was waiting in the hallway when I followed a few seconds later.

"Your friend, Sergeant Deavers, told me you'd be here," she said quietly. "I hoped I'd see you."

"You could see me in Atlanta if you needed to," I said. "Why here?"

She looked around. We could hear faint voices inside the Cherokee Rose Room.

"This isn't the best place to talk," she said.

"Then call me when you get back to Atlanta," I said, annoyed.

"No . . ." She hesitated. "All right. I came down because I've got to find out what really happened to Jackson. Deavers says Virginia Lee Mincey killed Jackson. And then killed herself. And that she was his stepmother. It's just unbelievable, all of it. Jackson never talked about this stuff. I didn't know his father had been killed, or that his stepmother had gone to prison."

She took a deep breath. There was a water cooler on the wall, the kind with the little paper cups. She got herself a cup, filled it, and drank the water in one long gulp.

"Why do you care?" I asked, deliberately blunt.

"It's not good business to get involved with somebody you work with," she said dispassionately. "Especially in the food business. But it happened. We kept it to ourselves. And I guess Jackson kept a lot of things to himself that I didn't know about."

"He never told you about his childhood?"

"Just that he'd lived in a small town in south Georgia and had been sent to boarding school in Virginia when he was in fifth grade. We didn't get around to talking about our pasts. What we were doing was so exciting, we were caught up in that. Opening a new business, starting a new relationship, all that was pretty intense."

"That still doesn't tell me why you came down here," I said. "Had you ever met Wuvvy?"

"I'd never even heard of her until Jackson was killed," Anna said. "Jackson said the tenant at Little Five Points didn't want to move out, so he got our lawyers busy with it. Every day we delay opening there costs us money."

"And you came down here because . . . ?" I prompted.

"Something wasn't right," Anna said. "Jackson called me Halloween afternoon. That woman, Wuvvy, was making a big stink, he said, but there was something else. He wanted to see about it himself. He was supposed to come by my place later that night."

Two of the Sunday school ladies came slowly out of the chapel, clinging to each other's arm, as though they were slightly tipsy. Their thick-soled shoes squeaked with each cautious step, and Anna gave them a brief smile before she resumed talking in a near whisper.

"I still don't understand what you were hoping to achieve down here," I said.

"What about you?"

"I found Jackson Poole's body," I said. "And I talked to Wuvvy. She insisted she didn't kill him. If she did kill herself, I'd like to know why."

"Nobody's paying you to do this?"

"No."

Anna's gaze followed the women as they wobbled toward the front door. "I'll pay you," she said. "Find out who killed Jackson. And why." She glanced down at her watch. "The funeral home director gave me directions to the house where Jackson grew up. I want to drive by there. He said it was in the middle of a pecan grove. Jackson used to talk about climbing this one tree. It was supposed to be over a hundred years old. I want to see it."

"Was there a funeral for him?" I asked. If there was, Bucky hadn't mentioned it. Or maybe I was too busy to look for the notice in the newspaper.

"No," she said. "He wasn't into that kind of thing. Jackson liked the idea of cremation. It was efficient. He liked efficiency."

She blinked rapidly, looked at her watch. "I've got to get going. I need to be on the road by four-thirty. Got to get back to Roswell to check on a new batch of hefeweizen, and talk about some menu changes with the chef. Will you do it?"

I needed three more house cleaners, four more hours in every day, a full-time bodyguard for my mother, quality time to spend with Mac. The last thing I needed was a murder investigation. But I knew enough about myself to know I'd pick at this thing like a bad scab, anyway. If Anna Frisch wanted to pay me to satisfy my own morbid curiosity, who was I to argue?

"Wuvvy probably did kill your boyfriend," I said. "She probably did kill herself, too. There's probably not much more to it than that. And I don't know a damn thing about microbreweries."

"I know enough for both of us," she said, handing me a business card. "Call me when you get back to Atlanta."

18

Hap came out of the chapel, spotted me, and walked rapidly toward the water cooler, where I was hanging out, waiting for him.

"It's over now, right?" he said, tugging at the narrow black necktie he'd worn with the Hawaiian shirt. "No cemetery or anything, right? Man, it's been a long time since I been to a funeral."

"I got the feeling burial was going to be private," I told him. "Yeah, I'd say it's over."

He yanked the necktie off, opened the drawer of the polished wooden end table nearby, and stashed the tie there.

"Poor old Wuvvy," he said. "Right back where she started. Man, she'd have hated that shit in there. She always said when she went she wanted a big party. No crying, just full-tilt boogie. Who were those people in there, anyway?"

"Old friends, I guess. You didn't know any of them?"

"I don't know anybody who lives outside I-285, Callahan."

"You'd think if Wuvvy meant to kill herself, she'd have

written down some specific instructions, about a party instead of a funeral, that kind of thing," I said.

Hap smiled fondly. "Wuvvy was big on ideas, short on follow-through. But what do you mean, *if*? You don't think she committed suicide?"

The minister came strolling out of the funeral chapel, Catherine Rhyne's arm linked through his. Her eyes swept over us, but she kept going.

I needed to talk to her. But I wanted to talk to Hap, too, away from the noise and commotion at the Yacht Club. "Are you going straight back to Atlanta?" I asked.

"I ain't sticking around here," Hap said emphatically. "This was all Miranda's idea. She would have come too, but it's our delivery day, and somebody's got to be at the bar. Small towns make me nervous. I keep expecting some hayseed sheriff's deputy to pull me over and tell me, 'You in a heap a trouble, boy.' They probably strip-search people down here for jaywalking."

Catherine Rhyne had stopped at the end of the hallway, in deep discussion with the minister. I wanted to catch her before she left Dubberly Brothers. It was time to abandon my normal tact and ask the questions I needed to ask.

"Did Miranda know about you and Wuvvy?"

Hap did a double take. "What about us?"

It was a guess, but a good one. "I heard things. A long time ago."

He shook his head. "I ain't believing this. Everybody in Little Five Points fucked Wuvvy. That's what she was like. If Wuvvy liked you, she slept with you. It didn't mean anything. I have no idea whether or not Miranda knew about it. Not that she'd care."

"Did Wuvvy get in contact with you? After Jackson Poole was murdered? While she was hiding out?"

"No. And I didn't go looking for her, either. Wuvvy was out of control. To tell you the truth, we were kind of nervous, with her running around loose like that. She killed a dude 'cause she thought he'd ruined her life. Maybe she would have come after me and Miranda next. She had that weird conspiracy idea in her head, you know. Everybody was out to get her."

"Somebody did."

Hap's mouth tightened. "That's why you're down here. You don't give a damn about Wuvvy. You just gotta play private eye. Who hired you to do that?"

"A seeker of truth," I said whimsically.

"Shit," he said. He was still shaking his head as he walked down the hallway. He shoved the front door of Dubberly Brothers Mortuary open, let it close with a resounding bang that made me jump. It was probably the loudest noise they'd heard in here in a long, long time.

Catherine Rhyne was sitting in one of the straight-backed chairs in the front parlor. The room was stifling, but she didn't seem to notice. She stood up as I approached, put out a hand to shake mine.

"Hello. Ah'm Catherine Rhyne," she said. The accent was pure South Georgia, thick and sweet as cane syrup, but it spoke of finishing school, not technical school. "Thank you for coming today. Were you a friend of Virginia's?"

"Yes," I said. It was simpler that way. "She asked me to help her. When the police thought she killed Jackson Poole. But I couldn't. I didn't know how. And then she was dead."

"Good Lord," she said, taking half a step away from me. "Who are you? Why would Virginia want your help?"

Catherine Rhyne was shorter and slimmer than I, with

thick dark brown hair that fell to her shoulders and stayed where she meant it to stay. Her eyes were bright blue, and her eyebrows were penciled in a determined arch. The beginnings of dewlaps around her chin told me she was older than she liked to admit, older than I, for sure.

I handed her one of my business cards. The private investigator one, not the House Mouse card.

She read it, knit her eyebrows together. "Virginia told me she'd tried to hire you. But I got the impression you turned her down. It's too late now, don't you think?"

"For Wuvvy, yes. But I have a client who wants to know who killed Jackson Poole and why. And I'd like to know why Wuvvy died. There's still time for the truth, if somebody cares enough."

"Don't call her Wuvvy," Catherine said, cringing. "Her name was Virginia Lee. Did she owe you money? If you'll submit a bill to my office, I'll see what I can do about paying you. There's not really an estate. She didn't have any insurance or anything. But I'm trying to settle her debts. It's the decent thing to do."

I'd been staring at her as she talked. She looked familiar. I thought maybe I'd seen her around Atlanta, a courthouse maybe. She certainly looked like a lawyer. But the context was all wrong.

"You were there," I said slowly. "At the Yacht Club. Halloween night. I saw you come in. You and Wuvvy went outside. When she came back, she was by herself. But she said she'd gotten the money to pay the back rent. You gave it to her, didn't you?"

She put a hand to her hair and smoothed it, unnecessarily. "It's not a secret," she said. "Virginia was an old family friend. She'd tried to call me down here. Mother told me she was desperate to talk to me."

The way Catherine said "mother," it came out "muthah." All her vowels had that softened, mushed-up sound.

"I just happened to be up in Atlanta. I keep a law office down here, too, you know, and most weekends I leave Atlanta by noon on Thursdays. But I had a hearing that kept me late Friday, and I'd intended to drive down to Hawkinsville in the morning. Poor Virginia," she sighed. "I was happy to lend her the money. But when I saw they'd started construction on that restaurant, I knew it was too late. Virginia just wouldn't face things. She was always like that."

"You'd known her a long time?"

"Since she married Broward Poole and moved to Hawkinsville. The Pooles were old family friends. My daddy and Broward were fraternity brothers at Tech. Virginia wasn't from here originally."

Catherine gave me an indulgent smile and patted my arm. "I've got to be getting along now. Mother has invited the ladies from church over for tea. She's been upset about all this awful mess. First Jackson, and now Virginia. This is a quiet little town, you know. We're not used to crime like you are up in Atlanta."

"Was Broward Poole's murder the only time anybody ever killed anybody else around here?"

I'd said it deliberately, to see if I could, as Edna would say, put a twist in her knickers. It had the desired effect.

Catherine Rhyne kept her hand on my arm, but her fingers dug into my sleeve ever so slightly. "That was all a long time ago," she said icily. "It was a horrible time for all of us. This isn't Atlanta. You can say anything you like to me. But you really can't go around here talking like that. Digging things up. Hurting people. Virginia's dead. She's been dead a long time. She tried to make herself into something else, but it didn't work. People can't really change."

She smiled again suddenly. "You just send that bill along to my office in Atlanta. If I were you, I'd hurry along now. You don't want to get caught in that Macon traffic at rush hour."

Catherine Rhyne didn't slam the door as she left the funeral home. She didn't need to.

19

Courthouses have the best secrets.

And the Pulaski County courthouse, with its crumbling stucco and gloomy old magnolias, seemed ripe with records of the kind of small-town transgressions and transactions that keep the machinery of justice churning.

If Catherine Rhyne wouldn't talk about Wuvvy's past, I could just look up the old trial transcripts. I found the court clerk's office easily—there were only four offices in the high-ceilinged courthouse lobby, and the hand-painted sign over the clerk's mahogany office door was impossible to miss. But there was another door—a weathered, rusted screen door. It had been pulled shut over the wood door, and fastened with a spring latch.

GONE TO LUNCH said a sign that had been written in pencil on a legal-sized file folder.

It was after three. Court clerks down here kept unusual hours, I thought.

But I hadn't had any lunch myself. I ambled out the door

and walked around the corner. There is an unwritten law in Georgia, maybe in all the Deep South, that provides that every county courthouse shall have a meat-and-three-vegetables café within a five-minute stroll of the halls of justice.

Half a block down Lumpkin Street I found the Red Hawk Café. Faded yellow gingham curtains were pulled halfway across the front window. A bell jangled when I pushed the door open, and my nostrils quivered at the comforting smell of hamburger grease and French fries.

The only soul in the place was a heavyset man in his fifties, who was slinging chairs on top of the Formica-topped tables. His graying black hair was brushed straight back from a high forehead. He wore baggy brown slacks and a white dress shirt with the sleeves rolled up to his elbows.

"We're fixin' to close," he said. "I thought Doreen had locked that door."

"She forgot," I said, and then, because I really was starving, "Couldn't I even get something to go? Please?"

He quit stacking chairs, looked at me with open curiosity. "Kinda late for lunch, ain't it? Most people around here are thinkin' about what's for supper. And you the second person stopped in here in the last thirty minutes."

"I'm from Atlanta," I said. "I came down for the funeral service for Virginia Lee Mincey, and I didn't have time for breakfast or lunch."

He moved behind the lunch counter. "I heard they was burying her today. That older lady, she was from Atlanta, too. Come down here for Virginia's service. Reckon that gal had more friends up there than she did down here. After what happened and all."

So Edna had already hit the Red Hawk. I was still starved.

"Griddle's been cleaned, so I can't fix nothin' hot." He opened the door of a glass-fronted cooler. "I got egg salad, tuna salad, chicken salad, and sliced hard-boiled eggs."

"Perfect," I said.

"Forget about the takeout," he said. "If you don't mind eating while I clean, you can just stay right here."

Five minutes later he plopped a green plate onto the lunch counter in front of me. It was the time-honored cold plate, the three paprika-frosted mounds arrayed around a scoop of cottage cheese with an iceberg lettuce leaf and a tomato slice on the side. He gave me a tall glass of iced tea, too, and three packages of cellophane-wrapped club crackers.

Mayonnaise! I'd been feeling like a pariah after my big brushoff from Hap and Catherine Rhyne, but things were suddenly starting to look up. I took a cracker and used it as a platform for the tuna salad.

"Did you know Virginia Lee?" I asked the man, who'd started sweeping behind the counter.

He kept sweeping, short, brisk strokes. As a cleaning professional, I always appreciate good technique.

"Sure," he said. "Virginia Lee come in here all the time when she come to town with Jackson. She was a cute little ol' thing. Never could see what somebody like her saw in Broward Poole."

"Did you know Broward?"

"Oh, yeah," he said dryly. "Everybody knew Broward. He made sure of that."

"How about Catherine Rhyne?" I asked, cutting off a piece of hard-boiled egg with the edge of my fork. "Do you know her?"

"Which one?" he asked, not looking up. "Big Kitty, Little Kitty, or Itty-Bitty Kitty?"

"You're joking," I said, temporarily slowing the fork-to-mouth action.

"It's a Rhyne family tradition. They ain't got but one name for the womenfolk, and that's Catherine."

He took a big plastic jug out of the cooler, poured himself a glass of iced tea, and came to stand by the counter in front of me. His big friendly face had an odd color to it, like flour, and there were huge puffy bags under his eyes.

A woman came bustling out of a door behind him. She wore a white rayon pantsuit, and she had her pocketbook in one hand and a key ring in the other.

"Robert Hickey, who in the world are you talking to out here?" she demanded. "We're supposed to be closed and on the way to your doctor's appointment in Perry."

He gestured toward me. "Doreen, this here's another lady from Atlanta. Come down here for Virginia Lee Mincey's funeral, and didn't have the first bite to eat today. So I fixed her a little something."

Doreen was at least ten years younger than her husband and not nearly as open-minded about nosy strangers from Atlanta.

"Tell the whole world somebody else's business," she muttered. "A man's a worse gossip than any biddy I ever met."

She grabbed a pad of paper, scribbled on it, and slapped it down on the counter in front of me. "That's five-twenty-five. Me and Robert got to go now."

Doreen stood right there while I gulped down a last bite of chicken salad and washed it down with a mouthful of tea, then counted out the six ones I handed her. She followed me to the front door, waited until I was on the sidewalk, then flipped the CLOSED sign on the door with a flourish.

Robert Hickey flashed me an apologetic grin before his wife pulled down the green shade on the door.

The gals in the clerk's office were a merry duo. They were both in their mid-fifties, one with a brownish-reddish bouffant, the other with a blondish-grayish bouffant.

The brown bouffant came to the counter and looked down her nose through her clear-rimmed bifocals at me when I told her I wanted the transcripts from Virginia Lee Mincey's murder trial.

"You mean Virginia Lee Poole," she said firmly. "That's how it's in the records, and I don't care if she did take back her maiden name. She was married to Broward Poole, and that made her a Poole, like it or not."

The blonde stopped rubber-stamping papers. "We know everybody lives in this county. And nobody around here is interested in Virginia Lee Poole anymore."

"They're public records," I pointed out.

The brown bouffant said, "You want to see them, you'll have to get an order from Judge Nyberg."

She went and sat back down at her desk and started rubber-stamping like mad. The blond bouffant gave me a smirk. "Anything else?"

"How do I apply for an order?" I said.

The brown bouffant just kept stamping. "Judge'll be back here in Pulaski the second week of January for criminal docket."

"January? But that's two months away!"

"Judge Nyberg is a busy man. It's a ten-county circuit," the blonde said. "This ain't Atlanta."

She was at least the second person that day to remind me that I was not in the capital of the New South, and that down here in Hawkinsville they did not care how they did things up there in Atlanta.

"How about a telephone book?" I asked, looking around the room. Three of the four walls were lined with old golden oak file cabinets, all of them stacked high with yellowing legal folders. Anna Frisch had mentioned going to see the Poole family homeplace before she left town. Maybe I'd have better luck out on the farm.

"There's a public phone out in the lobby," the blond bouffant said.

"Probably need a court order to use it," I said under my breath. For now, anyway, Hawkinsville's secrets were safe for another day.

20

I came out of the courthouse with a list of phone numbers and addresses for eight Pooles living in the greater Hawkinsville metropolis and no clear idea of how I would proceed from there.

A horn tooted at me and I jumped, halfway ready to be arrested for disturbing the peace.

It wasn't the sheriff, though. It was Edna, double-parked beside the sheriff's car right in front of the courthouse and waving me to join her.

I jumped in the front seat and she gunned the motor. "Damned strange town," she said, speeding down Lumpkin. "Good lunch plate, though." She patted a paper sack on the seat beside her. "And I picked up a nice blouse for your Aunt Olive's birthday at Genella's Fine Fashions. Only eight-ninety-nine."

"Where are the girls?" I asked, looking in the backseat.

"We're going to pick them up right now," Edna said.

"Where's that?" I asked.

"At the nursing home," Edna said. "And don't you go getting any ideas. You'll be ready for the nursing home a long
time before I am."

Azalea Acres was a small, olive-green cinder-block building two blocks off Hawkinsville's main drag. A painfully
manicured four-foot-tall hedge of azaleas hugged the building's profile, and a clump of pine trees provided the only
shade around. The residents had arranged their wheelchairs
and walkers in a circle under the trees, and as we pulled into
the gravel parking lot I could see that the only two ambula-
tory members of the group were Baby and Sister.

Edna tooted the Lincoln's horn again. Heads swung our
way. Baby and Sister took their own sweet time with their
departure. First they went around the circle, hugging and
kissing and patting various withered cheeks. Then they
leaned over a particularly frail person wrapped in a pink blanket in an old-fashioned high-backed wooden wheelchair, and
held a long conference with her.

"Whose idea was this?" I asked Edna.

"It was all our idea, if you really want to know," Edna said.
"We divided up the territory. I took the Red Hawk Café, and
they went to the bus station luncheonette. That's where black
people eat lunch down here," she explained. "We stopped by
the A.M.E. Church, then I carried them over here while I went
to the Feed and Seed and Genella's Fine Fashions."

"A nursing home?" I asked.

"The girls know what they're doing," Edna said tartly.
"What did you find out about Wuvvy and her family?"

"Not much," I admitted. "The natives weren't too friendly
today."

"Here they come now."

Sister clung to Baby's arm as they strolled toward the car.

Compared with the crowd taking the afternoon air under the shade of the pine trees, the two of them looked particularly perky.

I got out and, for the benefit of the watching crowd, made a big show of opening the back doors and helping them into the car. As we pulled away from Azalea Acres I caught the two of them waving at their newfound friends like a couple of travel-weary duchesses.

"Well?" Edna demanded.

"Ooh, honey," Sister said. "Me and Baby done heard all kind of wickedness about this town."

"Did you find out about the Pooles?" I asked.

"Sure did," Baby said. "There's two sets of Pooles down here. Mostly all the Pooles still living in town now are colored. All of that crowd is kin to Mrs. Frankie Poole. She works in the office over at the elementary school."

"What about the other Pooles?" I asked.

"I found out about them," Edna said proudly. "The white Pooles, the ones related to Broward Poole—they've been gone from here a long time. That boy Jackson, he was the last, and he got sent away to boarding school after his daddy got killed. There's some cousins up North, related to Broward Poole's first wife, but they never had anything to do with Hawkinsville.

"The pecan farm is still here," Edna continued. "Ain't nobody worked it since Broward Poole was killed. The lady in Genella's Fine Fashions said nobody goes out there. It was left just the way it was when they sent Wuvvy off to prison."

"You say a pecan farm?" Sister perked up. "Maybe we get some good pecans out there. This right now is pecan season, ain't it? Me and Baby, we could pick up some pecans quicker than a herd of squirrels."

"I know just how to get there," Edna said. "We came past the Poole place on the way into town. Dry Creek Road is on your right, and there's an old red mailbox before you get to the gate."

I turned the car back toward the road leading out of town. I wanted to see where Virginia Lee Mincey had lived before she reinvented herself as Wuvvy. And Anna Frisch, my new client, had mentioned a pecan tree Jackson had liked to climb near the old homeplace.

Slender fingers of sunlight pushed through the branches of the trees overhead.

Sister pressed her face to the window to watch the scenery. "Me and Baby met a nice lady at Azalea Acres. Miss Neola Scott. She told us all about how she worked for that Rhyne family, worked there until she was eighty-seven years old. Now she lives at Azalea Acres, and she has her food put in a blender 'cause her dentures gives her blisters.

"Neola said that Mr. Broward Poole was shot to death right out there in that pecan grove," Sister went on. "Them Rhyne ladies, all of 'em are lawyers. Big Kitty, she's the old lady, she's a invalid now, and then there's Little Kitty, and her daughter used to be called Itty-Bitty Kitty, only she come back from Atlanta and told people she wanted to be called Catherine, so don't nobody but family call her Itty-Bitty no more. And Little Kitty, she did some lawyering for the wife, Virginia Lee, after she killed Mr. Broward Poole."

"You girls did a great job," I said, watching the roadside for the red mailbox Edna had mentioned. "The biggest thing to happen to this town in twenty years was Broward Poole's murder," I said. "But nobody wants to talk about it officially. I couldn't get any local lips unzipped. Especially that Catherine Rhyne."

"That's 'cause you were barking up the wrong tree," Sister said. "You don't know 'bout the jungle telegraph."

"What's that?" Edna asked. "I don't know about it either."

"That's the way colored folks used to find out about white

folks' business. Used to be white folks didn't pay no attention to colored folks. Thought we were too stupid to figure out what was goin' on. But if you just keep your mouth shut and your ears open, you know who's been drinking too much whiskey and who's been sleeping in separate bedrooms and who can't pay their bills," Sister said.

"We heard all about them Rhyne women," Baby said. "Miss Neola, she run that family."

Five minutes out of town on the main road I saw the sign for Dry Creek Road, swung the Lincoln onto the potholed asphalt, and started looking for the gate and the red mailbox.

I found both, but Edna's sources had neglected to mention that the rusted cattle gate had an imposing new chain and padlock strung through it.

"Now what?" Edna said, getting out to try the lock. It held tight.

She got back in the front seat of the car. "Getting kind of late, isn't it?"

It was, but I still wanted to see the Poole place.

"You girls sit tight here," I said. "If anybody stops and wants to know what you're doing, tell them the car was burning oil and we pulled over to let it cool off."

I opened the trunk of the Lincoln and dug out the thick gray sweatshirt I'd thrown in with my cleaning supplies the day before. My shoes were plain black suede flats, not bad, but they weren't exactly snake boots either. I took off my wool blazer and pulled on the sweatshirt, then turned my back so Edna and the girls wouldn't see me stuffing my Smith & Wesson in the right pocket of my slacks. I had a suspicious-looking bulge on my right hip, but it couldn't be helped.

"Be careful," Edna called.

The gate was about four feet high, with metal slats. I took my time climbing it and still managed to scrape both my shins as I was hopping down onto the other side.

I spied a stout pine branch lying in the tall weeds at the edge of the sandy track that led onto the Poole property and immediately adopted it as a snake stick. As a kid I'd spent a summer on a distant cousin's tobacco farm in Lyons, Georgia. I'd learned then that you always get you a snake stick before venturing into the woods.

The pecan trees edging the road onto the Pooles' plantation made a leafy yellow canopy overhead. All I could see on either side of the road was pecan trees. Here and there pecan hulls studded the track, and dozens of gray squirrels leaped and chattered and jumped overhead from limb to limb, like a troupe of circus aerialists.

Mourning doves were perched on some of the low-hanging limbs, cooing softly to each other, and from the cool depths of the grove I heard the high-pitched twitter of a pair of whip-poorwills. More sandy tracks trailed off between the rows of pecan trees. At one time these would have been kept mowed and weed-free, but two decades of neglect had taken their toll on the place. Weeds were knee-high, and in places small shrubs had grown up in the middle of the tracks.

I trudged along for a quarter of a mile before I saw anything that looked like civilization.

People always think Tara when they think of plantations in the South—white columns, wide porches, smiling darkies offering silver milt julep cups. It looks fine for the movies, but Broward Poole obviously wasn't into antebellum chic.

Five hundred yards from the house the sand track switched to an asphalt driveway. The house was in a clearing in the pecan grove, surrounded by overgrown camellia and azalea hedges. What had once been a sweeping lawn was now a field of weeds, with pine tree seedlings poking up here and there. The house itself was a yellow brick split-level. Somebody's idea of cutting-edge fifties architecture, it had metal-framed two-story-high picture windows, a sharply peaked roof with orange tiles, and a one-story wing that jutted to the left of the front door, the brick walls punctuated with high transom windows. To the right of the front door the driveway led to an empty two-car carport.

Approaching the picture window made me nervous. Anybody inside could have seen me coming from a mile off. There wasn't anybody inside, I knew that, but I still skirted around to the side of the house, toward the wing with those high windows.

The back of the house consisted of floor-to-ceiling windows. Heavy curtains of rotted avocado-green fabric hung in shreds at the windows, and a yellow brick terrace wrapped around the space. Weeds poked up through the brick, and a heavy wrought-iron patio set had been piled up in one corner, the top of the table broken into a million pieces of frosted glass. A red dome-topped barbecue grill had been overturned onto the heap of patio furniture, all of it covered with a thick layer of pine needles.

Pine trees towered over the terrace, and their shadows cast it into deep shade. I shivered, looked around, tried to imagine the Wuvvy I knew in this setting. Hard to picture her in a domestic setting, in a miniskirt, holding a tray of hamburgers for her land-baron husband Broward.

"Cute little old thing," Robert Hickey, my friend at the café, had called her. Wuvvy?

21

A breeze stirred in the top of the pine trees, sending a shower of dried needles onto my shoulders. I brushed the needles off, looked up at the sky. Dark clouds scudded on the horizon. It was getting late. What was I looking for? Some sense that Wuvvy had lived here? Who she had been all those years ago?

Holding my breath, I tugged on the handle of a sliding glass door that led off the patio into the house. It held tight. Of course it would be locked. The front, too. Why bother trying?

Anna Frisch said the only time Jackson Poole talked about his childhood he'd mentioned an old pecan tree. She'd intended to look for it. Maybe I'd look, too.

The rows of trees in the pecan grove looked remarkably alike, of uniform size and age. How old, I wondered, were these blackened brooding trunks? How could somebody tell one from the other? On the way back to the car, off to the left of the dirt road, I noticed a slightly wider path cut through one of the rows. Here the trees were set farther apart. There were gaps in the row, too, where stumps were all that remained of long-gone pecan trees.

Get going, I told myself, it must be close to six. If I took too much longer, Edna and the girls would probably abandon ship and come looking for me.

But I've never been able to resist a dirt road. I swerved to the left and jog-trotted down the path.

I still hadn't seen much evidence that this had been a working farm. Maybe this was a service road. The house had been strictly residential. I had no idea what kind of equipment it took to grow and harvest pecans.

The trees seemed to go on forever. I was beginning to get some idea of just how big this farm was.

I'd just decided to turn around when I saw a flash of color up ahead.

Dull red through the browns and yellows and greens of the trees. Paint. I quickened my step again.

The red paint belonged not to the barn or equipment shed I'd expected. It was a tiny house, a wooden shack really, with more silvery wood showing than red paint. The corrugated tin roof had been blown off in places, and a single crude window had been boarded up with another piece of tin. There was no porch or doorstep, just a blank wall indented with the single window and a weathered plank door.

The shack drew me as the house had not. A tenant farmer's house, I thought. But there had been no tenants in a long, long time.

There was no doorknob left to turn. The door swung open easily. Swaths of cobwebs completely covered the inside of the doorway. I batted them aside with my trusty snake stick, started in, then backed out just as quickly.

The smell didn't retreat. It was the smell of mildew, of decay, of a place long shut away from sunlight and fresh air.

I took a deep breath, thrust my stick inside, and tamped the wood floor with it as loudly as I could.

"Okay, snakes," I announced. "Go away, little mousies and spiders and squirrels. And bats," I added as an afterthought. The shack was cavelike.

And empty.

With fading streaks of daylight creeping over my shoulder, the little house still refused to yield up any secrets. The crude wooden floor was carpeted with leaves and pine needles and clumps of dirt. A huge wasp's nest hung down from one corner of the single room, and broken glass and rusted beer cans were scattered around. I thought of an old Faron Young song that you hear only on jukeboxes these days. "Hello, walls."

Hello—who?

I went outside and walked completely around the shack. There was a kind of lean-to attached to the back of the shack, nothing more than a shed roof and four walls, none of which came to a right angle at any corner. If there had been a door, it was gone now. The floor was cement, and there was another door made from a single sheet of warped plywood. I pulled on it and found a combination bathroom and storage shed. A harvest gold sink and grungy white porcelain commode with a broken toilet seat took up one corner. So the tenants had plumbing. Broward Poole must have been a model of generosity. The other corner of the closet was stacked to the ceiling with wooden packing cases, broken bits of furniture, even a rusted green ten-speed bike. Hello, walls.

From a distance, I heard a car horn honking.

Jesus H. Christ! Had something gone wrong with the girls?

I turned so fast my foot slipped on something and I went down in a heap on the floor. I scrambled up and dashed outside and around to the front of the shack.

Nothing was there, of course. I hurried back to the car. Edna honked the horn again as I scrambled over the cattle gate.

"What?" I asked, out of breath and annoyed.

"Me and the girls need to get to a bathroom," Edna said.

"We're hungry too," Baby put in. "All this investigating makes folkses get an appetite."

I dusted off my shoes and slacks and started to open the car door.

"I'll drive," Edna said. "Genella told me there's a good steakhouse up on 341. That's what me and the girls want for dinner. Steak."

The parking lot of the Black Lantern steakhouse was so full that Edna had to let the girls off near the front door and park on the shoulder of the highway. The steakhouse obviously was Hawkinsville's hot spot. People stood shoulder to shoulder in the lobby. There was no lounge, but lots of brown paper sacks and plastic go-cups being passed around. The dark air was blue with smoke and thick with laughter and conversation. This was the Bible Belt all right, but at the Black Lantern, nobody appeared to be worried about the evils of tobacco, alcohol, or red meat.

It looked like we'd have a long wait for a table. Until Edna held a whispered conference with the hostess, who looked sympathetically at the girls, nodded her head, and five minutes later showed us to a table for four in the front room.

"Don't you worry," the hostess said, patting Edna's arm. "We'll get your daughter some food right away."

As soon as we were seated, a waitress appeared with wineglasses, a basket of steaming yeast rolls, and a large bowl of salad. Baby and Sister wouldn't drink wine in front of other people, but they fell on the salad and bread as though they hadn't eaten in a week. The waitress took the steak orders and promised to have them back "in a jiff."

"What did you tell her?" I asked Edna. "How come we're getting the royal treatment?"

Edna helped herself to a roll, broke it open, and started slathering butter across it. "Just that you're a very sick woman, that we checked you out of the hospital for the day, and that we're all your nurses. She has an aunt who gets low blood sugar too, and when that happens, her aunt has to eat real fast before she passes out."

I took a roll, too. "Someday somebody's gonna catch you in one of these lies of yours."

Edna smiled. "I'll just lie my way out of that, too. What did you see on the plantation? Did you see the shack where Broward Poole caught Wuvvy with the other man?"

I dropped my roll. "What other man? What are you talking about?"

"Oh yes," Sister said, pushing a piece of lettuce into her mouth with her fingertips. "Neola told us all about that. That Wuvvy was a real hussy. She was carrying on with some other man. And Mr. Broward, he found out about it and was gonna fix her wagon for good."

"The official story," Edna said, bending forward to be discreet, "was that Broward Poole was out in the pecan grove, shooting crows out of the trees, and somehow he tripped over a branch or something, fell, and the gun went off and killed him."

Baby hooted. "Edna, please. Nobody believed that mess."

"Why not?" I asked.

"That man in the Red Hawk Café knows a lot about guns and pecan growing," Edna said. "He used to work pecans until his heart give out. He told me it was all pretty obvious. Broward Poole was shot in the head, close range. The district attorney knew that wasn't right, and he confronted Wuvvy with that, but she kept right to her story, kept saying she'd heard the gun go off, and had gone looking and found his body."

"What else besides that?" I asked.

"For another thing," Edna said confidently. "Mr. Hickey at the café says you had to look at where it happened. Right out there by that tenant's shack. All those trees were old and diseased even then. Stinkbugs, pecan weevils, all kind of stuff. They hadn't been producing in years. Nobody messed with 'em. Especially not Broward Poole. When they had Wuvvy on trial, it came out that he'd told one of his workers he was gonna have 'em chopped down. He never got around to it."

"If he wasn't shooting crows, what was he doing?" I asked.

"Seeing what his pretty little wife was up to," Baby said.

"And what was she up to?"

"Shacking up in the shack," Edna said, laughing at her own little joke. "It was all over town, Wuvvy had a boyfriend. Little town like Hawkinsville, you can't just check into the No-Tell Motel. But that shack out there, he'd moved the tenant out a year earlier. Wuvvy was using it as a hangout. Broward wouldn't let her listen to rock 'n' roll in the house. He was strictly a country-music type. So she'd take her record player out there, hang out, party down."

"I heard about that shack," Sister said. She lowered her voice. "Neola went out there once, looking for Miss Catherine. She said Wuvvy and some other young folks were smoking that marijuana out there. They never proved it at the trial, but that's what everybody said. And Miss Kitty, she didn't want Catherine going over there, but Catherine snuck over there sometimes anyway."

The waitress brought our plates, slid them onto the table. My steak was so big it lapped over the side of the plate. The foil-wrapped baked potato was approximately the size of a cruise missile. "Okay, hon?" she asked.

"Fine," I said. "I can feel my blood sugar rising already."

"Broward Poole had a bad temper," Edna said. "Genella at the dress shop said everybody in south Georgia knew that. He'd as soon whip you as look at you. And that young wife of his was wild, Genella said."

"Hot stuff, that's a direct quote from Neola," Sister added.

I took dainty little bites of steak, dainty little nibbles of salad, mere morsels of baked potato, and waited while the girls entertained me with the facts and gossip they'd gathered that day.

"On the day Broward Poole was killed, Wuvvy called the sheriff," Edna said. "And when the sheriff got there, Wuvvy had bruises all over her face and up and down her arms. She was hysterical, said she'd had to run a long way to get to the phone after she found Broward, and she'd fallen and hit her head. Nobody believed it."

"Pretty obvious," I said.

"He caught his wife with another man and beat the tar out of her," Edna said. "Broward Poole probably threatened to kill 'em both with his shotgun. Somehow Wuvvy got it away, and turned the gun on him."

"What happened to the boyfriend?" I asked.

"Now that's a mystery," Sister said. "Couldn't nobody at the A.M.E. Church or Azalea Acres say who that boyfriend was."

"Genella always thought it was a man worked at the pecan warehouse," Edna said. "But Wuvvy never would say. When it was obvious she'd been caught in a lie, all she'd ever say was that he'd been beating on her for a long time. That day, he hunted her down out in the shack, beat her up again, held the shotgun to her head, and, uh, assaulted her."

"Raped her?" I asked.

"Shhh," Edna said, gesturing at the people whose chairs crowded around us in the dining room.

"Of course, Wuvvy was married to the man," Edna said.

"And Robert, the man in the café, he pointed out that Wuvvy never complained a single time before that that he was beating on her. But during the trial, after the other stuff came out, she changed her whole story. She said he raped her once and had the gun to her head and was going to do it again and she was scared he'd kill her, so she got the gun away and killed him instead. Then tried to make it look like some big hunting accident. Dumb. Not to mention it made everybody mad that she was bad-mouthing a dead man who couldn't defend himself."

"If it happened today, a jury would call it self-defense," I said.

"Maybe in Atlanta," Edna said. "Not down here. Anyway, her lawyer got her to plead guilty before it came to all that. She could have gotten the death penalty. Instead she got a life sentence. Wuvvy went to prison, Broward Poole went to the graveyard, Jackson Poole got sent to school up in North Carolina and never came back."

"And Virginia Lee Mincey never did either," I said.

"Folks down here got all riled up when the governor let her out of the jailhouse," Sister said. "Neola Scott said the white folks and the colored folks were ready to send a lynch party up there to the governor's mansion, they were so worked up about it."

The waitress came back to the table, clutching a coffeepot. "Folks ready for coffee?"

"You people got any pie?" Baby asked loudly. "Pecan pie?"

While the girls lingered over slabs of pecan pie and ice cream and decaf coffee, I brooded about all I hadn't gotten done. The girls had done their job, but rumor and gossip didn't fill in all the gaps. I still knew virtually nothing about Jackson Poole, or his relationship with Wuvvy.

I paid the check with my credit card because the girls had

used up most of my cash. "You all still want to spend the night in a motel?" I asked.

Edna made a face. She likes her own bed, her own coffeepot, and her own space. I waved the credit card around and promised to rent two rooms, so she could have her own bed.

The Regal Motel was only a mile outside of Hawkinsville. Its neon sign promised free color television, American ownership, and vacancies. I rented two double rooms for thirty-four dollars apiece and installed the girls in their room. Edna played solitaire for an hour before she went to bed, while I made notes about everything I didn't know about the tangled lives of Virginia Lee Mincey and Jackson and Broward Poole. "I'm getting up early in the morning to do some more interviewing," I told Edna.

"Just so long as you don't wake me up," she said. "These road trips are more work than I remembered."

Our thirty-four-dollar motel room came complete with a clock radio bolted to the bedside table. It said six A.M. when I opened my eyes. Edna never stirred as I climbed back into my sweatshirt, wool pants, and black flats and let myself out of the room as quietly as I could.

It was a foregone conclusion that I would go back to the pecan grove and Wuvvy's shack. All night long I'd pushed and pulled at the questions nobody could or would answer so far. Who was the other man in Wuvvy's life back then? What had he seen and why had she covered up for him all these years? Who stood to gain by Jackson Poole's murder so many years later?

It was still dark when I found Dry Creek Road and the red mailbox guarding the road to the Poole property.

I didn't relish the long hike back to the shack in the half-light of dawn. On a whim, I opened the red mailbox. Inside were yellowed newspapers, an abandoned wasp's nest, and at the very back of the box, a tiny key attached to a piece of string.

It was the first break I'd gotten in this town. Smiling to myself, I opened the padlock, pulled the Lincoln through the gate, then got out and shut it behind me.

I'd halfway thought about breaking into the big house to see what I could learn about the Pooles. Breaking in would have been a piece of cake. I parked the Lincoln in the driveway and studied the place. But those big yawning windows somehow made me feel vulnerable, exposed. I wondered if Wuvvy, the woman who'd lived for the last few years of her life in a single tiny room behind her shop, had felt the same way in Broward Poole's enormous house.

The shack, I thought. It was Wuvvy's place. The place where Broward was killed. I parked the Lincoln at the entrance to the path to the tenant farmer's shack, pulling far enough in that the car couldn't be seen by anybody who wasn't looking for it.

I ducked to keep the low-hanging branches off my neck. Something stirred in the dirt road ahead of me.

Wings flapped, and there was a flurry of movement.

CAAW. An enormous black crow rose up from the road, and another one flapped up to the branch of the nearest tree.

"Shoo," I said, waving my arms. The two crows looked at me with disinterest and stayed right where they were.

I picked up my snake stick where I'd left it the day before, and walked slowly around to the shack for another look.

I opened the plywood door as wide as I could and stood there a moment, waiting for the outside air to work itself into the musty, dirt-floored lean-to.

In the dim light of morning I could see the tall pile of haphazardly stacked wooden crates. If I pulled one down, the whole tower would probably come down on top of me. So I turned to the other stuff. A brown Naugahyde recliner with stuffing springing out of several places had been used as a resting spot for bundles of old magazines. *Georgia Crop Report, The Pecan Grower, Field & Stream, National Geographic.* The pages crumbled to the touch. An open carton was perched on the arm of the chair. I lifted the flap with the end of my snake stick. Faded fabric. I stepped closer, unable to resist the allure of an old textile. It was a homely thing, that quilt, made of dusty rose and pea-green squares of calico in a nine-patch pattern. A utility quilt, made for warmth, not show. I lifted it out and found another quilt, this one a nicely pieced Dresden Plate, done in lilacs, blues, pinks, and yellows. It was a Depression quilt top, made of old feedsacks, but its maker had never gotten around to giving it a filling and a backing, or doing the laborious job of quilting.

At the bottom of the crate were three leatherette-bound volumes. *The Rebel Yell—Pulaski County Consolidated High School* was embossed on each. The years were 1965, 1966, and 1967. I flipped open the cover of the top yearbook, the one for 1967.

"Virginia Lee Mincey—class of '67" was written in a looping flourish on the flyleaf. I time-traveled back as I flipped through the pages of black-and-white photos. Fierce-looking football players stared into the camera, cheerleaders with bleached, teased hair did backflips, goofy teenagers mugged. I found Virginia Lee Mincey's senior picture on page 136. Her hair was white-blond, parted straight down the middle, showing off a half-inch of dark roots. Unsmiling eyes were rimmed with black eyeliner, parted lips caked with some pale, frosty lipstick, and big white earrings dangled from her ears onto the shoulders that had been bared by the black photographer's drape.

"VIRGINIA LEE MINCEY," the caption read. "Ginny.

Vo-Tech 2, 3, Rebelettes, 1, 2, 3. Favorite quotation: 'All you need is luv!!'"

"Wuvvy," I said, surprised. "You were a slut way back then."

I leafed over to the page containing the group photo of the Rebelettes, who turned out to be the school's majorettes. Wuvvy was in the back row, dressed in a baton-twirler's getup that featured the Confederate flag picked out in sequins.

I put the yearbook aside and picked through the other boxes. Old clothes, schoolbooks, a cheap white plastic jewelry box filled with bits and pieces of dime-store jewelry, even a white baton with red, white, and blue streamers dangling from the ends. When she'd married Broward Poole, it looked like, Virginia Lee had packed up her teenage years and put them in storage. She was a wife now, married to a wealthy older man, stepmother to a little boy. She was a Poole.

I was restacking the cartons when I found the record player. I recognized it right away because my older brother Kevin had one just like it—heavy, gray, with a hinged lid that revealed the turntable and record changer. I lifted the lid. There was still a record on the turntable. It was a forty-five. I picked up the record to look at the label. I'd expected it to be one of Wuvvy's rock 'n' roll discs, but it wasn't. The paper label was white, the lettering, in no-nonsense type, said CROW-GO. Mid-South Enterprises. Hammond, La. Playing time, 4 minutes, 30 seconds.

I put the record back but picked up the yearbook and stowed it in the front seat of the Lincoln. As I was starting the car and driving slowly down the lane I remembered the boxes I'd picked up yesterday from Bucky Deavers. More of Wuvvy's stuff—the stuff she'd begged me to retrieve for her. When I got back to Atlanta, I promised myself, I'd take a look.

After I'd gotten out of the car and opened the gate on Dry

Creek Road, a dilapidated white pickup truck glided to a stop on the shoulder of the road. The driver raised his arm out the window.

"How you?" a man's voice called.

This was not, I hoped, somebody in a position of importance catching me trespassing on private property. Somebody who might notify the law. I closed the gate, popped the padlock in place.

"You doin' all right today?" the man called again.

I tramped over to the roadside to see what he wanted.

The driver wore faded blue overalls and a flannel shirt buttoned all the way to the top button. His mahogany-colored face was creased and weathered, and his ancient moss-colored fedora was tilted far to the back of his balding head. "Do I know you?" he asked.

"No, sir," I said. "I was just looking around the Poole place. Got a party might be interested in buying it." Edna wasn't the only liar in the family.

"Somebody gonna work pecans again?" he asked, grinning. "There's some good trees back in there. Some of them trees done a thousand pounds an acre, easy. Mr. Poole, he knew 'bout as much about pecans as anybody in the state of Georgia."

"Did you work for Mr. Poole?" I asked.

"I sure did," the gentleman said. "Helped plant a lot of them trees. Elliotts, Creeks, Desirables, Sumner. Mr. Broward, he liked to have about eight or ten different varieties. Them's good trees. You can tell the man thinking about buying this place, Harley Lutz is ready to go back to work. I'm a nut man, through and through."

"Did you know Mrs. Poole?" I asked.

He pushed his hat down on his forehead. "She didn't have a lot to do with the farm. She kept busy with that young'un, Jackson, and her friends, up in Atlanta."

Cars were whizzing by on the road now, and it had started

to drizzle, misty droplets ran down the neck of my sweat-shirt. "Did you believe it when she said she killed him because he was beating her?"

Harley Lutz looked as uncomfortable as I felt. "She was too young for Mr. Broward. He was thirty-five years old when he married that gal. And she didn't like living on a farm, noways. I can't say what happened with them two. Mr. Broward, he did me right. I come to work here when I was fourteen years old. Got paid two cents a pound for picking pecans, cash money, paid me at the end of every day. That's when money was money, girl."

I sighed. Time to get on up the road. But I had one more question.

"People say Mrs. Poole had a boyfriend. That Broward Poole caught her with the man that day. Do you know who the man was?"

He frowned. "None of that was none of my business. I didn't pay no attention to that gossip. I was trying to make me a living. But after Mr. Broward got killed, they just let the farm go. That was that. All them trees, nobody working it. When Mrs. Poole killed Mr. Broward, she didn't just kill him. She killed a lot of jobs for a lot of people. Folks around here don't forget that."

22

I found a service station, filled the Lincoln's bottomless gas tank, and added a quart of oil.

My stomach was growling, and I was getting a headache from the low blood sugar Edna had invented for me. The only food the gas station offered was Big Red chewing gum and a Pepsi machine. I don't drink Pepsi. It's an Atlanta thing.

I thought back to my interrupted lunch the previous day at the Red Hawk Café. Maybe my talkative friend Robert Hickey would be back behind the counter. I could pick up sausage and biscuits and coffee for the girls before I went back to the motel.

The Red Hawk Café wasn't open for breakfast. My shoulders sagged as I walked back to the car. I'd seen a McDonald's on my way through Perry, but an Egg McMuffin is sorry consolation when you've got your appetite set for country ham, biscuits, and deep-fried small-town gossip.

As I was opening the car door I glanced across the street. There was a drugstore and a diminutive white-painted cottage. The cottage was clearly the best-kept building in town, with pots of yellow chrysanthemums planted beside a cheerful bright red door. A polished brass plaque on the door said LAW OFFICES.

I crossed the street to get a better look at this civic marvel. By the time I was on the sidewalk outside the building I could see the smaller lettering on the brass plaque. RHYNE & RHYNE, it said.

Catherine Rhyne had been in no mood to talk to me yesterday. But that was then. She was in the middle of an old friend's funeral. Maybe it had been a tactical error to try to talk to her then. The sun had started to push through the gray clouds overhead, and it had quit drizzling. Maybe we could start all over again, Catherine and I.

Rhyne & Rhyne was unmistakably a family law office. The polished wooden floor in the outer office was covered with a threadbare Oriental carpet in deep reds and blues, and instead of framed law degrees, there were framed prints, florals and landscapes, and a sprinkling of what I assumed were family photos.

A very tiny, very elderly white woman sat erectly in a wheelchair that had been pulled behind the receptionist's desk. Her pink scalp showed through under a thin fuzz of white curls, and her lower jaw looked strangely caved in, as though the bones had just melted away with age. She wore a flowered white cotton housecoat, and her hands, on which she wore white cotton gloves, were folded demurely on the desk in front of her. Her head was tilted to one side, and she appeared to be having a long nap.

"Mother?" a voice called from one of the two open doors that led out of the reception room. "Mother, is there somebody there?"

"I think she's sleeping," I called back. "I wouldn't want to disturb her."

A younger woman popped her head around from the door on the left.

"Hello!" she said, as though we were old friends. She nodded at Sleeping Beauty. "Don't you wish you could sleep like that? Mother does that all the time these days—just drifts off for hours at a time."

She held out a hand to shake mine. "I'm Kitty Rhyne. Can I help you?"

So this was Little Kitty. And Big Kitty was taking a catnap. Kitty Rhyne was obviously the beauty of the family. Taller and slimmer than her daughter, she had hair of a lustrous silver, cut in a straight bob that fell across high cheekbones. Her flawless skin was lightly tanned, her brown eyes lively behind stylish tortoiseshell glasses. She wore Friday-casual duds: a hand-knit sweater and matching toffee-colored pants.

"I'm Callahan Garrity," I said. "I was actually looking for your daughter, Catherine."

"You're still here," Catherine Rhyne said, leaning against the doorway to her office. "I thought you'd gone back to Atlanta yesterday."

"I meant to," I told her, "but time got away from me. And I did want to come back and apologize to you for being so tactless yesterday. I realize you were under stress, losing Wuvvy so unexpectedly and having to deal with all these complications."

"How did you know Wuvvy?" Kitty Rhyne asked.

Catherine gave her an exasperated look. "She knew Virginia because she lives in the neighborhood where the shop was. Little Five Points."

Kitty Rhyne laughed. "You don't look like a hippie to me."

"I'm not," I said. "I'm a private detective. I'm afraid I upset your daughter by asking a lot of snoopy questions yesterday after the services. I was pretty insensitive."

"It's been a hard time for all of us," Catherine murmured. "There's so much none of us know."

"That's the truth," Kitty said, rolling her eyes. "It's hard to believe any of this has happened to that sweet little girl from out in the country. She's become Klondike's most famous—or should I say infamous?—native."

"She wasn't from Hawkinsville?" I asked.

"Lord, no," Kitty Rhyne said. "But then, nobody who's from Klondike ever says they're from there. It's just a little bump in the road. They don't even have their own mailing address. Wuvvy's people didn't have very much."

"She didn't have a pot to piss in when she married Broward Poole," a surprisingly sturdy voice piped up from the desk.

The senior Mrs. Rhyne was sitting up straight in her wheelchair, hands clutching the arms, wheels spinning furiously but going nowhere.

"Big Kitty!" Catherine yelped.

Kitty Rhyne smothered a giggle. "Now, Mother, be nice. This lady here is a private investigator. She was a friend of Virginia Lee's. You know, Virginia Lee is dead now. Jackson is dead too."

"He's the boy broke his arm in two places when he fell out of the swing at our house," Big Kitty said succinctly. "He's dead now. They say Virginia Lee Mincey killed him. Killed his daddy too."

"Did you ever hear the story of how she got the name Wuvvy?" Kitty asked, trying to change the subject. "That was Jackson. He was a toddler when Broward married Virginia. When he tried to say Virginia, it came out Wuvvy instead. We all thought it was the cutest thing."

"I never called her Wuvvy," Catherine said stiffly. "I never heard Broward call her that, either."

"After she got out of prison, Virginia had her name legally changed to Wuvvy," Kitty said. "No last name, just Wuvvy. I think she thought it was sort of—avant-garde."

"Broward caught her with another man," Big Kitty announced. "Never did say who it was. I always thought it was a nigger man. Or maybe one a them Mexicans Broward had working over there. That's why it was all hushed up."

"Come into my office, Callahan," Catherine Rhyne said hastily. "Big Kitty, would you like Mother to take you outside for some air? It's stopped raining now."

"No, thank you very much," Big Kitty said. "I'll stay right where I am and mind the phones."

Catherine motioned me into her office and Little Kitty followed us in. She closed the door, leaving it open a crack. Catherine sat at the chair behind her desk, and Kitty stayed standing in the doorway, openly amused at her daughter's disapproval of Big Kitty Rhyne.

I took a deep breath.

"My client believes there was some problem with the business that took over Wuvvy's store, Blind Possum Breweries, that could be connected to Jackson's death."

"What kind of problem?" Catherine asked, rolling a pencil between her fingers.

"We're not sure," I admitted. "Jackson called my client the day he was killed and said there was something wrong at the new location. I don't know that much about microbreweries, but I do know that it's a very capital-intensive business. Jackson and his investors spent close to half a million dollars to open their first pub in Roswell, and they will spend close to that by the time the Little Five Points store is completed."

"I didn't even know it was legal to make beer in this state," Little Kitty Rhyne said. "Guess that shows how long ago I went to law school."

"It's a fairly recent thing," I said, parroting some of the facts and figures Anna Frisch had reeled off during my visit to Blind Possum earlier in the week. "Microbreweries only started opening around the U.S. in about 1983, when some independent brewers started lobbying to have laws changed to allow beer to be brewed in the same place it's consumed. Brewing beer for anything more than personal consumption has only been legal for a couple of years in Georgia."

"The big beer distributors fought that law tooth and nail," Catherine Rhyne said slowly. "I didn't pay much attention to it at the time. But I do remember that the Bureau of Alcohol, Tobacco and Firearms regulates those kinds of places. Surely, if anything had been wrong, Jackson would have called them."

"Catherine has always been active in government," Little Kitty said proudly. "She was a delegate to the Democratic Convention way back when she was still in college. She was in the legislature, you know."

"That was a long time ago," Catherine said, dismissively. "One term only."

"Not that long ago," Kitty said.

"One term," Catherine said, interrupting her mother's proud recitation of the daughter's accomplishments. "The Georgia General Assembly is a circus. I didn't go to law school to be part of a sideshow.

"Besides," she said, glancing at Little Kitty, "I keep busy enough with my practice in Atlanta and the work Mother and I do down here. Mother was the politician in the family, really."

Catherine held up an old black-and-white photo of a young Kitty Rhyne speaking into what looked like a bank of microphones at a political function.

At her side were some of the stalwarts of the state's good-old-boy network. Two former United States senators, a former governor, even the wide-smiled man from Plains who'd made it as far as the White House. "Everyone in Georgia knows Kitty Rhyne," Catherine said.

Little Kitty bared a set of nonexistent fangs and flexed a set of exaggerated claws. "And they're afraid of me, too, if they know what's good for them."

Catherine Rhyne was chewing the end of the unsharpened pencil now. "Jackson Poole hadn't lived in Hawkinsville since his father died," she said thoughtfully. "He had absolutely no interest in the pecan business, which is why the farm hasn't been worked in so long. He inherited from Broward, of course, but the bank handled all that."

"I handled Broward's estate myself," Kitty Rhyne said. "We were totally blindsided when we discovered that Jackson was one of the investors in that brewpub that took over Wuvvy's place."

"Whoever killed him probably didn't even know Jackson was from Hawkinsville," Catherine added. "If someone other than Virginia killed him, it seems to me this would be the last place you'd find any leads for your investigation."

Everyone I'd met in Hawkinsville kept suggesting I should go back to Atlanta. It was enough to give a nice girl a complex. But I wasn't a very nice girl. And I wasn't ready to go home just yet.

"I found the body," I said. "Do you people understand that?

"When she was still hiding out from the police, Wuvvy called me and tried to hire me to help her. She swore she hadn't killed Jackson Poole," I said.

I looked from the mother to the daughter, to make sure they were taking my measure. I needn't have worried. Their eyes were riveted to me.

"I didn't believe her then, and I'm ashamed to admit it," I said. "Now, I don't believe she ever killed anybody. That's why I came down here. Having a client to pay me to find out is nice, but even if I didn't have a client, I would still need to know who killed Jackson Poole.

"Wuvvy told me she hadn't seen her stepson in years," I plunged on. "Not until Halloween night, when he walked back into her life. I was there. She didn't recognize him.

Afterwards, she couldn't understand why he'd want to come back and ruin her life."

"How typical," Little Kitty Rhyne said swiftly. "Virginia Lee Mincey ruined her own life a long time ago. And then she proceeded to ruin a lot of other lives, too.

"The Minceys were trash, all of 'em. She came to this town with nothing. But when she married Broward Poole, for the first time in her life, she had a chance to be somebody. People in Hawkinsville bent over backwards to accommodate her, but it wasn't enough. Nothing made her happy. Not a husband or an adorable little boy or the biggest house in town . . . "

"Mother," Catherine Rhyne said uneasily, "this is all old news."

"Excuse me, but I think it's time to air it out again," Little Kitty said unrepentantly. "I am a Christian woman, but if I hear 'Poor Wuvvy' one more time, I believe I will throw up. I really will." She glared at her daughter, and then at me.

Little Kitty Rhyne stalked into the hallway, into her own office, and slammed the door behind her.

Catherine Rhyne bit her lip, then took the pencil she'd been torturing and put it firmly in the top drawer of her desk.

"Anything else?" she asked, rising from her chair.

Never say die. "The court clerk won't give me the transcripts from Wuvvy's trial without an order from the judge, and that'll take weeks," I said. "I intend to track down the old newspaper accounts. In the meantime, you could save me some time if there's anything you remember from that time."

"I'm sorry," she said sheepishly. "I was away at school during all that. My freshman year at Duke. Mother followed the trial, of course, and she sent me clippings sometimes, but it was all so long ago."

"Yet you kept in touch," I persisted. "She called you when

she was in really bad trouble, and you came. You bailed her out. She must have talked to you about Broward's murder."

"No," Catherine said. "We were friends, but she never talked about that time."

She got up and walked to the door, too polite to tell me my time was up.

In the reception room, Big Kitty Rhyne was reading a dog-eared copy of *Reader's Digest*.

"Good-bye now," she said, looking up and smiling graciously, as though she were waving me off the front porch of some grand plantation. "Come again."

Catherine Rhyne followed me onto the sidewalk. She caught my elbow with her hand.

"Mother's a bit of a snob," she said, glancing back toward their shared office. "It was a class thing. She'd known Broward forever, and when he remarried, she was determined to make Virginia into a proper wife for him; you know, Junior League, Episcopal Women's Guild, all that. Virginia marched to a different drummer. She didn't even own a dress, let alone a hat and gloves."

Catherine Rhyne laughed. "Virginia was like a big sister to me. She took me to my first rock concert—at the Macon Coliseum. The Allman Brothers and Lynyrd Skynyrd. Later, after she went to prison, we kept in touch. And when she needed help, I tried to help her. But this last time, I was too late. That's what I've been trying to tell you, Miss Garrity. It's too late."

23

Too late, people kept telling me.

By the time I got back to the Regal Motel, Edna and the girls had already gotten themselves runny eggs and stale toast at the motel's coffee shop. But the dining room had stopped serving breakfast at nine A.M.

Too late, I told myself, steering the car back toward Atlanta.

It was autumn already. Mac and I had planned a trip to the north Georgia mountains, to trout-fish in his favorite stream near Clayton. But October had gotten away from us. Edna and I liked to take a weekend trip to visit her cousin down in St. Simon's in September, but it was too cold now for the beach. We were buried in work. I'd promised Baby and Sister to take them up to the mountains too, to look at the leaves and buy apple cider at the roadside stands, but the tornado had stripped the mountains of their fall color. Grocery store cider would have to do, I told myself bleakly.

It was still green in south Georgia, but the emerald blanketing the roadside was deceptive—kudzu, which crawled and crept and strangled the life out of every living thing in its path. For once, I was happy to get off the two-lane state highway and back on I-75. On the interstate, I could make up for lost time.

At Edna's insistence, I stopped at a farm stand in Perry, and the girls all trooped inside and bought five pounds of pecans for Christmas fruitcakes. On the way home the girls talked baking; lard versus vegetable shortening for pie crust, fruitcakes they'd known and loved, and the issue that kept them arguing all the way to Atlanta: whether or not dark corn syrup made a pecan pie too rich.

I'd expected to see C.W.'s van in the driveway when I got home. It wasn't there, and I cursed my old friend for breaking his promise and letting me down. I loved my mother, but I couldn't very well carry her around in my hip pocket every time I had to leave home.

The real irritant, of course, was that home no longer felt safe.

My foul mood lifted temporarily when I spotted Mac's Blazer down the driveway, and Rufus running around in circles in the front yard. Swannelle's truck was there, too, and he and Neva Jean were stashing tools in the back, packing up to go, it looked like.

On closer inspection, Rufus was the only one who looked happy to see me.

"Where've you been?" Mac demanded as soon as I got out of the Lincoln. "C.W. got here, and when you weren't around, he called me to see if I knew where you were. I called Neva Jean, and she didn't know anything, either."

Edna and the girls got quietly out of the car. "I'll take the girls home," Edna volunteered. She herded the girls into the house, calling Neva Jean to join them for a quick cup of coffee. It was the tactful thing to do.

"We went to Hawkinsville. To Wuvvy's memorial service," I said, hating the apologetic tone in my voice. Why should I apologize to Mac for doing my work? He certainly never hesitated to do what was needed to perform his job—even if it meant breaking promises to me.

"Edna and the girls rode along for company, and we spent the night there last night. We're all fine. Safe and sound."

"Nobody told me," Mac complained. "And nobody told C.W."

"I'm sorry we missed C.W.," I said, trying to hold my temper in check. "We got a late start this morning. Why'd he leave already?"

Edna had gone into the house, but now she was back on the front porch. "Power's out again," she called to me.

"It's all my fault," Swannelle hollered, throwing a pair of bolt cutters into the back of his truck. "Everbody blame Swannelle. They always do." He got in the front seat of the pickup truck and pounded the dashboard with a fist the size of a radiator. "Come on, Neva Jean, I got work to do."

Edna and Neva Jean came out to the driveway where Mac and I were glaring at each other.

"I'm real, real sorry, Callahan," she said. Her face was streaked with dirt, and her red McComb Auto Body T-shirt had a rip on the sleeve and shoulder. "Swannelle meant well, he really did. But he don't know no more about 'lectricity than a pig does about opera. You'd think he'd have learned after that time he wired our Christmas tree to light up and blink and twirl in tune to 'Santa Claus Is Comin' to Town.' But he don't like to admit defeat."

"What happened with the Christmas tree?" I should have known better than to ask.

She shuddered. "He picked a song that was too up-tempo. That tree got to twirlin' and the lights to blinkin' so fast, the tree just screwed itself right off the stand and up into the air, like one of them Challenger rockets. Then all the lights shorted out, and the sparks caught the tinsel on fire. Swannelle was about half lit himself by then, so he tried to put it out with a carton of eggnog."

"Some disaster," I said. Mac just stood there with his arms folded across his chest. His pissed-off position. Of course, I'd adopted the same stance.

"Yeah, it was something," Neva Jean agreed. "I got the videotape if you ever want to see it."

"No thanks," Edna said. "You better go, Neva Jean, he's backing down the driveway."

"Damn," she said, turning around to see her husband's red truck flash down the driveway. "He hates it when I tell that story."

Somebody had to bring the standoff to an end. It was getting cold out there in the driveway. "Has anybody called a real electrician?" I asked.

"We called Georgia Power," Mac said. "Somehow, between Swannelle and C.W., they've managed to cut the power not just to the house, but to the whole block. It was that damned chainsaw," he added. "Swannelle insisted that a branch of that pine tree in the back looked like it might fall on the house. C.W. tried to stop him, but you know Swannelle when he gets an idea in his head. He got the chainsaw your brother left behind, and he cut it down. It fell across the power line—knocked down the utility pole holding the transformer for the whole block."

"That's bad," I said.

"It gets worse," Mac said. "C.W. was trying to run some lines up under the house through the crawlspace, and Wash came along and started tickling his legs, and C.W. jerked his hand and cut some of the lines already under there. We think it was the phone lines," he said. "You probably didn't bother to try to call, did you?"

"My cell phone was ruined when the tree fell on my van," I said. "I was in a hurry to get back here to help C.W."

"You two better plan to spend the night at my place tonight," Mac said. "It's supposed to get into the thirties tonight, too cold to stay here without any heat or electricity."

Somehow the arctic tone in his voice didn't convey much of a welcome.

"Edna can go," I said stiffly. "I'll stay here tonight. There's plenty of wood. I'll make a fire in the fireplace and sleep in the den."

"I'm staying, too," Edna said quickly. "Even if it's ten below, there's no bed like my own bed."

"Suit yourself," Mac said. "You know where to reach me if you need me."

Mac had been right about the weather. It had been cloudy and fifty-five degrees when we got home around noon Saturday. The sun never did come out, and the mercury kept falling all that afternoon.

We made a fire in the fireplace, got Edna's tornado supplies back upstairs from the basement, and ate huge bowls of homemade soup for lunch.

Cheezer knocked on the back door as we were washing up the dishes.

"Can I talk to you a minute?" he asked.

"Get in here and quit letting that cold air in my kitchen," Edna said good-naturedly.

"Hi, Edna," he said, sitting down at the kitchen table. He looked at her closely as she bustled around the room, putting away dishes.

"What happened to you?" he asked teasingly. "Did you get in a fight over the bingo jackpot?"

Edna smiled wanly. "I got mugged."

"Right in the driveway," I told him. "We're going to have a security system put in. And I want you to keep your eyes open, especially when you're riding around this neighborhood on your bike. We've all fooled ourselves into thinking we're safe here. But we're not safe. This thug put a knife to her neck. He got Edna's purse and her bingo money. Even her St. Christopher's medal."

"The little gold one you wear around your neck?" He blanched. "Oh jeez. Jeez, Edna. I'm sorry. Did you get a good look at the guy?"

"Sort of," Edna said. "It was dark."

Cheezer doesn't drink coffee, but he did let me make him a cup of tea. I told him about our adventure in Hawkinsville, and Edna, eager not to discuss her attack, bragged about the snooping she and the girls had done.

I could tell there was something on his mind, but I waited until Edna went into the den to check on the fire to try to draw him out.

"Okay, Cheezer," I said. "You don't make social calls to us on Saturdays. What's up?"

"Well—I thought it was no big deal. But now that you tell me about this guy mugging Edna, maybe it's connected or something."

"Go ahead and tell me," I suggested.

"Last night," he said, "I was playing darts at the Yacht Club. It was late, but I was winning, and nothing else much was going on.

"You know, sometimes I walk home through the alley. It's a shortcut to the church. And, oh, Jesus, it makes me sick." His face did indeed get greenish, and he hung his head limply, like he would be sick.

"What?"

"I saw one of the street guys. Everybody calls him Spaceman, 'cause he always looks so spaced out. Spaceman was out of it. He was puking on a stack of boxes right by the Yacht Club's kitchen door. And all of a sudden, these two guys come blasting out of that door, and they grab Spaceman, and they're hitting him, and kicking him, and just beating the living shit out of him. I thought they were gonna kill him."

"What did you do?"

"I wasn't gonna mess with them," Cheezer admitted. "I was alone, you know? I know it sounds chickenshit. It feels chickenshit too. But there were two of them. And the one guy wasn't that much bigger than me, but the other guy was some kind of body builder. He had a gun. On a holster on his ankle. I'm pretty sure the dude's a cop."

"Which cop?" I said sharply.

"I don't know his name," Cheezer said miserably. "White guy. Dirty blonde hair, muscles, like he pumps iron. I try to avoid cops. I know some of 'em are your friends, but, man, it's kinda my own prejudice."

"What about the other guy?" I asked.

"Kind of squirrelly-looking. He was white, too, but he had his hair in a 'do,' you know."

"What kind of do?"

"That Jamaican shit," Cheezer said. "The braids with the beads and stuff."

"Dreadlocks? Did he have dreadlocks? Was he wearing a knit cap?"

"Yeah, dreadlocks," Cheezer said, looking surprised. "How'd you know?"

"The kid who attacked Edna had dreadlocks. He was wearing a purple and white knit cap," I said. I went to the hall to see if Edna was within earshot. "Don't tell her I told you. Edna had a pistol. A thirty-eight. He took that, too."

"Holy shit," Cheezer said. "You think it's the same guy?"

"Maybe. Did you call the police and report it?" I asked.

"I did," Cheezer protested. "I called from the pay phone in the bar and I told them two guys were beating the shit out of another guy in the alley. When I hung up, I went outside to see what was happening. And they'd pulled a car around, a black pickup truck. I saw 'em take Spaceman and toss him in the back. Like he was nothing. Like he was trash. They got in and took off."

"Did you get the license number?" I asked.

"I couldn't see it," Cheezer said. "But it was a black Chevy pickup. And it had a sticker on the window. I couldn't see the words, but it looked like one of those cop buddy associations. The kind you put on your car so you don't get a speeding ticket."

"Fraternal Order of Police," I said, feeling sick myself.

"I told Hap about it," Cheezer said. "He was pretty pissed off. He went running outside to see if he could stop the guys, but by the time he got there, they were gone. That's when I decided to get out of there, too. I'm sorry, but I didn't stick around to see if they'd send anybody."

I patted his shoulder. "You did the right thing."

"Those fuckers maybe killed Spaceman," Cheezer said. "They coulda killed Edna. Jeez. Man, I wish I'd have tried to stop them anyway."

"You want to do a little nosing around for me?" I asked.

"Sure," he said eagerly. "What do you want me to do?"

"Just talk to people around the neighborhood. You know a lot of those street kids. See if anybody's seen Spaceman since last night, or heard anything about it. See if any of the other street people have been roughed up."

I dug in my pockets and brought out a twenty-dollar bill.

It was all I had left after bankrolling Edna and the girls. "Here's some expense money. Sometimes you have to buy people a drink to get them to talk. You know?"

He looked at the bill in his hand. "Cool."

"No dope, though," I said hastily. "Nothing illegal."

He looked offended. "As if."

24

A couple times that night I rolled over in my sleep and threw my arm across Edna. She mumbled, pushed me away, and pulled the stack of quilts closer around herself. Some mother.

One of the benefits of having no electricity and no phone is that you lose track of time. Some time in the night I got up, pulled on another pair of wool socks, threw more wood on the fire, then fell immediately back to sleep.

To make it up to me for hogging all the covers, Edna let me sleep until noon. When I finally sat up on the sofa bed, pale yellow shafts of sunlight were streaming in through the window. I looked groggily out at the view, which I still hadn't gotten adjusted to. I blinked. A Georgia Power cherry picker was parked in our backyard, and three or four pissed-off-looking neighbors were standing around it, watching the workmen. I couldn't hear them with the windows closed, but I was sure they were muttering ominous threats against the Garrity women under their breath.

Edna came into the den with a cup of coffee. "Mr. Byerly's daughter called the power company and told them he might die unless his dialysis machine got hooked back up again," she said. "So they sent a crew right over. Phone company's already been and gone while you were asleep."

"Mr. Byerly doesn't have a dialysis machine," I pointed out.

"He doesn't have a daughter, either," she said, sipping her coffee. "But he does have a cell phone. I sure do like those new digital models."

As soon as I had enough coffee in me, I called my new client to give her a progress report. Anna Frisch wanted to talk to me as badly as I wanted to talk to her.

"Did you find out anything in Hawkinsville?" she asked.

"My assistants and I managed to talk to some people," I said cautiously.

She agreed to meet me at the Blind Possum in Little Five Points. "I want to see if my mash kettles have been set up yet," she said.

Some kids had made a fire in a wire-mesh trash barrel down at the Point, and they were huddled around it, passing a joint hand to hand. Most of the shop doorways had a shapeless blanket-wrapped bundle propped against them. Everyone in Little Five Points, it seemed, was enjoying the great outdoors today.

The regulars were sitting at their table in the window at the Yacht Club when I walked up. I knew them not by any names, only by their assigned seats. The fat guy with the sleeveless denim jacket always sat near the door. His girlfriend, who had enormous knockers and a missing front tooth, sat in the window to his right. Next to her sat the guy in the greasy red Winston Cup Racing Circuit cap, and on the side by the wall sat the oldest hippie in captivity.

It was only two-thirty. The Yacht Club had been open thirty minutes, but already the regulars' table was littered with empty longneck bottles and overflowing ashtrays. In the daylight like this, it struck me how ghoulish they all looked. Pale, bloated. The undead.

Hap was just coming out the front door. He had a length of garden hose with a nozzle attachment, a bucket of sudsy water, and a long-handled broom. As soon as I got close, I understood why the need for the cleaning supplies.

"Hey, Callahan," he said. "Watch your feet."

He took the bucket of cleanser and splattered it all over the sidewalk, then attacked it with the pushbroom. "The romantic life of the saloonkeeper, huh?" he said, pushing a wave of filthy water toward the curb. "Miranda hosed this down last night before we closed up, but you can see we've had nocturnal visitors."

He turned the hose on the granite front wall of the bar and I had to do a quick two-step to avoid being splashed.

"Sorry I lost my temper at that thing for Wuvvy," he said, looking a little ashamed. "I was an asshole. You got a right to do your job. You stick around long down there in Hawkinsville?"

"I spent the night," I said.

"Place is fucking depressing," Hap said. "No wonder Wuvvy hated it so bad. Prison was probably better than that place."

"Friendlier, at least," I agreed. "Hey, Hap—do you know anything about a plainclothes cop rousting street people down here?"

"That kid Cheezer, he told you what happened, huh?" Hap said. "He was pretty upset. I hate to say it, but maybe it was just some guys joking around. Hell, I don't want to see anybody get hurt, but, Christ, look at this mess." He gestured with the hose at the sidewalk and gutter. "We have to go through this routine two or three times a day. Maybe this cop was looking for the guy who mugged your mom?"

"No," I said quickly. "Cheezer described the guy with him. It sounds like the same kid who mugged Edna. A white kid with dreadlocks. Have you noticed anybody like that around the neighborhood?"

Hap thought about it. "I can ask Miranda, and some of my help. Doesn't sound like any of my regulars, though. I hope they catch the turd." He turned off the faucet, unscrewed the hose, and started coiling it in a thick roll.

"We're gonna start getting a whole different clientele down here when the Blind Possum opens," he confided. "Money brings money."

"They've definitely got money," I agreed. "The question is—who are they?"

Hap took the coiled hose and put it into the empty bucket.

"I don't know," he said. "I knew Poole, of course. He came over and introduced himself after he picked up Wuvvy's place. All he told me was, he was part of an investment group that was opening these brewpubs all over the place."

"You weren't worried about the competition? Right next door?"

Hap smiled. "It's a white tablecloth house. Fine dining. Whole different concept. It'll bring new business to the neighborhood, new business to the Yacht Club."

"It's so weird that he would end up here. Right here in Little Five Points—and take over YoYos, of all places," I said. "That still blows my mind."

"You still think he knew who Wuvvy was?" Hap asked.

"How could he not?"

"Wuvvy, man," he said, shaking his head. "That chick definitely had some bad karma. She could not catch a break."

I looked over at the storefront that had been YoYos two weeks ago. More miracles had been wrought since my last visit. The building had received a layer of stucco, one that had been painted a deep brownish-black. The plateglass window had been replaced with leaded-glass casement windows, and—this was a first for Little Five Points—a scalloped white wooden window box had managed to sprout overnight with blooming red and yellow pansies and curling strands of ivy.

"What next, cobblestones?" I marveled.

Anna Frisch popped her head out the door of the Blind Possum. "Cobblestones," she said. "Great idea. I'll mention it to the designer."

Hap went back to the Yacht Club to tend to his regulars, and I followed Anna back inside Little Five Points's latest dining concept.

"Wow," I said. Two brass and copper vats had been set up in a glass-walled brew room that had only been a blue line on a set of plans just last week.

Ann ran one hand over the gleaming metal. "They're the same kind you saw in the Roswell restaurant," she said. "But our space here is so much smaller, we'll have a fairly limited production. The beer will be just as good, though. Totally up to Blind Possum standards."

"Who is Blind Possum?" I persisted.

"I told you before," she said, shrugging. "Investors. Restaurant people and money people. The president of Blind Possum is a man named Reuben Sizemore. He lives in Birmingham. I've only met him at the openings of the other restaurants."

"One person doesn't put up all this capital and start an operation on this scale, Anna," I said. "Tell me who they really are, or I can't help you."

Anna looked out at the workmen in the dining room who were rolling cream-colored paint on the walls.

"We're supposed to be a totally self-contained entity," she said. "Home grown. That's the whole concept. That's why we have owner-managers and owner-brewmasters."

"But," I prompted.

"Total Entertainment Systems," she said in a half whisper. "They're us. We're them."

"The cookie people?" I asked. I'd read about TES. And they weren't just cookies anymore. From a family-owned bakery in Birmingham, the company had gone into manufacturing video arcade games, which is where they'd made their first big money. The company had gotten swallowed up by a bigger company a few years back, and now, to my knowledge, they owned an upstart cable television system, a minor league baseball franchise in Memphis, and a gospel music theme park in Texas. Total Entertainment Systems was one of those conglomerates that had steamrolled in a dozen different directions in the late eighties.

"Video games, cable television, pro sports, and now beer," I said admiringly. "All that's missing is a popcorn company."

"Grandma Sue's Ole-Timey Movie Show Popcorn," Anna said. "We own them too."

"And how did Jackson Poole fit into the company?"

"He was working for TES, marketing video games in Portland. That's where we met," Anna said.

"When TES decided to start up Blind Possum, Jackson was picked to be part of the management team for the new division. I'd already graduated from brewschool, and this was a great opportunity for both of us. Jackson moved down here a year ago to start the real estate acquisitions."

"Why live in Atlanta?" I asked. "I heard Blind Possum is opening brewpubs all over the place. And TES is headquartered where?"

"Birmingham," Anna said. "I don't know. He liked it here, I guess. And I thought, maybe, he was a little homesick for Georgia, but he didn't want to admit it."

"He's the one who did the real estate acquisitions?" I asked. "He picked this location: YoYos, which just happened to be the place where his long-lost stepmother was trying to eke out a living?"

"I guess," Anna said weakly. "It sounds strange now, I know. But as soon as TES talked about expanding into other markets, Jackson knew he wanted to come to Atlanta. And he always talked about wanting to have a presence in Little Five Points. Jackson knew his stuff. He said this was a hot neighborhood. I was just in charge of making the beer. I didn't care where we made it, as long as it was good beer."

She was getting teary-eyed now. I didn't know if it was over Jackson Poole's murder or the prospect of making a really bitchin' brew.

"Never mind," I said, trying to head off the tears before they gained momentum. "You said Jackson told you something was wrong here. Have you looked around? Can you give me any idea what he could have been talking about?"

"No," she sniffed. "I mean, yes, I've checked the place from top to bottom. It looks fine. It looks great. We're ahead of schedule, even. That's how TES does things. You have a schedule, you have a plan, you have goals, and you perform."

"Even when there's a murder. Damn," I said admiringly. "I wish I could get my business to operate like that.

"What about Jackson's office, or his apartment?" I asked Anna. "Did he keep any business papers relating to Blind Possum?"

Her face fell. "He was working out of his condo. I was living with him. It's on Greenwood, near Piedmont Park."

"Can we go take a look?"

"It's no good," she said despairingly. "I cleaned it out.

After Jackson was killed. The company's attorney called me
and asked me to box up all his files and things. They've hired
a new manager, and he's actually supposed to start work this
week."

"You sent everything?" I asked incredulously.

"Sergeant Deavers told me they were going to arrest that
Wuvvy woman," Anna said. "Our lawyer called me and told
me he'd have a messenger pick up the boxes. It didn't occur
to me to keep anything."

"What about personal papers? Bills, correspondence, that
kind of thing?"

Anna put out a hand to steady herself against one of the
vats. The cool feel of the metal seemed to comfort her.

"I got rid of everything," she said. "It was so depressing
having it around. I'm still living there, see, until everything
is settled. In the meantime, I'm paying rent," she said, as if I
cared.

"I'll need the name and phone number of the company
lawyer," I said. "And a list of everybody who's had anything
to do with this restaurant. Contractors, suppliers, vendors,
drivers, delivery people, anybody you can think of."

"All right," she agreed. "We're closed tomorrow. Everybody
else is off, but I always go in on Mondays because it's a good
day to have the place quiet and to myself. I think we used a
lot of the same people at both restaurants. I'll get the list
together and call you tomorrow."

25

The power was on again when I got home, and Edna was working the phones, apologizing for creating a blockwide blackout and organizing her Commando meeting for that night.

"We're going to discuss security systems," I heard her saying. "I've got a close personal friend who'll give us a group discount."

I groaned and went back out to the car to start bringing in the boxes of Wuvvy's stuff.

It was obvious Wuvvy's belongings had been more or less tossed at random into the cartons, by somebody who had other things on their minds. The cops had been tidy, though. Each of the cartons was sealed with tape, with a typed inventory list attached.

The list had been compiled by someone with little or no sense of rock and roll history. T-shirts, 20, the list would say.

Or Record albums, 116, or Posters, 32. The inventory didn't say that one of the T-shirts was from Captain Beefheart's debut tour, or that the albums were mostly mint and all classics of the genre, including copies of everything ever recorded by Frank Zappa and the Mothers of Invention. There was even a Claudine Longet album. A real collector's item.

At the bottom of a box of mildewed T-shirts, I found what I'd been looking for, papers. And I literally mean papers. There must have been ten cartons of Zigzag rolling papers. Underneath them were the papers that could tell me something about Wuvvy's life—and maybe her death.

I sat cross-legged on the floor of my bedroom, dumped out the box, and started sorting things into piles. Most of the stuff related to YoYos. Wuvvy didn't seem to have much of a life or an identity outside her shop.

There were copies of purchase orders, catalogs from toymakers, packing sheets, canceled checks, and a thick stack of bills that looked like they'd never been paid.

Rubber-banded together in one thick packet were what she must have considered her most pressing debts: the power bill, phone bill, insurance statement, gas bill, a form letter from the IRS inquiring about her nonpayment of income tax for the past year, some bills from suppliers notifying her that her accounts had been placed on "hold" until they received payment, and a notice from her landlord that her lease had been terminated.

I found three notices, in all, from her landlord, starting in July. Month by month, they notified her in formal detached language to pay up or get out.

Why? I wondered. Why, if she'd had that much notice, had Wuvvy refused to do anything to keep the roof over her head? She'd known since the summer that she was in trouble. And from what little I could tell from her sloppy records, she'd been going deeper into debt with each passing day.

The landlord's name was Restoration Properties, Inc. The letters threatening eviction were all signed by someone named Rutledge Gross.

I called Restoration Properties, but got an answering machine telling me that business hours were Monday through Friday, nine A.M. to four-thirty P.M. And for emergencies I could call another number. Which I called. Which gave me a tape recording telling me to leave a message.

I did leave a message, asking to have Rutledge Gross call me in reference to the property at 362 Euclid Avenue.

Back to the bills. I took a calculator and added up all Wuvvy's unpaid debts. They came to more than twelve thousand dollars, a huge chunk for someone with a marginal business like YoYos. And at the same time she'd been struggling financially, Wuvvy's store seemed to have been under siege from shoplifters and burglars.

When I called Bucky and caught him at his desk—on a Sunday—I was surprised. Wasn't this football season? I asked.

"I've got a case working," he said, sounding exhausted. "Jane Doe found in the kudzu behind the Carter Center Library. Don't tell me you're still trying to free Virginia Lee Mincey?"

"I won't tell you that," I agreed. "But do you have time to answer a couple questions? If I ask nice?"

"You never ask nice, that's why I love you," Bucky said. "What do you need?"

"A couple things," I said. "Remember you told me that Wuvvy had reported all kinds of break-ins and burglaries and simple thefts in the last couple months before she died? What I'm wondering is, when did all this start to escalate? I'm looking through all these boxes of stuff from the store, and from her records, it looks like she started getting in financial trouble in June or July."

"You want uniform crime statistics for Zone Six," Bucky said. "I can get you that, if you wait till tomorrow."

"Will it have complaints broken down by each address within the zone?" I asked.

"If I have the computer analyst run it that way," he said. "But why?"

"Hap said something to me today," I said. "About what shitty karma Wuvvy had. How all this stuff was happening to her. I want to know if Wuvvy was the only person in Little Five Points who was experiencing a crime wave."

"All the stats have been up in L5P, I can tell you that right now," Bucky said. "Marge Fitzgerald, that new chief I told you about, has been busting everybody's chops about it. Assaults alone are up thirty percent over there."

"Edna was assaulted," I said. "But Wuvvy wasn't the victim of an assault. She was being nickel-and-dimed to death with petty thefts. That's what I'm interested in."

"Okay," he said. "What was the other thing?"

I took a deep breath. "Do you know a street guy named Spaceman who hangs out in the neighborhood?"

"Guy wears a space helmet made out of a plastic milk jug, has a walkie-talkie made out of an old television remote control," Bucky said. "What about him?"

"Cheezer, one of my associates? He was at the Yacht Club Friday night. He saw two guys grab Spaceman, kick him senseless, and throw him in the back of a truck. Cheezer said he thinks one of the guys is a cop who hangs around the Yacht Club, a body-builder type with blond hair. The description of the other guy fits Edna's attacker."

"Half the cops in this town pump iron in their spare time," Bucky said. "And if Edna will look at some mug shots, maybe file a complaint, we could do a little more about the guy who robbed her. Besides, Garrity, maybe it was just a couple righteous citizens who got tired of having the

Spaceman crawling into their vehicles and shitting all over the place. That's his specialty, you know. Car-shitting."

"He wasn't in a car when Cheezer saw him, he was in an alley," I said angrily. "And the pickup truck had an FOP sticker on the windshield. Come on, Bucky. You must know this guy. What's going on? Is this part of the new chief's plan to cut crime in Little Five Points? By yanking helpless winos off the street, beating them up, and trucking them out of there?"

Bucky laughed, but not a hearty ha-ha. "You're complaining? Callahan Garrity? The same person who comes crying to me because you've got a Peeping Tom one night and then your own mother is mugged in your own front yard the next night—and you don't want the cops to clean up the scum living in the gutters over there? Are you going to give me a lecture now on the constitutional rights of lowlife scumbag maggots?"

"I'm going to tell you that what I heard about this Spaceman guy makes me want to puke," I said. "Cheezer said he was unconscious when those guys threw him in the back of that truck. What if he's dead?"

"Then that's one less scumball committing crimes against tax-paying citizens like you and me," Bucky said. "I gotta go now, Callahan, before you piss me off so bad I forget we're friends."

I hung up the phone and kicked the nearest box. The cardboard seam caved in and an album slid out. It was Country Joe and the Fish. What were the words to their big song? Something about whoopee I don't give a damn, next stop is Vietnam?

The album underneath was another classic. The Woodstock quadruple album. My brother Kevin had that one. In fact, looking at it reminded me that it had been one of his favorite places to hide his dope stash—not from my mother, who had no idea a stash existed, but from my other brother, Keith, who would have ripped off Kevin's dope in a minute.

I opened the album and Wuvvy's stash came drifting out, several small yellowed pieces of paper that fluttered to the floor like so many dying butterflies.

They were newspaper clippings. Nothing long or sensational. No trial stories, to my disappointment. The first one was the smallest, just two paragraphs.

"GOVERNOR APPOINTS PANEL TO INVESTIGATE BATTERED WOMEN'S SENTENCES," the headline said.

> Gov. George Busbee today appointed a three-person panel to look into several controversial murder cases involving battered women who were convicted of killing the men who allegedly abused them.
>
> Chairing the panel will be G. H. "Buddy" Hughes of Conyers, former head of the State Department of Corrections. Also serving on the panel will be Gail Samford, former mayor of Banbury Cross, and Joseph P. Mengino, professor of forensic psychology at the Medical College of Georgia in Augusta.

The other two clippings weren't much longer. One announced that the panel had spent a year analyzing sentencing patterns for women convicted of homicide when the victim had a history of abusing his murderer, and that three cases had been chosen by the panel for reconsideration of their sentences. Two of the women, Shelley Diane Moore and Virginia Lee Mincey Poole, were serving life sentences for the murders of their husbands; the third, Ruth Barrett, had been on death row since 1981 for the fatal poisoning of her stepfather and two uncles.

The final clipping was the biggest. It looked like it had taken up the top half of the front page of the *Atlanta Constitution*, and it announced:

GOVERNOR SETS ASIDE BATTERED WOMEN'S SENTENCES: MOORE, BARRETT & POOLE ORDERED RELEASED FROM PRISON

The story had photos too, old prison mug shots of the three women that made them look tough and incorrigible. Wuvvy was unrecognizable. Her hair was dark, pushed behind her ears, eyes heavy-lidded and wary. There was also a photo of a group of picketers standing outside the gates at Hardwick, the state prison for women. One picketer was a pigtailed little black girl who grinned for the camera and held aloft a sign that said GO TO HELL SHEL—YOU KILLED MY DADDY.

I lined the stories up on the floor and read them over again. Wuvvy had been delivered from prison. She and two other women. I wanted to know how. I wanted to know why. The only name in the news stories I recognized was Gail Samford. She'd been the first female mayor of a city in Metro Atlanta. I'd seen her on television news. A ballbuster back then, unafraid to speak her mind. Maybe, I hoped, she still liked to talk. I'd had it with people with secrets. It was time to let some light onto the tired old story of Broward and Virginia Lee Mincey Poole.

26

Banbury Cross was a dot-sized town fifteen minutes from downtown. Physically, it was just another of Atlanta's countless bedroom suburbs, but technically, it was an incorporated town, with its own city council, police force, and school system. I'd passed through there before, but had never crossed the six-foot-high hedge that separated the town from Covington Highway, which ran through it.

Even though she'd given me detailed directions to her house when I'd called, it was dark by the time I'd navigated the winding confusing maze of streets in Banbury Cross to find Gail Samford's sprawling Tudor-style house.

I didn't even have to ring the doorbell. She switched on the porch light and opened the door as I was walking down the front path.

She was short and round, with long blond hair and wire-rimmed glasses perched on an upturned nose, and she was dressed like a lumberjack, in worn blue jeans, a plaid flannel shirt, and work boots.

"After you called, I realized it was probably a rotten idea—talking to you about the Hughes Three," she said, showing me through a darkened living room and into a cavern-sized den.

The room smelled like a forest. A twelve-foot live fir or spruce or something like that had been erected in front of a cathedral window, and cartons of decorations were scattered all over the room. It was only the first week of November. We still had a bag of Halloween candy in our living room.

She saw me staring and laughed. "I'm a Christmas nut," she said. "There's a place up in Hiawassee where they grow my tree every year. I went up there to the mountains today and chopped it down. I'll keep this one up until the end of January. I collect Santa Clauses, too. There's about a hundred and fifty in those boxes. I have to start this early because it takes me the whole month to get them all unpacked and set up the way I like. Crazy, huh?"

She motioned me to sit in one of a pair of armchairs beside a fireplace and took the chair opposite mine.

"I appreciate your seeing me," I told her.

"When you said you'd known Virginia Lee after she got out of prison, I was curious," she admitted. "I've read the newspaper stories, but I'd like to hear from you how things really were with her. Maybe we made a mistake with Virginia Lee," Gail Samford said. "That's what I've been wondering."

"I don't think so," I said. "She started a business, made friends and a new life. And I'm not sure she was ever guilty of murder."

"So," she murmured. "I'm glad you came. I'll talk. You'll talk."

She poked the fire with a piece of kindling from a stack on the hearth. "My lawyer would kill me if he knew I was talking to you. He's always telling me people love to sue elected officials. But hell, I'm retired now. What do you want to know?"

"Your committee recommended that the governor pardon three women, including Virginia Lee," I said. "Why those three?"

"We looked at about fifteen cases, as I recall," Gail said. "But a lot of those women were real hard cases, with long criminal histories and a previous history of violence, alcohol or drug addiction, shoplifting, bank robbery, you name it." She shuddered a little. "I'm a die-hard feminist, but some of those broads we looked at—they needed to be locked up for life."

"But not Virginia Lee Mincey," I suggested.

"No," Gail said. "I liked her. I liked the other two women, too. We interviewed them all, looked at the trial transcripts, talked to the district attorneys, the prison warden, gave them psychological tests up the wazzoo. You know something?" she asked. "Until she committed suicide, Virginia Lee was the last of the Hughes Three who was still alive."

"Really? What happened to everybody?'

She didn't have to hesitate to think about it. Gail Samford had kept up with the women whose lives she had helped to change.

"Virginia Lee Mincey Poole you already know about. Shelley Moore? She was the one who stabbed her common-law husband, after he beat her and assaulted her with a beer bottle and burned her repeatedly with cigarettes. Great little gal. After she went to prison, she got her GED, took a correspondence school course in hairdressing. Hers was the first case we chose and the only one we all agreed on was worth a second look."

Gail shrugged. "How wrong could we be? Two years after she was released, she died of a crack overdose."

She held up a second finger. "Ruth Barrett was the most unlikely murderer you'll ever meet. Very shy and quiet. Extremely religious, devoted to her family. Nursed first her stepfather and then her uncles through two long, horrendous illnesses. And then it came out that she'd fed them rat poison in their coffee for two years. Her attorney was a serious drunk. He never mentioned during her trial that her step-father and uncles had taken turns screwing Ruth since she was in diapers."

"And what happened to Ruth Barrett?" I wanted to know.

"All the paperwork had been done for her release, and as part of the regular procedure, they gave her a physical. Totally routine. Until the nurse found a mass. On her neck, the size of a walnut. She went right from Hardwick to the hospital, to have surgery. But the cancer had spread too far, to her brain, kidneys, lungs, everything. She died in that hospital a week after her surgery. We never did get her home."

As Gail Samford was discussing Ruth Barrett's cancer I found my own hand clenched tightly across my chest, like a shield that would protect me from a recurrence of my own breast cancer. If she noticed, she didn't mention it.

"Who came up with the idea to get the cases reconsidered?" I asked.

"A bunch of us," she said. "It was the eighties, and there were a bunch of us loudmouthed feminists who wouldn't shut up or take no for an answer. We kept reading about those kinds of cases, women who killed after suffering years of abuse. So we started agitating. Going down to the capitol, lobbying the General Assembly, writing letters. Ruth Barrett was the final straw, I guess. After she got the death penalty from an all-white, all-male jury in Stephens County, we really put up a stink. The next thing I know, Governor Busbee had appointed me to the Hughes Committee."

A cat wandered into the room then. It was a calico, scrawny, with yellow eyes that gleamed in the firelight. It crept up to me, rubbed against my legs, and meowed beguilingly.

"Dookie likes you," Gail said, surprised. "Usually when I have company she goes into hiding."

I wished Dookie would go back into hiding, but I kept that to myself.

"You said you and your colleagues got organized after hearing about Ruth Barrett," I said. "What about the other two? Shelley Moore and Virginia Lee? How did they get on the committee's list?"

"It's been a long time," Gail admitted. "Probably through one or another group that had an interest in social justice issues. Legal Aid, the Southern Poverty Law Council, Georgia Women's Political Caucus. All those folks were working behind the scenes. Quietly, of course, because back then you didn't want to alienate the good ol' boys."

From my experience, you still didn't want to alienate the good ol' boys. Unless you had so much clout the good ol' boys couldn't mess with you . . .

"Did you know Catherine Rhyne back then?" I asked abruptly.

"Little Kitty?" Gail smiled widely. "Sure. I knew Big Kitty, too. Everybody did. Talk about a dynasty!"

She picked up Dookie and stroked the cat's head absent-mindedly. "They had a real power base down in Hawkinsville. Wait," she stared at me. "I see what you're getting at. Hawkinsville. It's not that big a place. Virginia Lee was from there. And Itty-Bitty, well, Catherine, she was a member of the Women's Political Caucus. She was still in the General Assembly back then, I guess."

I leaned forward. "Did Catherine Rhyne ask the Hughes Committee to take a look at Virginia Lee Mincey's case? Would she have lobbied to have Virginia's sentence commuted by the governor?"

Gail stood up and the cat jumped down. "Catherine Rhyne never liked to ask for favors. It was Little Kitty who called me and sent over the case file."

27

I borrowed Gail's phone so that I could call home and check on my mother. Edna hated to be checked on. She hated to be coddled or patronized in any way. But it was either phone checks or taking her along with me every step of the day. Neither of us could have stood that.

Cheezer answered the phone at my house.

"Oh, good," I said. "In the middle of everything else, I realized we still need a bodyguard for Edna, since the burglar alarm didn't get installed. What are you doing there? Mooching groceries again?"

"You asked me to do some checking around the neighborhood, remember? I've been kind of making rounds, riding past your house every so often, just seeing if everything's cool."

"And is everything cool?"

"You're not gonna like this," Cheezer warned. "Edna just left."

"Did my sister pick her up?"

"No. When I got here, Edna was in the middle of some neighborhood commando meeting," Cheezer said. "Some cop buddy of Deavers's showed up, to give them tips about crime prevention."

"Was it Jeff Kaczynski? The same guy Deavers sent over before?"

"Yeah, I think that was his name," Cheezer said. "And he brought some more photos for Edna to look at. I think maybe she recognized the guy who beat her up and stole the medal your dad gave her. But she was real quiet. Then, after everybody else went home and I was getting ready to leave, too, she went in her bedroom. I thought she was getting ready to take a nap or something. I was writing a note to leave for you when she came out of the bedroom. She was dressed all in black. I asked her where she was going, and she got this funny look. She told me she and Neva Jean were going out for a nightcap. The next thing I know, Swannelle's truck is in the driveway and before I can stop her or make her let me come along, she's gone. Adios. Outta here."

"Shit," I said. "Neva Jean McComb with Edna Mae Garrity riding shotgun. This is not good."

"I'm sorry," Cheezer said. "You thinking what I'm thinking?"

"I'm thinking you better meet me at Little Five Points."

When I got to the PitStop I decided to have another quart of oil put in the Lincoln's crankcase. The Iranian clerk, who sat behind a bulletproof glass booth, went so far as to offer me a paper towel to clean up. The guy must have had an ownership interest in the place, because I'd never seen anybody else working the cash register there.

I put my money in the retractable slot in the window, then tapped on the glass.

"Jess?"

"Were you working here last Monday night?" I asked.

"Jess. My wife, she works Monday mornings."

"Do you remember Wuvvy, the woman who owned YoYos, over there in Little Five Points?" I pointed toward the store.

He shrugged. "She does beezness wit me."

"I heard she bought gas here that night, a full tank. Was that unusual for her?"

Another shrug. "She buy five dollars gas, a wine cooler, cheeps, that's all usually."

"But last Monday?"

"Beeg night," he said sarcastically. "Full tank of gas, windshield wiper blades, ham sandwich. I have to change fifty-dollar bill for her." He scowled. "Sign say no bills over twenty dollars."

Deavers had told me Wuvvy'd bought a full tank of gas that night. He'd assumed she'd wanted to make sure she didn't run out of gas before the carbon monoxide fumes did their job. But the last time I'd seen her at YoYos she'd told me she was leaving town. Maybe she really had intended to leave town, to literally keep on truckin'.

"Did you tell all that to the police?" I asked.

"I answer the police questions," he said. "You want anything else?"

Cheezer walked up as I was walking back to the Lincoln. He was dressed in green army fatigues three sizes too big for him, and he was sipping from a quart bottle of Gatorade. He jumped in the Lincoln's front seat. "What was that all about?" he asked.

"Nothing," I said. "Let's go find Edna and Neva Jean."

"You think Neva Jean might have a gun?" he asked.

"This is a woman who wore a derringer tucked into the garter belt at her own wedding," I said. "Let's just hope Edna and Neva Jean don't find the guy who mugged Edna before we find the two of them."

We cruised the Lincoln across the street to Euclid Avenue, turned down the alley behind the organic food coop, and cruised slowly back up Moreland again.

"Right there," I said, pointing to the left, toward the parking lot in front of the Junkman's Daughter, a sprawling vintage clothes boutique located in an old supermarket.

Swannelle's battered truck was parked with its nose facing Moreland. But it was empty, no sign of Annie Oakley or her sidekick, Ma Barker.

"What now?" Cheezer asked.

"Let's walk down Moreland," I suggested. "They couldn't have gone far."

As we got closer to the point where Euclid, Moreland, and McLendon intersected, we could hear music pumping out of the Vortex. A low, twangy baritone backed by steel guitar. People were spilling out of the Vortex and onto the plaza beside it. There was a long, final wail, a prolonged riff on the steel guitar, and then a crescendo of applause for the big finale.

"Ed's Adenoids and Concrete Dreams," Cheezer said, nodding at the marquee announcing the night's double bill. "They rule."

Cheezer picked up the pace, and I struggled to keep up with him. "Hey, uh, Callahan," he said, craning his neck to see over the throng. "You, uh, don't really think they'd, uh, do anything if they saw the guy who mugged Edna, do you? I mean, they wouldn't really shoot somebody, would they?"

I was so tired I could barely pick up my feet and put them down again. "Maybe not."

Cheezer plowed into the crush of people departing the Vortex. I had to hang on to a fold of his baggy pants to keep from getting separated from him.

"Hey, Cheez," I heard somebody exclaim. Cheezer offered a high-five and a "How's it going, man?" but he kept moving.

"I can't see anything," I complained.

"This way," he said over his shoulder, shouting to be heard in the din. Somebody stepped on my foot, and somebody else jostled me. The combined aroma of incense, dope, beer, puke, and sweat made me feel giddy and slightly nauseous.

"Look," Cheezer said, pointing toward the tiny roped-off patio outside Fellini's Pizza. All I could see was a yellow-gold bouffant hairdo. It was enough.

They'd staked out a table at the edge of the patio. A cardboard box held remnants of pizza crust, and there was a half-empty pitcher of beer on the table. Neva Jean had a pair of binoculars trained on the crowd coming out of the Vortex, and Edna was busy scribbling away on a notepad. They didn't notice me until I pulled out the vacant chair at the table, scraping the metal legs against the concrete.

"Jesus!" Edna said, doing a double take. Her hand fluttered nervously in her lap. Neva Jean dropped the binoculars and grabbed for her suitcase-sized purse.

"Hi, girls," I said.

Cheezer smiled nervously. "Hello, ladies."

"What do you want?" Edna glowered at Cheezer.

"First, I want Neva Jean to take her hand off that gun," I said. "Then I want you to call off the dragnet and go home before somebody gets hurt."

"It's not a gun," Neva Jean said. She reached in her purse and brought out a blunt black object. "It's my phone. We were gonna call the cops when we spotted that guy who robbed your mama. I wouldn't bring a gun over here to this neighborhood. Somebody might try to steal it."

"What about you?" I asked Edna. "What are you so busy writing down?"

"Descriptions," she said. "That nice Detective Kaczynski told the Commandos tonight that if we wanted to clean up this neighborhood we had to be on the lookout at all times for criminal activity." She held up the notebook and leafed through three pages of notes.

"Jaywalking, underage drinking, dope dealers, public intoxication, public indecency, prostitution . . . it's all right here. Time, date, and details."

I peered over her shoulder at the notations.

"Very nice," I said. "But I don't think this is exactly what Kaczynski had in mind. He probably didn't mean for you to go out on patrol looking for crime."

Edna snapped her notebook shut. "I don't care what he meant," she said peevishly. "I'm not going to just sit around the house and wait for something else bad to happen. Those cops are nice and polite because I'm an old lady and because they know you used to be a cop, but I know damn well they're not going out looking for the kid who robbed me. So *I* will," she said, slapping the table. "And you're not going to stop me."

Neva Jean and Cheezer both waited to see what my reaction would be. I pulled up one of the empty chairs and sat down.

"All right," I said, my voice calm. "You're right, Ma. You're an adult. I can have Cheezer babysit you and have C.W. install all the burglar alarms and video cameras in the world, and there's still no guarantee it'll keep you safe. And I can carry a gun, and you can get another gun. But it doesn't make a difference. Bad people are out there. If they want to take something, they will. If they want to hurt us, they'll do that, too, if they really want to. All I'm asking is, don't go looking for trouble. Kaczynski's right. You should be watching and paying attention to what's going on around you. "

Neva Jean was nodding her head vigorously in agreement. "I told her she shouldn't carry that gun in her purse," she said. "Ought to have a bra holster, like the one Swannelle got me."

Her hand went to her bra strap, and I looked at Cheezer to see what his reaction would be. But Cheezer wasn't there.

I swung my head around to see where he'd gone. Out of the corner of my eye, I caught a glimpse of green camouflage melting into the crowd.

"Where'd that boy go to?" Edna said. "There's plenty of pizza and Neva Jean just ordered another pitcher of beer . . . "

"Take her home, Neva Jean," I said, and I plunged into the crowd after Cheezer.

The streetlights blinked on at dusk. But most of the store-fronts in L5P were dark after six P.M. on Sunday. People still milled around, cars drove past, and every other human being I saw, male or female, seemed to be dressed in baggy green fatigues.

I searched the faces for one that looked familiar. And for the first time, I noticed that the lost children of Little Five Points weren't all alike and anonymous after all. They could have been faces from my own high school. Teenage boys with bizarre haircuts and cheeks rosy from the cold, sallow-faced girls with heartbreaking acne, dyed blond hair, short butch cuts. Blue-eyed, brown-eyed, bloodshot-eyed. The main difference, aside from the shocking shaved heads, was the number of multiply-pierced ears, nostrils, eyelids, and upper lips.

But none of these kids was Cheezer. I pushed through the clots of people on the sidewalk, got pushed back, shoved a little harder, watching, scanning faces for the right one. I was in front of the incense store when a kid on a skateboard careened directly in front of me. Moments before we would have collided he hopped off the back of the board, flipped it, and caught it in midair with one hand. "Get the fuck outta the way," he growled at me. I bared my teeth and snarled, but he put his board down and continued down the middle of the sidewalk.

I hurried into the Yacht Club and caught Hap's eye as he was filling a glass from one of the taps. "Callahan!" he said, surprised to see me twice in one day. "You meeting some-body?"

"Cheezer?" I said urgently. "Did he come in here just now?"

"Haven't seen him," Hap said. "You want me to tell him you're looking for him?"

"I'll find him," I said, and raced back out.

I stood in front of the bar, facing the street, trying to decide which way to turn.

Suddenly, I heard the squeal of tires, a burst of accelera-tion, and then a blur of black paint and shiny chrome shot out of the parking lot across the street and veered hard right, across Euclid and down Colquitt. A truck. Shiny. Black. I ran to the corner of Colquitt, but all I could see was the truck's red taillights speeding in the other direction.

A black truck. I ran across Euclid, darting between cars, ignoring shouted insults and blaring horns. The parking lot beside Sevananda was half-empty, the attendant's booth aban-doned.

"Cheezer?" I shouted. The name came echoing back from across the asphalt and concrete canyon. "Cheezer?"

A pair of androgynous black-clad kids Rollerbladed up the hill toward me. "Have you seen a guy in green fatigues?" I asked.

They looked at me blankly, locked arms, and kept rolling, headphones firmly in place.

The parking lot sloped down at the back and was lined with rows of tractor-trailer-sized recycling containers. I was running toward the bins when he called me. "Over here." The voice was faint, but unmistakable.

I veered to the right. The back of the old Euclid Theatre faced the parking lot. A high chain-metal fence had been erected outside the rear entrance to what was now the Variety Playhouse. Even the avant-garde need to fence out the riffraff.

Cheezer had managed to pull himself up to a sitting position, his back propped up against the chain-link fence. His eyes were closed, his head tilted back, knees bent double.

He was breathing, I noticed. No visible blood. His hands were clamped on his knees.

"Cheezer?" I knelt down in a greasy puddle beside him. His eyes fluttered, then opened. When he smiled, I saw the missing tooth and the split lip. He held something out in his hand. It was dark, but there was a little moonlight, and it shone on a thin gold chain with a small oval medallion dangling from it.

"St. Christopher protect us," he said. "And fuck all the bad guys."

28

We found Cheezer's missing tooth in a rain puddle. I picked it up and handed it to him. "I heard that if you lose a tooth and put it in milk, the dentist can put it back in," I said, pulling him to his feet.

"Hey, it's no big deal," he protested. "Besides, I think that's only good for baby teeth. Man, you should see that other dude, the one that beat up Edna. He's toast, Callahan." He wrapped the tooth in a bit of tissue and tucked it in the pocket of his fatigues.

"If his buddy hadn't come along in that truck, it could have gotten radical," Cheezer told me. "I mean it. He was walking along, like he was some badass or something, and he didn't even see me come up behind him. I waited until he was on this side of the street, by the juice bar. Nobody around. Put him in a neck lock, he didn't know what hit him."

"He wasn't armed?" I asked. "No gun? No knife?"

Cheezer reached in the pocket where he'd just stashed his

tooth and brought out a small ugly chrome-handled knife. "Not any more he ain't."

"I thought you were nonviolent," I said. "I can't believe the risk you took confronting that thug. I can't believe you took off like that on your own, without even telling me."

"Violent times call for violent responses," Cheezer said serenely. "You were talking about bad people doing what they want to," he said, "and it was pissin' me off. I look up, and there's the guy, the same one I saw beat up the Spaceman, coming out of the Star Bar. I saw the pictures that cop showed your mom, and it was definitely him. And the dude had a gold chain around his neck. I just started following him."

"You couldn't have told me what you were doing?" I groused.

"There wasn't time," Cheezer said. "I didn't want him gettin' away. And I didn't want to get Edna involved. Like you said, there's no tellin' what she'd have done."

I put my arm around his child-sized waist, and we trudged up the slope from the parking lot, toward my car.

"And you just took the St. Christopher medal away from him, and the knife? So how'd you lose the tooth and split the lip? Did you forget about that part of the incident?"

Cheezer blushed. "I ripped the medal off his neck while I had him in the head lock. That's when he brought out the knife. I, uh, got mixed up with knives a couple times when I lived in New Orleans. And the main thing I learned there was, if somebody's concentrating on stickin' a knife in you, they might not be payin' attention to what else you're doin'. First, I bit him on the knife hand. That's when he hauled off and slugged me in the mouth. So I kicked the dude in the, uh, the nuts. And while he was dealing with that, rolling around on the ground, I stomped on his hand four or five times."

Cheezer raised one of his feet. His fatigues were tucked into Doc Martens, the favored footwear of Little Five Points.

"I got the knife, and I was getting ready to see if he had Edna's pistol on him, when the black truck comes out of nowhere. It pulls up right next to us, and the driver's-side window rolls down, and there's a gun pointed at me."

"Was it the same guy you saw the other night?" I asked. "The cop?"

Cheezer shook his head. "The windows were tinted, and you saw how dark it is back there. I saw the barrel of the gun. I backed away, the kid got up and got in the truck, and they peeled off."

"And it headed down Colquitt," I said thoughtfully. "These guys know the neighborhood. Come on, I know you don't much like cops, but I think we ought to have a conversation with Bucky Deavers."

After I told him what had been going on, Deavers reluctantly agreed to meet with us. "Starbucks?"

It's sad when a street cop tries to be what he ain't. "Someplace else," I suggested. "I don't do cappuccino. I need grease and grits."

We agreed to meet at the Majestic, a diner on Ponce de Leon whose rooftop sign proclaims it to have the world's finest apple pie. I've never known anybody who ever ordered pie at the Majay. We got there first and ordered the works: eggs, bacon, grits, toast, hash browns.

Bucky had bags under his eyes, but he wore a snowy white dress shirt and a lime green necktie with acid yellow daisies. His hair was still damp from the shower. He gave Cheezer a curt nod, then sat down at the booth with us.

"What's this about some bad cop in a black truck?" he

asked. "I thought you were going to stay home and keep your mother from getting murdered in her bed."

"She won't stay home," I said. "And the thing with the black truck is for real. I saw it myself tonight, Bucky. It definitely had an FOP sticker on the window. I think these guys are connected to Jackson Poole. And to Wuvvy."

"How about the missing-and-murdered kids?" Bucky goaded me. "And the Olympic Park bombing? Maybe you can connect up all of this stuff, Garrity. Come down, look through my files, really give my clearance rate a boost."

"Shit," Cheezer said, disgusted. "I'm outta here. This cop ain't no different from any other cop." He got up and stormed out of the diner.

Bucky looked immensely amused and pleased with himself as he watched Cheezer go.

"Seems like your boy's kinda thin-skinned," he commented. "Not to mention he's got a bad attitude about law enforcement. Now, what was that you were telling me?" he asked, turning his attention back to me.

I considered following Cheezer out. Bucky loved to pull his macho cop crap on anybody he thought it might impress. It didn't impress me.

"Wuvvy didn't kill Jackson Poole," I said flatly. "And she didn't kill herself either. I think whoever killed Poole made her death look like a suicide."

"Since you know so much, tell me whodunnit," he suggested. "I'm all ears."

"For starters, I think Poole deliberately forced Wuvvy out of YoYos. She was doing fine until about three months ago—coincidentally the same time Jackson Poole decided to open Blind Possum Brewing in Little Five Points.

"Poole was involved with Anna Frisch. Remember her? The brewmaster we met at the Blind Possum in Roswell?

They were living together in his condo in Midtown." I felt it unnecessary to mention that Anna had hired me to find Poole's killer.

"It turns out that Poole and Anna had only a minority ownership interest in the Blind Possum. It's actually owned by TES, the big conglomerate."

"TES—they own a minor league baseball team in Memphis," Bucky said.

"Among other things," I said. "Jackson Poole was in charge of site selection. He came to Atlanta and decided on Roswell, and on Little Five Points. Anna says Poole thought L5P was the hot place to be. And the very hottest place in L5P just happened to be the shop owned by his stepmother."

Bucky reached in his jacket pocket and brought out a sheet of folded paper. "I almost forgot. Here's the crime stats you asked me for. The analyst said she charted it out for the past year. Wuvvy definitely had a crime wave going on, but she wasn't the only one in the neighborhood. A couple other places were hit hard, too. Take a look at the stats for Lolita's, for example. Somebody broke in and stole their cash register in June, then they had a fire in July. The place has been empty ever since. So it wasn't just Wuvvy. Hell, you're a crime stat yourself. You gonna blame that on Jackson Poole?"

"I'm gonna blame it on whoever killed Poole," I said. "Somebody doesn't want me rocking the boat. None of this stuff that's happened to us, the Peeping Tom or the mugger, is random, Bucky. It's somebody trying to shut me down, scare me off."

"You're too stupid to scare," Bucky said, chewing on a piece of toast.

"Suppose Poole did try to put Wuvvy out of business. Did Poole ever talk to his girlfriend about anything that had happened in Hawkinsville? About his father's murder? Did he ever talk about wanting revenge?"

"No," I said. "Anna says he was too busy working on opening the Blind Possum on time. He never talked about his childhood."

"Crazy," Bucky said. "His stepmother murders his father, and he just clams up about it all these years?"

"Something weird went on down there in Hawkinsville," I told Bucky. "Nobody wants to talk about Broward Poole's murder. When Wuvvy finally confessed to killing her husband, she said it was in self-defense. Yet the rumor is that he beat her because he caught her with another man."

"Sounds right," Bucky said.

"Then who's the other man?" I asked. "Nobody will say. It's a small town. I don't think that's the kind of secret people keep all these years. You remember that lawyer down there, Catherine Rhyne? The one who made Wuvvy's funeral arrangements?"

"Yeah," he said.

"She's the woman I saw at the Yacht Club the night Poole was killed," I said. "She was there, Bucky. And she admitted to me that she gave Wuvvy the money to try to pay her back rent. I think she's mixed up in this whole thing."

"Because she loaned money to an old friend?"

"There's more to it than that," I said, and I told him about Gail Samford's recollection that Kitty Rhyne had lobbied to have Wuvvy's prison sentence commuted.

"Somebody's hiding something," I said. "And I think those Rhyne women are involved somehow. They're a couple of operators. I think Poole knew something and tried to use it against them. And it got him killed. Then it got Wuvvy killed."

"Nothing you've told me connects up to anything else," Bucky said. "You think—you don't know. And what's this crap about Wuvvy being murdered? It's a suicide and you know it."

"I don't know it," I said stubbornly. "I talked to the gas station attendant over at the PitStop. The one who sold Wuvvy the full tank of gas that night."

"So she could kill herself."

I shook my head violently. "So she could leave town, get away from the heat. She bought windshield wiper blades and a sandwich. Does that sound like somebody who was planning to kill herself?"

"The attendant never told me about any food," Bucky said.

"You didn't ask, did you?"

He ate quietly. "Will you at least take a look at what I've come up with?" I begged. "Catherine Rhyne shares a law office with her mother down in Hawkinsville, but she's got an office in Atlanta, too. Come on, Bucky. At least look at whether or not she was in town when Wuvvy supposedly killed herself. I'd do it myself, but Catherine's a lawyer. She's smart. She knows she doesn't have to talk to some rinky-dink private investigator."

He made no promises. We finished our food and chitchatted about nothing. His new girlfriend. My old boyfriend. Politics. We talked about the weather. There was a raw wind blowing and streaky white clouds were in constant motion in the ink-dark sky outside.

In time-honored Southern tradition, I asked about his mama and he asked about mine.

"I was gonna tell you before you and your buddy jumped all over me about this so-called cop in the black truck," Bucky said, trying to sound casual. "Kaczynski told me Edna ID'd the mugger. He's a dipshit named Stahlgren. Josh Stahlgren. Only nineteen, but he's got a sheet. Burglary, auto theft, theft by taking. He did twenty months for the last car theft, then was released to his uncle. Supposed to be living with him and working on some tree-trimming crew, but the uncle claims he hasn't seen the kid lately. The uncle lives in Kirkwood. On Hooper Street."

Only a couple miles from our house. "He's got Edna's gun now," I reminded Bucky. "Is he likely to use it?"

"He might," Bucky admitted. "There's a warrant out for him. Aggravated assault. He got in a beef with a guy in the parking lot at the Austin Avenue Lounge, bashed the guy's head in with a tire iron."

I winced involuntarily. The Austin Avenue Lounge was a blue-collar beer-and-shot joint on the fringes of our neighborhood. Josh Stahlgren was becoming a neighborhood menace.

"Kaczynski's looking for him," Bucky said, offering cold comfort. "And I've got him checking around to see if any Atlanta detectives own a black pickup with an FOP sticker."

29

Monday morning's staff meeting, such as it was, had already started when I saw Cheezer's mail truck come lumbering up the driveway. It was windy and drizzly outside, but I threw on a raincoat and ran out to meet him.

"How's your mouth?" I asked.

He grinned. "Doesn't even hurt."

"I don't want you telling Edna what really happened last night," I told him hurriedly. "The cops know the guy's name. It's Josh Stahlgren. They know where he lives, so it's just a matter of time until they pick him up."

"What about St. Christopher?" he asked. "Aren't you going to give Edna back her medal?"

I took it out of my pocket and showed it to him. "See? The chain is broken. I'll have it fixed, then you can give it back to her as a surprise, after this whole thing settles down."

"If you say so," he said, ducking his head. I could tell he was disappointed. He'd been looking forward to regaling the girls with his tales of derring-do.

Edna and Ruby were looking over the day's schedule, trying to fit all Ruby's jobs in, when we went into the kitchen.

"Look who's here," Edna said, rolling her eyes at him. "Where did you get off to last night? You had us worried, young man."

"Sorry," Cheezer mumbled. "I saw a chick I know."

My sharp-eyed mother saw the gap in Cheezer's mouth immediately.

"Your tooth!" she exclaimed. "That must have been some chick. Did she knock that tooth out last night?"

Cheezer blushed. "No. Uh, that was her old boyfriend who did that. I guess he's the jealous type."

"I guess he is," Ruby said, patting Cheezer's hand. "And shame on him for ruining your pretty smile. Did you put the tooth in some milk? You know, they can make a tooth take root again if you keep it in a glass of milk until you get to the dentist's office."

"Not milk," Edna corrected her. "Alcohol. You're supposed to keep it in rubbing alcohol."

"Never mind," I said. If Ruby and Edna got started debating old wives' tales, we'd never get any work done. "We're covered up in work," I reminded them. "We've still got to make up for all the jobs we canceled because of the tornado, plus all the new business Edna's got us lined up with."

I heard a car door slam. A few moments later, Neva Jean, Baby, and Sister came bursting through the back door.

They were out of breath and drenched to the skin from the rain.

"Hey there," Neva Jean said, panting. "The girls wanted me to bring them by so they could pick up their paychecks."

I looked at Edna. Hadn't we just paid the girls last week?

Baby was fumbling with the snaps on her yellow vinyl slicker. "We are fixin' to get evacuated again," she said. "The police come to the high-rise this morning and tell everybody we got to get out 'cause the roof got a bad leak and might collapse and kill every last one of us. So we are fixin' to go to the hotel again tonight," she said, smacking her lips in anticipation. "We just wanted to get us a little draw on our paycheck before we get home and pack our valises."

Sister had managed to get out of her raincoat, but she was tugging ineffectively at her gray rubber boots. Finally she plopped down on a kitchen chair, thrust her legs out in front of her, and said to me, "Take these off, please, Callahan."

I knelt down and slid the boots off. She wore another pair of shoes underneath, black Converse All-Stars, with thick red wool hunting socks pulled up over her knobby knees.

"Ask Miss Baby what she's fixing to take to that hotel and strut herself around in," Sister said, flexing her feet.

Baby tossed her head and preened a little. "Can so get my butt in it," she replied.

"In what?" I asked loudly.

"My new one-hundred-percent nylon, midnight-blue baby-doll pajamas," Baby said, flicking her fingers down her tiny stick-straight torso. "Size six, ain't that right, Neva Jean?"

Neva Jean blushed. "They were just sitting in my dresser drawer, Callahan. She said she wanted lingerie for Christmas. And Swannelle, he paid good money for 'em at Victoria's Secret. I never had the heart to tell him I ain't been size six since I was six."

"That's the kind of Christmas present Miss Negligee likes all right," Sister said, still scandalized. "Not writing paper or dusting powder or a nice box of handkerchiefs like a decent girl wants. Oh no. Miss Boudoir asks for lingerie."

"Whose fiancée?" Baby asked. "I never told that old man I'd get engaged to him. If he said that, he told a lie."

Edna went to the old metal bread box where we keep petty cash, got out two twenties, and handed one to each of the girls. "Y'all want to do some work before you check into Sin City?" she asked.

Between the two of us, we dealt out a full day's worth of jobs to everybody, including me and Edna, who insisted she was feeling strong as an ox, and that if she went along with Baby and Sister their many hands would make light work.

I had a couple of Edna's storm specials on my docket, but first, I pulled out the file I'd started on Virginia Lee Mincey, a.k.a. Wuvvy. Somebody was hiding some dirt somewhere, I knew, and if the cops wouldn't clean it up, then it was up to me. I owed it to Wuvvy to find out the truth.

I read over the crime statistics for Zone Six that Bucky had given me the night before. For months, it looked like, the area had been plagued with petty crimes: burglary, purse snatchings, theft by taking. Then, in April, when the weather had gotten warmer, the crime rate seemed to slack off a little. Except for a couple of exceptions in Little Five Points. YoYos, and the now defunct Lolita's. Every week, it seemed, there was an incident reported at 362 Euclid, the address for YoYos. It was no wonder Wuvvy hadn't been able to pay her bills. She'd been picked clean by thieves. Had Jackson Poole been behind Wuvvy's run of bad luck?

The phone rang. It was Anna Frisch. She was agitated, upset. It sounded like she was making an effort not to cry.

"I'm at the Blind Possum," she reported. "I went through the condo this morning, like you asked me to do." She sniffed. "Jackson loved beautiful clothes. He had so much! Expensive shoes, so many shirts. I don't know what to do with all of it."

"Give it to Goodwill," I said. "What about papers, letters, anything personal?"

She hesitated. "Oh, God. There's a checkbook. I found it in a shoebox at the back of the closet."

"Was it his regular account?"

"We had separate accounts, but at the same bank, so I could deposit his check for him and do his banking because he was always so busy," Anna said. "I didn't know he had another account." Silence. "There's a balance of twenty-five thousand dollars. Where would Jackson get that kind of money? Why would he keep it in a checking account?"

I felt my pulse quicken. "And why would he hide it from you?"

She was crying again. "I don't understand any of this."

"It's hard," I said, trying to be sympathetic. "What else was with the checkbook? Were there any statements or canceled checks?"

"A computerized statement," Anna said. "Deposits and withdrawals. Not that many. Two deposits of ten thousand, another for five thousand, between September 15 and October 15. And there's a withdrawal, for five thousand, on October 15."

"No canceled checks or other statements?" I asked. "You're sure? You looked everywhere?"

"There's nothing else," Anna said. "I swear. My God, what was he doing with all that money?"

"Blackmail," I said softly. "Somebody was paying Jackson to keep their secrets."

"Wuvvy?" she asked wildly. "Where would she get that kind of money? And why? I don't understand any of this."

"I don't think it was Wuvvy," I told Anna. "I think it was somebody else down in Hawkinsville. Somebody who knew the truth about who killed Broward Poole. But the five-thousand-dollar withdrawal is kind of odd. Unless he was paying off somebody himself."

Somebody, I thought, like the thieves who'd driven Wuvvy out of business. Somebody like Josh Stahlgren and the cop in the black pickup truck.

Anna sniffed and cried a little bit more.

"I'm sorry," she said finally. "You think I'm a jerk because I knew so little about somebody I was supposed to be in love with. But you don't understand the restaurant business. There's so much money on the line. The competition is unbelievable. Only one out of every five restaurants that opens stays in business past its first year. Everybody's out to screw everybody else. Brewmasters steal each other's recipes, restaurants hire each other's chefs away, the vendors demand kickbacks. You have to be tough to survive. Jackson knew that. He was good at what he did."

So she realized her lover's ethics were somewhat elastic. "Would Jackson pay bribe money?" I asked. "Do you think he was capable of blackmail?"

It was a question she wasn't ready to deal with yet. She knew the truth about Jackson Poole, but it would be a while before she'd be able to speak it.

"You didn't know him. He could be wonderful sometimes. So funny. He was a great mimic. We loved to cook together, just the two of us, on our nights off. Jackson had a horrendous childhood. I know that now. It explains so much. I don't think he trusted people. He didn't like having a lot of people around him."

I thought about how uncomfortable Jackson Poole had looked the one time I'd seen him; Halloween night at the Yacht Club, with the mob of drunken partiers.

"That's odd," I commented. "Somebody in the hospitality business who doesn't like people."

"He never called it hospitality," Anna offered. "It was the food business.

"Is there anything else? Do you know who killed him?"

"I've got an idea," I said. "Keep looking through the papers at the restaurant. Jackson made a five-thousand-dollar payment to somebody. It would help if we knew who."

After Anna hung up, I took out the packet of papers I'd

found among Wuvvy's belongings and called her landlord at Restoration Properties, Inc.

The woman who answered the phone said she was Rutledge Gross, and, yes, she'd gotten the message that I was interested in the building at 362 Euclid Avenue.

Ms. Gross was a cautious lady. Good business practice. Made me repeat my name twice, spell it, and read off the serial number on my private investigator's license.

"I'm interested in anything you can tell me about your dealings with Virginia Lee Mincey," I said.

"Oh," she said. "Her."

"She's dead," I pointed out. "So there shouldn't be a confidentiality issue."

"I realize she's dead," Ms. Gross said briskly. "We evicted her, you know. I don't have the file on that property in front of me, but I can tell you that she was in arrears on her rent, and had been for some time. Before that, she didn't actually miss payments, but she was always a late pay. The owner was fed up and directed us to start eviction procedures."

She'd taken me by surprise. "You're not the owner?"

"No," Ms. Gross said. "We manage the property. Or we did until recently."

"Who is the owner?"

"That's not really something I can discuss," Ms. Gross said.

"Did you handle the transaction with the Blind Possum brewpub?" I kept at her.

"No," she said regretfully. "The owner handled all that. I've driven by since it changed hands," she added. "Looks like a money-maker. A good deal. YoYos was a marginal tenant at best. Hardly worth the trouble. Retail space over there is renting now for eighteen dollars a square foot. She was paying a quarter of that and she still had three years to run on the lease, or would have, if she hadn't defaulted."

"Who was the owner, Ms. Gross?" I repeated. "It's really important."

She sighed. "Gemini Properties. We don't manage anything for them anymore. I dealt with the secretary. Miranda something."

"Miranda?" I knew a Miranda. Hap's girlfriend. His business partner. What was her last name? I couldn't remember if I'd ever known Miranda's last name. Last names weren't an issue in Little Five Points.

I looked down at the crime statistics, and another business name popped up. "Ms. Gross, did Gemini Properties own any other buildings in Little Five Points?"

"Everything they own is in that area, as far as I know," she said. "I don't have the file, but there were several parcels."

"What about the building that housed a place called Lolita's? Does Gemini Properties own Lolita's?"

"Another marginal tenant," she sighed. "Vacant since the fire. Not our fault, but again, we no longer manage the property."

30

Gemini Properties. Was Miranda into astrology? I was trying to look up the phone number for Gemini when the phone
rang. The connection was a bad one, the line full of static, the
voice far-off. Or maybe it was just that Mac and I had found
yet another way to put distance between us.

"I need a favor," he said, cutting right to the chase. "Are
you still mad at me?"

"To tell you the truth, I haven't had a lot of time to think
about you in the past two days," I said evenly. "You're not the
only thing going on in my life, McAuliffe. I'm working a case,
you know. And I've got a cleaning business I'm trying to run."

"I know that," he said, his voice tense. "And I wouldn't ask
if it wasn't an emergency."

"What kind of an emergency?" I asked. "Are you all right?"

"I'm fine," he said. "I'm in Tifton for a planning conference. It's Maybelline I'm worried about. She was acting funny
when I got ready to leave this morning. I put some blankets
out, and some extra food, but I've worried about her the

whole way down here. I'm wondering if she isn't getting ready to have the puppies."

"Did you call your vet?" I asked.

"He just called me back," Mac said. "I think he thinks I'm another hysterical owner. Dogs have puppies by themselves all the time. But not Maybelline. And she's so big. There must be at least eight puppies."

"Maybe she'll wait until tonight," I said.

"Our agenda just got pushed back by two hours," Mac said. "There's no way I'll be home before ten o'clock at the earliest."

Poor Maybelline. Mac had pushed my agenda back lots of times. I knew what it felt like. "What do you want me to do?" I asked.

"Could you go out to the cabin and stay with her?" he asked. "Make sure she's all right? You've got the key. And the vet's phone number is on the refrigerator door. He's part of a twenty-four-hour clinic, so if Maybelline looks like she's in trouble, you could take her over there. It's on Old Alabama Road."

I bit my lip. I had enough on my platter without playing midwife to a skittish black Lab. My fingers were itching to call Gemini Properties and find out who and what they were, and what their connection was to Wuvvy and Jackson Poole. I was so close. And yet the thought of Maybelline alone tugged at my conscience. Mac and I had a lot of stuff we needed to work out yet, but that wasn't her fault.

"I'll go out there," I said finally. "You'll be home by ten?"

"Absolutely," he promised.

I hung up and sat at the kitchen table, brooding. On Halloween night, Wuvvy had accused her old friends of greed and betrayal. I'd written it off as part of Wuvvy's paranoia. She'd had too much to drink, too much to smoke. Maybe so.

One thing was certain—once again she'd been too loyal and too trusting of the wrong people. Now she was dead. She'd trusted me, too.

Why, I wondered, what was it about me that made people count on me for things I couldn't deliver? I started throwing my files into a shopping bag. I could make my phone calls from Mac's house, call Deavers and try to persuade him I'd unraveled at least part of the puzzle. I wrote a note and left it on the kitchen table for Edna and was outside, locking the back door, when the phone's insistent ringing brought me running back inside.

"Callahan?" With the crackling on the line, I could barely make out the voice. "It's Anna. You told me to call you back if I found anything."

"What?" I said. "What did you find?"

"A list of the vendors for the restaurant," Anna said. "It might not be anything. But Jackson was using a different beer distributor over here. Not the same one we use out in Roswell."

"Is that unusual?" I asked.

She sounded uncertain. "Maybe. Well, sort of. Beer distributors divide the market into territories. One distributor handles certain brands in his territory. If you want Coors, you have to deal with the Coors guy in Atlanta. And he can make you take the five or six other beers he handles, too. But the distributor Jackson signed with over here doesn't really make sense for us. It's a lot of imports we don't need."

It didn't make sense to me, either.

"There's something else, though," Anna said. "Listen. I think I figured out what was bothering Jackson the night he was killed."

She paused to let that sink in. "It's the water pipes. They're useless."

I sat up straight and tried to concentrate.

"What do you mean?"

"The water lines," Anna said. "I've been here all morning.
The Southern Bell guys were here right after I talked to you,
putting in another line. While they were rooting around in
the walls, I got to looking at the plumbing fittings and the
other stuff, and that's when I figured it out. The water lines
are all wrong. There's no way I could make beer here."

"Why not?" I said, trying to remember our conversation
about the niceties of brewing. "You said you use mountain
spring water, trucked in."

"We do," Anna said. "For the end brew. But we use city water
for the other processes. It takes a three-inch main. I can only see
a three-quarter-inch main stubbed out from the wall here. And
I came over here, to the Yacht Club, to ask Hap about it. He's
out running an errand. I told Miranda you'd asked me to check
on that kind of thing. Miranda says she doesn't know anything
about the water pipes, but Hap is on his way back."

Miranda. The woman who'd engineered Wuvvy's ruin.
Who had been the one to discover Wuvvy's body.

"Anna?" I took a deep breath. "Where are you now?"

"I'm at the Yacht Club," Anna said. "Miranda gave me a
sandwich and some iced tea for lunch. What's wrong with
you, Callahan? You don't sound right."

Anna was the one who didn't sound right. She'd been so
emotional earlier. Now her voice was oddly buoyant. As
though she were just a little drunk, even.

"Is Miranda standing there? Can she hear what you're
saying?"

"No," Anna said. "She went back to the office."

"Hang up the phone. Tell Miranda you left a message, that
I was out. Then I want you to leave there. Right away. Do
you understand? Get in your car and drive over to my house."
I gave her the address and directions.

"All right," Anna said gaily.

31

I gave Anna fifteen minutes. When she didn't show up I called Jeffrey Kaczynski at Zone Six. I got his voice mail. Left a message that there was a crime in progress at the Blind Possum Brewery on Euclid. I tried to beep Bucky, left my number on his pager. Then I put a clip of bullets in my Smith & Wesson, pulled on my hooded rain slicker and ran for the Lincoln.

Maybe Anna wasn't clear on my address. My right hand rested lightly on the Smith & Wesson I'd placed so carefully on the front seat. Maybe Anna was already dead, and I'd helped get her that way.

I parked the Lincoln at the end of the alley. The black pickup truck with the FOP sticker was parked behind the Yacht Club. I stuck the pistol in the waist of my jeans and ran for the shelter of the garbage Dumpster. The Blind Possum's back door was propped open. There was a two-foot space between the building and the Dumpster, and the building's eaves jutted out just enough to keep the rain off. I squeezed into the gap, scraping my hip against the rough brick of the wall.

Voices inside. My hand went to the gun.

Hap's voice, strained somewhat. "I've got a customer next door. She's had too much to drink. You could give her a ride home."

"Shit!" It was Miranda. "Hap, she just threw up all over the place. I can't get her to keep it down."

The third voice must have belonged to Hap's enforcer.

"I don't want somebody puking all over my truck. Forget about it."

"We'll give you a towel," Miranda said. "Hap, tell him what he needs to do."

Rain dripped from the eaves onto the hood of my jacket and under my collar. I pulled the collar tighter and squeezed forward. What had they done to Anna?

Hap's voice lowered. "She's taken a lot of pills. She's depressed. Suicidal. All you have to do is take her to Poole's condo in Midtown, walk her in, and dump her."

Pills. They'd found drugs in Wuvvy's system after she committed suicide. I wondered if these were the same kind of pills. If they took Anna away, I knew, she'd die too.

"No way," the other voice insisted.

"Make him do it," Miranda said shrilly.

It was now or never. I pulled the pistol out of my waistband, said a prayer, and made the move for the doorway.

I would have had the drop on them all, could have been a big hero. If I hadn't stepped on a beer can as I made the dash for the back door.

The hollow sound of aluminum squashing underfoot seemed to echo louder than a thunderclap.

The blond cop met me at the door. He didn't even have a gun. Just a fancy tae kwan do kick that sent my gun spinning into the alley, and me howling with pain.

He yanked me inside the restaurant.

Hap and Miranda stood over Anna, who sat on the floor,

her head drooped between her knees, eyes dilated. Miranda looked more annoyed than surprised to see me. "I told Hap you'd be snooping around here somewhere. He didn't think you'd put it all together. Hap has a surprisingly low opinion of women, don't you think?"

Hap stepped into the alley and came back with my pistol. "You dropped something, Callahan."

I looked him in the eye. "Bastard."

He winked at me, the bastard. Like he'd just played some big practical joke. "Look here, Jimmy," he said, turning to the cop. "Here's another customer."

Jimmy wouldn't look at me. He had wavy dark blond hair, a wispy goatee, and the overdeveloped bulges of a career bodybuilder, his black T-shirt stretched taut over the pecs and biceps. "Not me, man," he said. "She's got cop friends. Deavers has already been hanging around, asking questions about me. I'm out of this. You want her done, do it your-self."

He turned and walked out the door. A second later I heard the truck's engine roar, and then go splashing down the alley.

"Why'd you let him go?" Miranda asked, turning on Hap. "He knows everything."

"Davis can't touch us," Hap said. He stroked her arm. "Don't worry, baby. I'll take care of it."

Anna Frisch groaned and pitched forward, limp as a rag doll. Miranda stepped away from her body, as though she might be contaminated by it.

"Good stuff, huh?" Hap said.

"What did you give her?" I asked.

"Just a couple beers," Hap said. "The little lady is fasci-nated with beer. Knows all about it. She was telling Miranda about her big plans for this place. Same kind of big plans her boyfriend had, that asshole." He winked at me again. "You ever hear of roofies?"

"Rohypnol," Miranda said. "Callahan knows everything. She must know about roofies."

"Doesn't ring a bell," I said, trying to look passive.

"The looove drug," Hap said. "All the kids know about it. It's the nineties equivalent of blotter acid. Direct to you from old Mexico."

He reached in the pocket of his baggy olive-green shorts, calm and unruffled, like he was reaching for a stick of gum. He held his hand out to show me two small white tablets.

"Swallow these, please," he said. "Everybody says it's great stuff." He shoved it at my face.

"Fuck you," I said, swatting his hand away. The pills went flying, and Hap slapped me with the open palm of his hand.

"Don't," he shouted, his face contorting in anger. "Don't make me hit you. I hate that."

"Hap?" Miranda's voice was a whisper. "I'm going back to the Yacht Club. You'll take care of everything, right?"

"Oh yeah. I'll be over in a few minutes. Put the sign on the door, okay? Anybody asks, we've got a malfunction in the water lines. Health Department won't let us stay open. Go on, baby. I'll handle this."

He had the tenderest expression on his face as he watched her step delicately over Anna's limp body and out into the alley. Then he reached in his pocket and brought out two more roofies.

"I'll fuckin' slap you senseless if you try that again," he warned me.

"You're going to hit me," I said. "You're going to kill Anna, if she's not already dead. You killed Wuvvy. But you don't like to hit. What a goddamned hypocrite you are, Hap."

He held my gun out and turned it back and forth, like he'd never seen one before. "I'm not a violent man, Callahan. You know that. I'm a businessman. It's not like I get off on hurting people. I'm nothing like Jackson Poole. He enjoyed watching people squirm. You've got a business. You know how it goes. Sometimes you have to make the hard choices."

Hap took a step closer. He grabbed me by my hair, jerked my head backwards, and tried to shove the pills down my throat. I gritted my teeth. He put the pistol in his pocket and then held his free hand over my nose until I gasped for air. With the other hand, he popped the pills in my mouth, then clamped my jaws shut.

I gagged, and he kept his hand over my mouth. "I can put it in some beer and make you swallow that," he said, his lips close to my ear. "But you're gonna take that roofie."

I felt the pills slide down my throat. He shoved me and I went sprawling on the floor. It was thick with sawdust and Sheetrock dust. I could hear Anna's breathing, shallow and labored. Her eyes were open but unfocused.

Hap pulled the back door closed and locked it. "Now it's just us," he said, pointing the gun at me.

"Why?" I said, asking the question only he could answer. "You've got a good business, enough money. Why go down this road?"

He walked over to the gleaming copper-clad brew kettle, then to the control table. There was a computer screen, and a row of switches and buttons. He frowned as his hand hovered over each button.

"It was Poole," Hap said. "He screwed me over, the son of a bitch. He screwed everybody. It made him happy. But he fucked with the wrong person when he came knocking at my door."

"He came to you?"

Hap nodded. "He knew I owned Wuvvy's building. He'd looked it up in the deed records. Poole had waited a long time to mess with her. Like I told you, Wuvvy was a victim looking for a crime. I just helped things along a little. To protect my investment. Everything would have been cool if he hadn't done me like he did. Wuvvy would have gotten along. But he had to try to screw me."

"So you killed him. Over some beer distribution deal."

He shrugged. "You figured it out. I'm impressed, Garrity. Poole thought he had me by the balls. He came in here, to my neighborhood. My building! Cut a deal with my import beer distributor to give Blind Possum exclusive rights to all my premium imports. Paulaner, Haufbrau, Bass, every yuppie brand I sell. Bribed my distributor! I would have been out of business in a month. He told me just before he left the bar that night. Slimeball! I followed him over here, picked up a piece of galvanized pipe the plumbers had left lying around. He went down without a sound."

"And then Wuvvy came looking for him," I said.

"She had a talent for disaster," Hap said. "Nothing I could do."

He turned back to the control panel and punched a button. I heard a clicking noise, and then the sound of water rushing. Hap turned and pointed the gun at me. "Stand up," he said. "You'll feel much better after a hot bath."

I had to grasp the ladder rails tightly to keep from falling. I was already feeling drowsy, dizzy. The copper and stainless steel brew kettle loomed blurrily above me, and Hap was right behind me, jabbing the pistol into my leg. "Go on," he said. "Or I'll blow your head off right here. Either way, you're going in."

My legs weren't working right. It took forever, but I finally pulled myself up the top rung and flopped over onto the metal platform. At the top of the ladder a catwalk stretched between the two kettles. Through the open rectangular manhole of the kettle on the right, the brew kettle—Anna had called it—I could hear the water flowing in.

"Get in," Hap said, standing on the catwalk beside me. "Go on. Poole told me all about these kettles, you know. He said brewmasters sometimes fill them up and use them for their own personal hot tubs, with their girlfriends, you know?"

"This is insanity, Hap," I said, but my lips weren't moving just right, and it came out garbled. "They'll catch you. You're going down."

He put his hand on my back and shoved.

It was the oddest sensation, falling into that kettle, like a slow-motion dream, sliding down the slick stainless steel side and coming to rest in the bottom, in about ten inches of lukewarm water. Water flowed into the vat from a valve near the top of the tank. I moved lazily to one side, to keep it off my head. Hap stuck his head over the edge and looked down at me.

"It'll look like Anna the brewmaster was trying out her tanks and fell in. Then the busybody private eye came along, tried to save her client, but instead fell in, too. So tragic!" I could swear he winked. "See, it's kind of fun, isn't it? Relax. I'll be back in a minute."

Everything was so slow and stretched out. I slapped my face, trying to get alert, but I could already feel the loss of coordination. Whatever was in the roofies, it was definitely fast-acting. I had to get rid of it before any more got into my bloodstream. I rammed three fingers as far down my throat as I could, gagged, then retched. I could hear Hap's feet on the ladder rungs outside. Water splashed around me, and I could feel the side of the tank warming where the heat elements were. He was moving slowly, must have been carrying Anna. I gagged and retched so hard I thought my ribs would crack open, but quietly, hoping Hap wouldn't hear me. I splashed water on my face and whimsically wished my mother was there to hold my head.

"Here she comes," Hap called.

Anna's body fell straight down, like a pebble into a fast-moving stream. The water was waist-high on me, but she was so petite, barely five feet, and probably didn't weigh ninety pounds. She fell forward and I struggled to hold her upright, to keep her head out of the rising water.

Hap's head peered over the side. "I haven't tried one, but the roofies are basically supposed to paralyze you, Callahan. It's like a super tranquilizer. Respiratory depression, coma, then nothing. Not a bad way to go at all. See? I told you I'm not a violent man."

"Don't let him close the lid," I prayed. "Please don't let him close the lid."

He flipped the manhole doors shut.

I heard him climb back down the ladder, and then it was quiet, if you didn't count the rush of the water, which was getting much warmer. During our tour of the other Blind Possum, Anna had told us how hot the brew kettle got. How many degrees? My mind wouldn't focus on numbers. But the word *boil* came to mind.

Anna's head kept slipping under the water, and she was so limp, so pale. I tried to remember more of what she'd told us on that tour, about the kettles. I flailed around in the water with one hand, looking for something to catch hold of, to anchor me in one spot. My sneakers felt like they weighed a thousand pounds apiece. I leaned back, tried to grasp one, to take it off, but my fingers fumbled with the wet laces. Useless to try to untie them. I tugged, and one and then the other came loose. Peeling off my socks took a Herculean effort. Finally, I stood, felt around the bottom of the tank with my toes, found two agitator blades. Thank God Hap hadn't been able to figure out how to turn them on.

I peered up toward the top of the tank. It was about ten feet deep and seven feet wide. The water level was nearly shoulder high on me. Anna bobbed around, and I kept one hand on her shirt to keep her head from slipping under the water.

There were two handholds, but they were high up in the wall of the tank, over my head. So high. And I was so tired, so groggy. The water was bath temperature now, and I wanted to let go, just lie on my back and float, with my toes sticking up and my hair fanned out around me, like I used to do at the beach as a kid. Dead man's float, we called it.

Dead man. I shook my head, stood upright, my toes curving under the agitator blades to gain a grip. I let go of Anna's shirt, tried to stand on my tiptoes and reach. My fingertips touched the bottom rung, then slipped off. I lost my balance and fell off the blade.

The water was getting hotter. We had to get out. I plucked at the buttons on my work shirt, but my fingers were so stiff and unyielding. I yanked harder, tearing the topmost buttons off, then pulling the whole shirt off over my head. I twisted the shirt into a long, bulky roll, positioned myself on the agitator blades, and tossed one end of it up, toward the lower of the rungs. It fell back, slapping me in the face.

"Goddamnit," I cried. I'd held out some hope that I could float as the water level rose, but my heavy cotton turtleneck and waterlogged blue jeans kept pulling me down, and I was getting groggier.

Once more, I perched on the blades, tossed the shirt upward. My vision was fuzzy, but I could see the sleeve slipping over the edge of the rung. I steadied myself, fed more of the sleeve through it, until I had a complete loop through the rung.

That work shirt was my favorite one, Gap, one hundred percent heavy cotton denim. I tugged hard on the makeshift rope, braced my feet against the side of the brew kettle, and somehow did what I'd never been able to do in four years of high school gym class. I rope-climbed, hand over hand, three feet probably, until the fingers of my right hand wrapped themselves all the way around the lower rung.

I wanted to scream, or cry, or shout, but I didn't have the energy. I felt for the highest rung, managed to pull myself up to a crouch. The manhole cover was directly over my head. If I let go of the rung, I'd fall back down into the kettle. And there was no more energy to do the impossible twice in one day. I tucked my chin into my chest and then heaved my head and shoulders upwards, directly into the stainless steel manhole cover.

For fifteen seconds or more—a lifetime, really—I hung there, half in and half out of the kettle, flopping around like a mullet on a dock. Screw this, I thought. I wriggled a little more, and dropped headfirst onto the platform.

The headache was a good hurt. It brought tears to my eyes. At least it was a sensation, a feeling. I pulled myself upright, looked back down into the kettle. Anna was floating face-down, her legs kept dragging her down. She was so rigid, unmoving. I had no idea whether she was still alive.

Somehow, I managed to drag myself down the ladder. I stood with difficulty, lurched over to the control panel.

The computer screen had a color diagram of the kettle, with all the parts labeled. But my vision was so blurred, I couldn't read the print below the buttons. I'd seen the button Hap had pushed to fill the kettle. I pushed it, waited. The water stopped. Thank God. Now to make it drain. I rested my head on the control panel, squinted, found a button beneath the one I'd just pushed. I put my thumb on it and left it there, and then I sat down on the floor to take a little nap. Soon, I promised myself, I'd go back and drag Anna out.

* * *

"Callahan?" Somebody was tugging at me. It was always like that. Somebody always wanted something. Why wouldn't they let me alone? Let me sleep? I was so tired, and my head hurt. God, it hurt.

"Callahan!" Now they were pulling at my shirt, trying to make me sit up. I tried to push the hands away. "No," I mumbled. "Sleep."

"Wake up!" Hands patting my face, slapping me. Slapping hard. I opened my eyes. Cheezer. Good old Cheezer. He looked silly without that tooth. Why was he slapping me? "Go away," I said.

"Callahan!" he yelled. "Edna was worried when you didn't answer the phone. She sent me out to look for you, and I saw the Lincoln out in the alley. I called the police. What happened? What's wrong with you? Are you sick?"

"Roofies," I said in a singsongy voice. He held my face between both his hands. I smiled. "Roofies make me ralph." I threw up all over both of us.

32

It would take a twisted mind to think of a drug like Rohypnol as "the love drug." Later on, while I was in the emergency room, waiting for the antidote, a drug called Romazicon, to take effect, Cheezer told me roofies were known among the college set as the date rape drug.

They kept me at Grady Memorial Hospital overnight, feeding me the antidote at twenty-minute intervals, the same way they do patients they're bringing out from under general anesthesia. I was still nauseous, and I had a splitting headache, which the doctor, a cute Korean resident named Dr. Soo, warned me was one of the side effects of Rohypnol.

"Something else, too," he said. "Rohypnol is a powerful sedative. It's one of a class of drugs called benzodiazepam, although it's been outlawed in the U.S. since 1996. I don't want you to worry if you can't remember anything that happened after you were given the drug. That happens. It induces short-term memory loss. Luckily, you seem to have regurgitated part of the tablets, so you didn't really get a full dosage."

Anna. "What about Anna?" I asked. "She was with me. What happened to her?"

The doctor frowned. It didn't suit his pleasant, round face. "Anna Frisch? She was given a much larger dosage. As many as three or four tablets. And her body mass was so small." He shook his head.

"She has not regained consciousness. Her pulmonary function is not good." He wouldn't tell me anything more.

Cheezer rode in the ambulance to Grady's emergency room with me. His was the first face I recognized, once I could focus. He smiled that gap-toothed smile, which I was getting very fond of, and told me he was glad I was all right. Before I succumbed to the big sleep, I told him he was getting a raise for finding me.

Edna brought Mac to the hospital with her. He brought me flowers and a Polaroid of Edna holding all eight of Maybelline's tiny black puppies in a bath towel. She'd gotten my note and rushed out to Mac's cabin with Baby and Sister. They'd gotten Maybelline home and settled just before the puppy onslaught began.

"We're gonna need a new sofa in the den," Edna told me.

"I'm buying," Mac said. He didn't say a lot else, but he slept in a chair beside my bed all night and only let go of my hand when I told him he was giving me a cramp.

Deavers showed up in the morning, with a dozen Krispy Kreme doughnuts and a hangdog expression. He and Mac shook hands and Mac went out to get me a Diet Coke to go with the doughnuts.

I made Deavers tell me everything that had happened. "The last thing I remember is Hap telling Miranda to leave," I told him. "This doctor says the drug does that."

"I should have listened to you," Deavers said. "Christ. Hap Rudabaugh. The guy was a Jekyll and Hyde. You know, he and Miranda were so cool. Unbelievable. They left you and

Anna there to die, went home, packed their bags, and booked a flight to Grand Cayman. We stopped them at the airport. Hap was talking on his cell phone to his lawyer when one of our guys stopped them."

"You got them?" I said.

Deavers fidgeted. "We're holding them on drug charges. We found Hap's stash in the back room of the bar. Roofies, steroids, speed, a real smorgasbord of goodies."

"What about the murder charges?" I asked. "He killed Poole. He killed Wuvvy. He tried to kill me. Anna Frisch could still die. And all you've got is drug charges?"

"It ain't over yet," Deavers said. "There were enough drugs in the bar that we can get them under one of the federal racketeering statutes. Rudabaugh and Miranda weren't just selling dime bags. They were smuggling the roofies and steroids in from Mexico and using the bar as a distribution point. It turns out Hap was a model capitalist."

"What's that mean?" I asked irritably. My mouth felt awful, and I still had a searing pain over my left eye.

"He was reinvesting all his profits. In Little Five Points," Deavers said. "They've been quietly buying up buildings for the past five years."

"Gemini Properties," I said. That part I could remember. "They bought up Wuvvy's building, but she had a dirt-cheap, long-term lease. They were in the process of forcing her out of business when Jackson Poole showed up."

"We think Hap originally tried to sell him the building across the street, Lolita's," Deavers said. "But Poole had done his homework. It wasn't just about business. He wanted to get at Wuvvy."

"Revenge," I said.

"Excuse me." Dr. Soo poked his head in the doorway of my room. "Your friend is better. Maybe in the morning, you can talk to her."

"Thanks," I told him. I looked back at Deavers. "The doctor told me they fed her a huge dose of roofies. They said earlier she might not make it."

"That's good news," Bucky agreed. "You know, we've still got blood samples from Wuvvy's autopsy. The state crime lab's backed up, but the DA wants a drug screen done, to see if they can find traces of the Rohypnol. Once that's done, we'll add murder charges against Hap and Miranda."

"But you need a statement from me," I said, guessing at what he was getting at. "And Anna."

"You're the glue that holds it together," Deavers admitted. "But we've got time. Hap and Miranda aren't going anywhere anytime soon. We've also figured out the cop was a guy who used to work not in Atlanta but for the Fulton County P.D. His name is Jimmy Davis. We're looking for him and Stahlgren. When we find them, I guarantee they'll spill their guts about Hap and Miranda."

The nurses wouldn't let anybody stay for very long. They kept giving me the Romazicon and taking my pulse and messing with me.

At ten o'clock that night, just before visiting hours were over, Edna chased everybody else out of the room.

"I'm going home to get some sleep," she announced. "If those puppies don't keep me up all night." She reached inside her new leather pocketbook and fumbled around and finally brought out a small package wrapped in toilet paper and scotch tape.

She pressed it into my hand. "The doctors found this in your pocket when they brought you into the emergency room," she said, blinking rapidly. "I think you better keep it. Your daddy would want you to have it." My small motor coordination was still knocked loopy by the pills, so I handed it back and let her undo the wrappings.

It was the gold St. Christopher's medal. The chain was still broken, and wisps of toilet paper were still stuck to it.

"That's yours," I said, taking her palm and closing her fingers over it. "It's still got a lot of protection left in it. Better than a thirty-eight, even."

33

After everybody had gone home for the night, I had a lot of time to think. My headache was better, and they'd given me something for the nausea. I was woozy but wakeful.

At midnight, I got up and got dressed in the clean clothes Edna had brought me. The nurses fussed at me, but I told them I was just going out for a stroll. What could they do?

The motor skills were still not quite up to speed. I hailed a cab and I'm sure the driver thought I was drunk or drugged, because he made me show him my money before he'd pull away from the curb at Butler Street.

He was even more surprised when I gave him Catherine Rhyne's address. Atlanta cabdrivers probably don't take a lot of fares to that part of town at midnight.

Catherine Rhyne lived in Morningside, a cozy neighborhood of close-set homes in one of Atlanta's better in-town neighborhoods. Morningside by moonlight had a quaint, almost Norman Rockwell feeling that night, with the cottages dressed up with autumn decorations of hay bales, cornstalks, scarecrows, and lighted jack-o'-lanterns. Gas lanterns glowed in every doorway, planters brimmed with gold and crimson chrysanthemums.

I wondered if this was how Candler Park would look once the yuppies had gotten a firmer toehold there. Probably none of the nice ladies who lived in Morningside toted loaded thirty-eights in their purses or rode wino patrols at night.

Catherine Rhyne's house looked cared for—lawn mowed, shrubs trimmed. The Saab in the driveway had Pulaski County license tags. I gave the driver a five-buck tip and he gave me his number and promised to come back for me when I was ready.

I leaned hard on the doorbell. I hadn't called ahead for an appointment, and I was another of those tacky Candler Park residents with a gun in my purse—my Smith & Wesson.

Catherine Rhyne was still tying the belt of her bathrobe when she answered the door. It was a low-crime area; she hadn't bothered to arm herself or ask who was at the door before opening it.

At first, she was too astonished at seeing me there to say anything. She gathered her robe tighter, put her hand on the door, and started to close it firmly in my face.

She didn't get the chance. A dog, part beagle, part cocker spaniel, brown with white spots and short fat legs, scooted out the front door and onto the stoop. It barked and jumped up on my legs—probably smelled Rufus and Maybelline on my clothes.

I bent down and scooped it up in my arms and held it up for Catherine to see.

"Brownie—isn't it? Great little Frisbee dog. Wuvvy spoiled him outrageously, wouldn't you say?"

Catherine scowled and tried to snatch the dog away, but I stepped back.

Brownie wriggled in my arms, stretched out his neck, and licked my chin.

"See? He remembers me from YoYos."

"What do you want?" she said coldly.

"I want to talk about how your mother got Wuvvy's prison sentence commuted," I said. "I want to talk about all those dirty little secrets you people have been keeping all these years."

There was no furniture in the living room or the dining room. We went into the kitchen. I sat on a barstool at the counter, and Catherine put a kettle of water on the stove to boil. She opened a canister, got out a dog biscuit, and flipped it toward the dog.

Brownie did a neat vertical leap—straight up, a canine Michael Jordan—and swallowed the biscuit in one midair gulp.

"Good boy," Catherine said, patting Brownie's head. "Good boy."

Then she turned around and got out heavy pottery mugs and teaspoons and napkins and herbal tea bags. She waited, her back turned away from me, for the water to boil, then she made the tea, fixed the cups just so, and handed one to me.

"Why does any of this matter to you?"

"Three people are dead. Somebody tried to kill me too, earlier tonight. I know those deaths are connected and I know that you know how they're connected."

"You don't know a goddamned thing," she said fiercely.

"I'm a helluva guesser," I said. "Jackson Poole had a secret bank account with an extra twenty-five thousand dollars rattling around in it. I think you and your mother gave him that money."

I had another idea. "Where was your mother Halloween night? Up here in Atlanta? You know, you two make a very determined pair. One of your mother's old friends called you all a real dynasty. I'd like to have seen Big Kitty in her day. Man, talk about a family of ballbusters."

Catherine sipped her tea calmly. Me, I was so pumped with adrenaline that I could see my own hand shaking so badly, the tea sloshed all over the side of the cup. Her hand was rock steady.

"I didn't kill Jackson Poole," she said. "You can drag my family's name in the mud and I can't stop you. But it doesn't change the facts. I didn't kill him."

"You would have," I said. "Jackson threatened you both. I wonder why he waited all these years to make you pay?"

She set the cup down. "He wanted us to suffer," Catherine said. "The money was secondary. Mother thought we could just pay him off. That's how things were always done in Hawkinsville. But I knew he wouldn't be happy until he'd degraded and utterly ruined us all."

"Especially Wuvvy," I said.

"Oh yes," she said sadly. "Poor Wuvvy."

I drank four cups of tea while she told her story. She stood by the stove, very straight-backed and matter-of-fact. I sat on that damned barstool and drank tea and listened until my ass ached and my bladder screamed for relief.

"Broward Poole was a horrible person," Catherine said. "And he raised a son who turned out to be just like him. Everybody in Hawkinsville always said how wonderful he was, but I always, always knew there was something evil about those two.

"Virginia Lee was so naive. She had a job at the pecan ware-house, writing tickets for the brokers, I think. That's where they met. Broward had a big shiny car and he took her on a weekend trip down to Fort Lauderdale. She said he treated her like a princess. It didn't occur to her until the morning they got married that they didn't know anything about each other, and that she didn't particularly love him.

"By then it was too late. She really did care about Jackson. But he was so distant all the time. Off playing in the woods or reading a book by himself.

"Broward wouldn't let Virginia keep her old job. Wouldn't let her listen to her music, or have her young friends over. He bought her a car, a black Trans Am, as a wedding present, but she wasn't allowed to take it to Atlanta or Macon or anywhere. And he knew everybody in town, had everybody spying on her for him.

"He was a mean old man, that's all. And the meaner he got, the wilder she got."

"Did he really beat Wuvvy?" I asked. "Or was all that just made up for the trial?"

"The first time he slapped her was after he found out she was smoking marijuana out in that tenant farmer's shack."

Catherine smiled ruefully. "You know who told on her? My mother. Little Kitty found some rolling papers in my purse, after that time I'd gone with Virginia to that concert in Macon. Mother just knew Virginia Lee was turning me into a raving dope fiend. She marched herself right over to Broward's office and threatened to call the sheriff and have Virginia Lee Poole arrested for contributing to the delinquency of a minor.

"But Broward didn't confront her right then. No. He sniffed around and figured out why Virginia Lee spent so much time out in that shack. She had her little stereo out there, and some candles, and she'd party with her friends out there. It was her own little hidey-hole.

"Broward waited and watched, and then he went out there and caught her. It was just one little joint. But he carried on like he'd caught her with a needleful of heroin stuck in her arm. He called her a junkie whore and slapped her so hard it dislocated her jaw."

"Were you there when he hit her?" I asked.

"No, ma'am," Catherine said. "Little Kitty Rhyne saw to that. She threatened to put me in juvenile detention hall if I so much as turned in the Pooles' driveway. That was in the summer. I went off to Duke that fall.

"Virginia called me in Durham and told me Broward had put her in the emergency room. Of course, they said she'd fallen off a horse or some lie like that.

"Afterwards, I think Broward felt guilty for hurting her so bad. Or he was still afraid she'd tell people he was a wife beater. He was sweet to her for a while after that. Even let her drive the Trans-Am up to see me in Durham and gave her money for a hotel room."

Catherine started straightening the canisters on the counter, lining them up, big to small. She frowned, changed them around small to big, but still wasn't happy with the results.

"I am not a homosexual," she said adamantly. "I lost my virginity at a rush party at the SAE house the weekend of the Wake Forest football game. And I was engaged my third year of law school, but my fiancée wanted me to move with him to Chicago and I wouldn't do that."

"Tell me what happened with Wuvvy," I said. "When she came up to see you in Durham."

"Not what you think," Catherine said. "We did smoke some marijuana. And I fixed Virginia up with my boyfriend's roommate, and we, um, we all used Virginia's hotel room to have sex, because I was living in the dorm, and we weren't allowed to have men in the room after midnight."

"Did she suggest something kinky, or was that your idea?" I asked.

"For God's sake!" Catherine said, blushing. "It was Virginia's date's idea. I thought he meant he wanted to have sex with me, and I said no, right away, because he was repulsive. But he said he wanted to watch. I mean, watch Virginia and me. And my boyfriend got really, really mad and disgusted. So we—my boyfriend and I—we left right then and there."

"But the subject came up again, didn't it?"

"When I came home at Thanksgiving break," Catherine said. "I saw Virginia while I was at the IGA picking up some sweet potatoes for Mama. Virginia said she'd bought some good marijuana down in Savannah, and I should meet her at the shack."

Catherine's eyes were closed as she described the scene.

"I could hear that music playing as soon as I turned my car down that path. Santana. She always played that same spooky album when she got high. I've forgotten what it was called."

"*Abraxis*," I said. "'Black Magic Woman.' Music to get loaded. Or laid."

Catherine winced and swallowed hard.

"That marijuana she'd gotten down in Savannah was stronger than anything you could get in Hawkinsville. She was so stoned. And so was I. She hadn't forgotten what that boy wanted us to do in Durham. She said she'd had sex with girls before. It was a hoot. Didn't mean a damn thing. Didn't turn you into a queer. Just try it, she said. And I wanted to. I was curious."

Catherine took her mug and rinsed it out in the sink. She dried it and put it in the cupboard, folded the dish towel a couple of times, and put it away. When she ran out of things to do with her hands and places to hide from me, she finished the story.

"The music was so loud, we didn't hear Broward drive up. We were naked, dancing around, giggling. And then he was in the doorway. He had a shotgun.

"He called us sluts. Dykes. Awful words. He held that shotgun on me. Made me get dressed while he stood there and watched and called me filthy names. And I noticed he had an erection. He did. He was enjoying the whole show. Then he told me to get out. He said he was going to deal with his slut wife and then go up to my house and tell Little Kitty Rhyne and Big Kitty what kind of degenerate perverted whore they'd raised. And he slapped me so hard he knocked me down.

"Then Virginia jumped on him, and was scratching him and hitting him and telling him to leave me alone. He dropped the shotgun and went to hit her.

"I picked up the shotgun. My grandmother taught me to shoot. Did you know that? Big Kitty shot a snake out of a tree one time. I saw her do it. With my granddaddy's deer rifle.

"I shot Broward Poole.

"Virginia Lee hugged me around the neck. And then we got scared. We dragged him out into the middle of the pecan grove. Virginia got the idea that we would make it look like a hunting accident. She went and got the record and put it on, and I shot a couple crows with Broward's gun. And we thought we were really smart."

"What record?" I asked. And then I remembered the forty-five I'd found. "'Crow-Go'?" I asked. "What was it for?"

"Horrible, excruciating," Catherine said. Now she was shaking, her hands trembling uncontrollably, tears streaming down her face.

"Sweet Lord. I'll never forget that sound. When I have nightmares, it's never about Broward. It's that record. Those crows." She held her hand up to her ears, as though she could shut out the memory of the sound.

"I don't understand," I said.

"Pecan growers despise crows, almost as much as squirrels," she said. "Crows travel in these huge flocks. Their beaks are so strong, they just peck open the nuts on the ground. They can strip a grove in no time. The growers tried all kinds of things. Poison, cannons. They'd shoot off these big carbine guns to scare the crows away. But crows are smart. They'd get used to the cannons and come right back. So Broward sent off for this record. It was a recording of an owl attacking a crow. The crow caws and calls, and the owl makes this screech, and they make a terrible racket and when the other crows hear it, they swarm into the area to help the one being attacked, and that's when you get out the shotguns. An ambush. You kill as many as you can. And then the other crows won't come back to that part of the grove again."

Catherine sat down on the kitchen floor. She gathered Brownie up in her arms and buried her face in his fur and sobbed and sobbed until he squirmed out of her reach and sat on his haunches and whimpered right along with her.

"Hundreds of crows came," she whispered, looking up at me. "The sky was black with them. Cawing and screeching."

"And Jackson saw the whole thing," I said. "From his favorite climbing tree."

"He never said a word to anybody," Catherine said. "We didn't know."

She was shaking like a leaf. I went to the stove and put another pot of water on to boil. This time I found some tea bags with caffeine. It looked like we'd be here a while.

There was a soft click out in the hallway, and then the sound of a door closing. Brownie's ears quivered and he trotted into the hallway to investigate. We heard water running. A toilet flushing. Water again. And a door opening.

"Catherine? It's late. I heard voices. Is someone here?"

Kitty Rhyne wore a navy blue satin robe piped in white, with matching blue slippers. Even the ugly snub-nosed revolver in her hand was blue steel.

"Mother," Catherine started.

"You shut up," Kitty said, her voice hoarse. "Not another word out of you. Is that clear?"

"Hello, Kitty," I said, my own voice cracking. The teakettle had started to whistle. I turned the burner off and moved the kettle to keep it quiet.

"It's Ms. Rhyne to you," Kitty said. Her lips compressed in a tight white line, and under the kitchen's fluorescent lights, her golden tan looked unnaturally dark, the skin cracked and dried like old leather. Her hair was thin as cornsilk and clung to her scalp, and she squinted without her eyeglasses.

"I've been listening to you talking out here, and I finally had to go in the bathroom and be sick to my stomach," Kitty said, glaring at Catherine. "None of this ever would have happened if you had listened to me in the first place. If you'd stayed away from Wuvvy, like I told you."

"But it did happen," I said. "Catherine killed Broward Poole and you covered it up for her. Years later, Jackson came back and threatened to spill the whole nasty story unless you paid him off." I was feeling unreasonably brave. Too many pills, too much caffeine. I wished I hadn't sat my purse on the counter near where Catherine stood. Wished I was the one pointing a gun at Little Kitty Rhyne.

"What are you going to do? Shoot me?" I asked. "This isn't Hawkinsville, Kitty. You can't just kill somebody in Atlanta and get away with it."

"Watch me," she snapped. "I'm a very competent woman. All the Rhyne women are competent. Except her," she said, motioning with the gun toward her daughter. "All her education—and she's got no more common sense than a flea."

"This isn't going to work, Mother," Catherine said patiently, as though she and her mother were discussing a new chicken casserole instead of my life. "Put the gun away. I'm not going to let you keep up this insanity."

"I told you to shut up!" Kitty screamed as Catherine reached for the pistol. She slammed the snout of the gun down hard on the back of her daughter's neck. Catherine screamed, then fell to the floor in a heap, banging her head on the edge of the counter.

"I warned her," Kitty said matter-of-factly. Brownie began to bark. Short, unhappy yaps dissolving to loud mournful howls. "You shut up too," Kitty muttered to the dog. She aimed a swift vicious kick at the pooch, but he skittered out of the way, backed himself up to the door and took his stand. He was full-out baying now. Blood was pooling on the white tile floor around Catherine's neck. Kitty bent down and touched her daughter's cheek. "Catherine?" she said, alarmed. "Come on, honey. It's Mama. Sit up and talk to Mama."

I took the heavy pottery tea mug in both hands, ready to defend my life for the second time in two days.

Kitty cradled her daughter's head in her lap, caressed the pale cheek. "Itty-Bitty," she crooned. "Pretty Itty-Bitty." She picked up the little pistol. I felt myself tense, tried to concentrate on aiming the mug.

She tucked the little blue pistol snug against her right ear and fired.

Not such a loud sound, really. Brownie howled for a long, long time.

I would have given anything right then for my own bed and some peace and quiet. But I was the one who had insisted on having all the answers. I had them all now, probably, but two more people were dead.

I used the telephone in Catherine's bedroom. It was so late, I decided to give Deavers a break. Somebody else could call him, in the morning, I hoped. After all, Kitty and Catherine weren't going anywhere. After I called 911 I sat down on the living room floor and held Brownie in my arms and waited for the questions to begin again.

The murder of a politician, even a former politician, is a high-priority item. Major Mackey himself came to the scene, arriving at the same time as the ambulance and the patrol cars.

By the time we got outside to go to the homicide office so I could give my statement, the press had gotten wind of the fact that a prominent former politician and her mother were dead. There were two helicopters hovering overhead and four television camera crews along with half a dozen miscellaneous reporters waiting outside, trampling Catherine Rhyne's immaculate lawn.

Brownie bared his fangs and growled viciously the first time one of the television reporters stuck a microphone and a camera in my face.

"Bite 'em, boy," I hissed.

All the reporters backed away from me then, like I was the one responsible for the two corpses inside on the kitchen floor. "It wasn't me," I wanted to tell somebody. "It all started a long time ago." Instead, Mackey put his hand on my back and pushed me gently through the throng. "No statements," he told them.

EPILOGUE

By the week before Christmas, the banner on the front of the Little Five Points Blind Possum brewpub was torn and gray and sagging. The OPENING SOON! had been crossed through and one of the locals had scrawled NEVER beneath it. I heard through the grapevine that TES had the building up for sale.

The regulars sat in their same places in the window at the Yacht Club, wreathed in flashing red and green Christmas lights and strands of sparkly silver garlands. Miranda's lawyers got the charges against her dropped. My sources tell me she stands silently behind the bar most days, nursing a Fresca and a grudge against the world. Hap wasn't scheduled to go to trial until the spring. They never have found the Spaceman. Bucky keeps hoping his body will turn up so that they can get another shot at nailing Miranda for being an accessory to his murder. I'm in the market for a new watering hole.

Edna had me shelling pecans for her last big push of

Christmas baking. She'd promised me my own pecan pie—a new recipe that called for a cup of Jack Daniel's.

When the phone rang she wiped her floury hands on her slacks and answered it, "Merry Christmas from the House Mouse."

I winced at the cutesy greeting, mouthed the words: "I'm not here."

"She's right here," Edna said.

It was Anna Frisch. She wanted to know if I could come out to the Blind Possum in Roswell. "To settle up accounts," she said.

I let Brownie ride in the front seat of the van on the way out there. He's good company, and somehow having a watchdog makes me feel a little safer. False security, probably. If I have a client who likes dogs, I sometimes take Brownie on a cleaning job with me. We both know it's not permanent. A dog like Brownie needs a real family, with kids, and maybe a yard to run in. Edna has put the word out among her commandos.

The parking lot at the Blind Possum was full and people stood around outside in a new courtyard, waiting to be served. Everybody had a pint of beer in their hands. Nobody was complaining. They'd strung red and green Christmas lights on the old brick walls outside, and the neon possum had been given a set of glowing red antlers for a festive holiday touch.

Anna was standing inside, near the hostess stand, waiting for me. She'd cut her hair since the last time I'd seen her, which was the day they'd released her from the hospital. It was very short, a lot redder. It made her look older, more businesslike.

She gave me a hug, which surprised me. Anna hadn't seemed like the hugging type.

We went into her office. She sat behind a desk piled high with files and menus and sample beer bottles.

"Looks like it's going good," I said.

"Amazingly well," she said, smiling. "The company's been very decent to me. The business has exceeded their wildest expectations, we're on target to be in the black by March, so that doesn't hurt. You know, a month ago, I thought I'd never come back to this place. After all I found out—about Jackson, about me, I wanted to quit."

"You were pretty sick," I said. "We were both pretty sick." I shuddered at the memory of it.

"I'm tough, I got over the physical part pretty quickly," Anna said. "And I'm finding out that the emotional part is just going to take some time. Having work I love to do helps a lot. Friends do, too. I've made some good friends here. People in the restaurant community have been wonderful. It's a part of the business I didn't know about. Jackson was so suspicious of competition, he never would have anything to do with those people."

I tried to think of something nice to say about the dead. But I still hadn't heard anything that would make me think good thoughts about Jackson Poole.

Anna helped me out. "He was complicated. But he did do something for me, you know."

"What's that?"

"He had a will. He left me everything, named me beneficiary on his company life insurance policy. It's a lot of money, Callahan."

"You deserve it," I said. "Every penny."

"So do you," she said. "It's payday, Callahan."

She handed me an envelope. My name was written on it. It was a Christmas card, bright red with the Blind Possum reindeer logo on the outside. "Merry Christmas to Brew!" it said. There was a check inside, made out to me, for twenty thousand dollars.

"I was going to send you an invoice," I said, embarrassed.

"Uh, it's probably more like six hundred. Eight hundred tops." I held the envelope out to her.

"It's the exact right amount," she said firmly. "That's the money that was left in Jackson's checking account. The money he extorted from Catherine and Kitty Rhyne."

"I don't want this," I said, puzzled. "I've got no right to it."

"Who does?" she said lightly. "Wuvvy, probably. But she's dead. I can't give it back to Catherine or Kitty. Anyway, it was about time they paid for what they did all those years ago."

"What about Big Kitty Rhyne?" I asked. "She probably inherits anything from her daughter and granddaughter."

"She's in a nursing home," Anna said. "Azalea Acres. It sounds nice. No, I've thought a lot about this. You did what I asked you to do. You earned your fee. So take it, please?"

The bills had started coming in for the new roof, the new porch, and the new security system. I had my eye on a secondhand van. And Edna wanted a cell phone for Christmas.

I put the envelope in my purse. "All right," I said. "I'll send you an invoice and mark it paid. For your records and mine."

"Good," Anna said, standing up. "Now, can I buy you a beer?"